"**Y**ou know the system we have now, unchanged since the mid-twentieth-century. Copyright ceases to exist fifty years after the death of the copyright holder. But the size of the human race has increased drastically since the 1900s—and so has the average human lifespan. Most people in developed nations now expect to live to be a hundred and twenty, you yourself are considerably older. And so, naturally, S. '896 now seeks to extend copyright into perpetuity."

"Well," the senator interrupted, "what is *wrong* with that? Should a man's work cease to be his simply because he has neglected to keep on breathing? Mrs. Martin, you yourself will be wealthy all your life if that bill passes. Do you truly wish to give away your late husband's genius?"

She winced in spite of herself.

"Forgive my bluntness, but that is what I understand *least* about your position."

"Senator, if I try to hoard the fruits of my husband's genius, I may cripple my race. Don't you see what perpetual copyright implies? It is perpetual racial memory! That bill will give the human race an elephant's memory. *Have you ever seen a cheerful elephant?*"

Books by Spider Robinson:

SPIDER ROBINSON

MELANCHOLY ELEPHANTS

A TOM DOHERTY ASSOCIATES BOOK

MELANCHOLY ELEPHANTS

Copyright © 1985 by Spider Robinson

First printing: June 1985

A TOR Book

Published by Tom Doherty Associates
8-10 West 36 Street
New York, N.Y. 10018

Cover art by Jill Bauman

ISBN: 0-812-55231-8

Printed in the United States of America

To *Jeanne*,
of course, and to *Beth Meacham*, in both cases
for the patience, and to all the sf writers,
past, present and future

Contents

Introductory Note

If a few of the stories in this volume seem familiar to you, congratulations! You must be a fanatical Spider Robinson fan, a compleatist collector, or a Canadian—any of which is cause for congratulation. Which is to say that four of these twelve stories are reprinted from the Dell paperback *Antinomy* (1980), and nearly all of them are reprinted from a Penguin Canada trade paperback which is also called *Melancholy Elephants* (1984).

But the chances are excellent that they are all new to you.

The week that *Antinomy* was released, Dell made the decision to drop its science fiction line—making it one of the only books ever to be remaindered *during* publication. Although a few copies apparently did sneak out of the warehouse, they were not so numerous as to earn me dime one of royalties, and the collection as such is stone dead, never to be reprinted—so I feel justified in raiding it here. If you already have it, you own a rare book: seal it in nitrogen and keep this copy to reread and loan out.

The Penguin Canada edition of this book has been available in Canada for a year—but nowhere else. (Book traffic across the longest undefended border in the world seems to flow only one way.) And even if you are a Canadian, and in possession of a copy of the Penguin volume, you'll find that this version contains two stories which are not in that edition.

This seems as good a place as any to mention that the title story of this collection won the Hugo Award for Best Science Fiction Story of 1982. My thanks to those who voted for it.

—S.R.

Melancholy Elephants

This story is dedicated to
Virginia Heinlein.

She sat zazen, concentrating on not concentrating, until it was time to prepare for the appointment. Sitting *seemed* to produce the usual serenity, put everything in perspective. Her hand did not tremble as she applied her make-up; tranquil features looked back at her from the mirror. She was mildly surprised, in fact, at just how calm she was, until she got out of the hotel elevator at the garage level and the mugger made his play: she killed him instead of disabling him. Which was obviously not a measured, balanced action—the offical fuss and paperwork could make her late. Annoyed at herself, she stuffed the corpse under a shiny new Westinghouse roadable whose owner she knew to be in Luna, and continued on to her own car. This would have to be squared later, and it would cost. No help for it—she fought to regain at least the semblance of

1

tranquillity as her car emerged from the garage and turned north.

Nothing must interfere with this meeting, or with her role in it.

Dozens of man-years and God knows how many dollars, she thought, *funnelling down to perhaps a half hour of conversation. All the effort, all the hope. Insignificant on the scale of the Great Wheel, of course . . . but when you balance it all on a half hour of talk, it's like balancing a stereo cartridge on a needlepoint: It only takes a gram or so of weight to wear out a piece of diamond. I must be harder than diamond.*

Rather than clear a window and watch Washington, D.C. roll by beneath her car, she turned on the television. She absorbed and integrated the news, on the chance that there might be some late-breaking item she could turn to her advantage in the conversation to come; none developed. Shortly the car addressed her: "Grounding, ma'am. I.D. eyeball request." When the car landed she cleared and then opened her window, presented her pass and I.D. to a Marine in dress blues, and was cleared at once. At the Marine's direction she re-opaqued the window and surrendered control of her own car to the house computer, and when the car parked itself and powered down she got out without haste. A man she knew was waiting to meet her, smiling.

"Dorothy, it's good to see you again."

"Hello, Phillip. Good of you to meet me."

"You look lovely this evening."

"You're too kind."

She did not chafe at the meaningless pleasantries. She needed Phil's support, or she might. But she did reflect on how many, many sentences have been worn smooth with use, rendered meaningless by centuries of repetition. It was by no means a new thought.

"If you'll come with me, he'll see you at once."

"Thank you, Phillip." She wanted to ask what the old man's mood was, but knew it would put Phil in an impossible position.

"I rather think your luck is good; the old man seems to be in excellent spirits tonight."

She smiled her thanks, and decided that if and when Phil got around to making his pass she would accept him.

The corridors through which he led her then were broad and high and long; the building dated back to a time of cheap power. Even in Washington, few others would have dared to live in such an energy-wasteful environment. The extremely spare decor reinforced the impression created by the place's very dimensions: bare space from carpet to ceiling, broken approximately every forty metres by some exquisitely simple objet d'art of at least a megabuck's value, appropriately displayed. An unadorned, perfect, white porcelain bowl, over a thousand years old, on a rough cherrywood pedestal. An arresting colour photograph of a snow-covered country road, silk-screened onto stretched silver foil; the time of day changed as one walked past it. A crystal globe, a metre in diameter, within which danced a hologram of the immortal Shara Drummond; since she had ceased performing before the advent of holo technology, this had to be an expensive computer reconstruction. A small sealed glassite chamber containing the first vacuum-sculpture ever made, Nakagawa's legendary Starstone. A visitor in no hurry could study an object at leisure, then walk quite a distance in undistracted contemplation before encountering another. A visitor in a hurry, like Dorothy, would not *quite* encounter peripherally astonishing stimuli often enough to get the trick of filtering them out. Each tugged at her attention, intruded on her thoughts; they were distracting both intrinsically and as a reminder of the measure of their owner's wealth. To approach this man in his own home, whether at leisure or in haste, was to be humbled. She knew the effect was intentional, and could not transcend it; this irritated her, which irritated her. She struggled for detachment.

At the end of the seemingly endless corridors was an elevator. Phillip handed her into it, punched a floor button, without giving her a chance to see which one, and stepped back into the doorway. "Good luck, Dorothy."

"Thank you, Phillip. Any topics to be sure and avoid?"

"Well . . . don't bring up hemorrhoids."

"I didn't know one could."

He smiled. "Are we still on for lunch Thursday?"

"Unless you'd rather make it dinner."

One eyebrow lifted. "And breakfast?"

She appeared to consider it. "Brunch," she decided. He half-bowed and stepped back.

The elevator door closed and she forgot Phillip's existence.

Sentient beings are innumerable; I vow to save them all. The deluding passions are limitless; I vow to extinguish them all. The truth is limitless; I—

The elevator door opened again, truncating the Vow of the Boddhisatva. She had not felt the elevator stop—yet she knew that she must have descended at least a hundred metres. She left the elevator.

The room was larger than she had expected; nonetheless the big powered chair dominated it easily. The chair also seemed to dominate—at least visually—its occupant. A misleading impression, as he dominated all this massive home, everything in it and, to a great degree, the country in which it stood. But he did not look like much.

A scent symphony was in progress, the cinnamon passage of Bulachevski's "Childhood." It happened to be one of her personal favourites, and this encouraged her.

"Hello, Senator."

"Hello, Mrs. Martin. Welcome to my home. Forgive me for not rising."

"Of course. It was most gracious of you to receive me."

"It is my pleasure and privilege. A man my age appreciates a chance to spend time with a woman as beautiful and intelligent as yourself."

"Senator, how soon do we start talking to each other?"

He raised that part of his face which had once held an eyebrow.

"We haven't *said* anything yet that is true. You do not stand because you cannot. Your gracious reception cost me three carefully hoarded favours and a good deal of folding cash. More than the going rate; you are seeing me reluctantly. You have at least eight mistresses that I know of, each of whom makes me look like a dull matron. I concealed a warm corpse on the way here because I dared not be late; my time is short and my business urgent. Can we begin?"

She held her breath and prayed silently. Everything she had been able to learn about the Senator told her that this was the correct way to approach him. But was it?

The mummy-like face fissured in a broad grin. "Right away. Mrs. Martin, I like you and that's the truth. My time is short, too. What do you want of me?"

"Don't you know?"

"I can make an excellent guess. I hate guessing."

"I am heavily and publicly committed to the defeat of S. 4217896."

"Yes, but for all I know you might have come here to sell out."

"Oh." She tried not to show her surprise. "What makes you think that possible?"

"Your organization is large and well-financed and fairly

efficient, Mrs. Martin, and there's something about it I don't understand.''

"What is that?''

"Your objective. Your arguments are weak and implausible, and whenever this is pointed out to one of you, you simply keep on pushing. Many times I have seen people take a position without apparent logic to it—but I've always been able to see the logic if I kept on looking hard enough. But as I see it, S. '896 would work to the clear and lasting advantage of the group you claim to represent, the artists. There's too much intelligence in your organization to square with your goals. So I have to wonder what you *are* working for, and why. One possibility is that you're willing to roll over on this copyright thing in exchange for whatever it is that you *really* want. Follow me?''

"Senator, I *am* working on behalf of all artists—and in a broader sense—''

He looked pained, or rather, more pained. ". . . 'for all mankind,' oh my *God*, Mrs. Martin, really now.''

"I *know* you have heard that countless times, and probably said it as often.'' He grinned evilly. "This is one of those rare times when it happens to be true. I believe that if S. '896 does pass, our species will suffer significant trauma.''

He raised a skeletal hand, tugged at his lower lip. "Now that I have ascertained where you stand, I believe I can save you a good deal of money. By concluding this audience, and seeing that the squeeze you paid for half an hour of my time is refunded pro rata.''

Her heart sank, but she kept her voice even. "Without even hearing the hidden logic behind our arguments?''

"It would be pointless and cruel to make you go into your spiel, ma'am. You see, I cannot help you.''

She wanted to cry out, and savagely refused herself

permission. *Control*, whispered a part of her mind, while another part shouted that a man such as this did not lightly use the words, "I cannot." But he *had* to be wrong. Perhaps the sentence was only a bargaining gambit. . . .

No sign of the internal conflict showed; her voice was calm and measured. "Sir, I have not come here to lobby. I simply wanted to inform you personally that our organization intends to make a no-strings campaign donation in the amount of—"

"Mrs. Martin, please! Before you commit yourself, I repeat, I cannot help you. Regardless of the sum offered."

"Sir, it is substantial."

"I'm sure. Nonetheless it is insufficient."

She knew she should not ask. "Senator, *why*?"

He frowned, a frightening sight.

"Look," she said, the desperation almost showing through now, "keep the pro rata if it buys me an answer! Until I'm convinced that my mission is utterly hopeless, I must not abandon it; answering me is the quickest way to get me out of your office. Your scanners have searched me quite thoroughly, you know that I'm not abscamming you."

Still frowning, he nodded. "Very well. I cannot accept your campaign donation because I have already accepted one from another source."

Her very worst secret fear was realized. He had already taken money from the other side. The one thing any politician must do, no matter how powerful, is stay bought. It was all over.

All her panic and tension vanished, to be replaced by a sadness so great and so pervasive that for a moment she thought it might literally stop her heart.

Too late! Oh my darling, I was too late!

She realized bleakly that there were too many people in

her life, too many responsibilities and entanglements. It would be at least a month before she could honourably suicide.

"—you all right, Mrs. Martin?" the old man was saying, sharp concern in his voice.

She gathered discipline around her like a familiar cloak. "Yes, sir, thank you. Thank you for speaking plainly." She stood up and smoothed her skirt. "And for your—"

"Mrs. Martin."

"—gracious hos— Yes?"

"Will you tell me your arguments? Why shouldn't I support '896?"

She blinked sharply. "You just said it would be pointless and cruel."

"If I held out the slightest hope, yes, it would be. If you'd rather not waste your time, I will not compel you. But I am curious."

"Intellectual curiosity?"

He seemed to sit up a little straighter—surely an illusion, for a prosthetic spine is not motile. "Mrs. Martin, I happen to be committed to a course of action. That does not mean I don't care whether the action is good or bad."

"Oh." She thought for a moment. "If I convince you, you will not thank me."

"I know. I saw the look on your face a moment ago, and . . . it reminded me of a night many years ago. Night my mother died. If you've got a sadness that big, and I can take on a part of it, I should try. Sit down."

She sat.

"Now tell me: what's so damned awful about extending copyright to meet the realities of modern life? Customarily I try to listen to both sides before accepting the campaign donation—but this seemed so open and shut, so straightforward . . ."

"Senator, that bill is a short-term boon, to some artists— and a long-term disaster for all artists, on Earth and off."

" 'In the long run, Mr. President—,' " he began, quoting Keynes.

"—we are some of us still alive," she finished softly and pointedly. "Aren't we? You've put your finger on part of the problem."

"What is this disaster you speak of?" he asked.

"The worst psychic trauma the race has yet suffered."

He studied her carefully and frowned again. "Such a possibility is not even hinted at in your literature or materials."

"To do so would precipitate the trauma. At present only a handful of people know, even in my organization. I'm telling *you* because you asked, and because I am certain that you are the only person recording this conversation. I'm betting that you will wipe the tape."

He blinked, and sucked at the memory of his teeth. "My, my," he said mildly. "Let me get comfortable." He had the chair recline sharply and massage his lower limbs; she saw that he could still watch her by overhead mirror if he chose. His eyes were closed. "All right, go ahead."

She needed no time to choose her words. "Do you know how old art is, Senator?"

"As old as man, I suppose. In fact, it may be part of the definition."

"Good answer," she said. "Remember that. But for all present-day intents and purposes, you might as well say that art is a little over 15,600 years old. That's the age of the oldest surviving artwork, the cave paintings at Lascaux. Doubtless the cave-painters sang, and danced, and even told stories—but these arts left no record more durable than the memory of a man. Perhaps it was the storytellers who next learned how to preserve their art. Countless more generations would pass before a workable method of musical notation was devised and standardized. Dancers only learned in the last few centuries how to leave even the most rudimentary record of their art.

"The racial memory of our species has been getting longer since Lascaux. The biggest single improvement came with the invention of writing: our memory-span went from a few generations to as many as the Bible has been around. But it took a massive effort to sustain a memory that long: it was difficult to hand-copy manuscripts faster than barbarians, plagues, or other natural disasters could destroy them. The obvious solution was the printing press: to make and disseminate so many copies of a manuscript or artwork that *some* would survive any catastrophe.

"But with the printing press a new idea was born. Art was suddenly mass-marketable, and there was money in it. Writers decided that they should own the right to copy their work. The notion of copyright was waiting to be born.

"Then in the last hundred and fifty years came the largest quantum jumps in human racial memory. Recording technologies. Visual: photography, film, video, Xerox, holo. Audio: low-fi, hi-fi, stereo, and digital. Then computers, the ultimate in information storage. Each of these technologies generated new art forms, and new ways of preserving the ancient art forms. And each required a reassessment of the idea of copyright.

"You know the system we have now, unchanged since the mid-twentieth-century. Copyright ceases to exist fifty years after the death of the copyright holder. But the size of the human race has increased drastically since the 1900s—and so has the average human lifespan. Most people in developed nations now expect to live to be a hundred and twenty, you yourself are considerably older. And so, naturally, S. '896 now seeks to extend copyright into perpetuity."

"Well," the senator interrupted, "what is *wrong* with that? Should a man's work cease to be his simply because he has neglected to keep on breathing? Mrs. Martin, you yourself will be wealthy all your life if that bill passes. Do you truly wish to give away your late husband's genius?"

She winced in spite of herself.

"Forgive my bluntness, but that is what I understand *least* about your position."

"Senator, if I try to hoard the fruits of my husband's genius, I may cripple my race. Don't you see what perpetual copyright implies? It is perpetual racial memory! That bill will give the human race an elephant's memory. *Have you ever seen a cheerful elephant*?"

He was silent for a time. Then: "I'm still not sure I understand the problem."

"Don't feel bad, sir. The problem has been directly under the nose of all of us for at *least* eighty years, and hardly anyone has noticed."

"Why is that?"

"I think it comes down to a kind of innate failure of mathematical intuition, common to most humans. We tend to confuse any sufficiently high number with infinity."

"Well, anything above ten to the eighty-fifth might as well be infinity."

"Beg pardon?"

"Sorry—I should not have interrupted. That is the current best-guess for the number of atoms in the Universe. Go on."

She struggled to get back on the rails. "Well, it takes a lot less than that to equal 'infinity' in most minds. For millions of years we looked at the ocean and said, 'That is infinite. It will accept our garbage and waste forever.' We looked at the sky and said, 'That is infinite: it will hold an infinite amount of smoke.' We *like* the idea of infinity. A problem with infinity in it is easily solved. How long can you pollute a planet infinitely large? Easy: forever. Stop thinking.

"Then one day there are so many of us that the planet no longer seems infinitely large.

"So we go elsewhere. There are infinite resources in the *rest* of the solar system, aren't there? I think you are one of the few people alive wise enough to realize that there are *not* infinite resources in the solar system, and sophisticated enough to have included that awareness in your plans."

The senator now looked troubled. He sipped something from a straw. "Relate all this to your problem."

"Do you remember a case from about eighty years ago, involving the song 'My Sweet Lord' by George Harrison?"

"Remember it? I did research on it. My firm won."

"Your firm convinced the court that Harrison had gotten the tune for that song from a song called 'He's So Fine,' written over ten years earlier. Shortly thereafter Yoko Ono was accused of stealing 'You're My Angel' from the classic 'Makin' Whoopee,' written more than thirty years earlier. Chuck Berry's estate eventually took John Lennon's estate to court over 'Come Together.' Then in the late '80s the great Plagiarism Plague *really* got started in the courts. From then on it was open season on popular composers, and still is. But it really hit the fan at the turn of the century, when Brindle's *Ringsong* was shown to be 'substantially similar' to one of Corelli's concertos.

"There are eighty-eight notes. One hundred and seventy-six, if your ear is good enough to pick out quarter tones. Add in rests and so forth, different time signatures. Pick a figure for maximum number of notes a melody can contain. I do not know the figure for the maximum possible number of melodies—too many variables—but I am sure it is quite high.

"I am certain that is not infinity.

"For one thing, a great many of those possible arrays of eighty-eight notes will not be perceived as music, as melody, by the human ear. Perhaps more than half. They will not be hummable, whistleable, listenable—some will be actively unpleasant to hear. Another large fraction will be so similar to each other as to be effectively identical: if you change three notes of the Moonlight Sonata, you have not created something new.

"I do not know the figure for the maximum number of discretely appreciable melodies, and again I'm certain it is quite high, and again I am certain that it is not infinity. There are sixteen billion of us alive, Senator, more than all the people that have ever lived. Thanks to our technology, better than half of us have no meaningful work to do; fifty-four percent of our population is entered on the tax rolls as artists. Because the synthesizer is so cheap and versatile, a majority of those artists are musicians, and a great many are composers. Do you know what it is like to be a composer these days, Senator?"

"I know a few composers."

"Who are still working?"

"Well . . . three of 'em."

"How often do they bring out a new piece?"

Pause. "I would say once every five years on the average. Hmmm. Never thought of it before, but—"

"Did you know that at present two out of every five copyright submissions to the Music Division are rejected on the first computer search?"

The old man's face had stopped registering surprise, other than for histrionic purposes, more than a century before; nonetheless, she knew she had rocked him. "No, I did not."

"Why would you know? Who would talk about it? But it is a fact nonetheless. Another fact is that, when the increase in number of working composers is taken into account, the *rate* of submissions to the Copyright Office is decreasing significantly. There are more composers than ever, but their individual productivity is declining. Who is the most popular composer alive?"

"Uh . . . I suppose that Vachandra fellow."

"Correct. He has been working for a little over fifty years. If you began now to play every note he ever wrote, in succession, you would be done in twelve hours. Wagner wrote well over sixty hours of music—the Ring alone runs twenty-one hours. The Beatles—essentially two composers—produced over twelve hours of original music in *less than ten years*. Why were the greats of yesteryear so much more prolific?

"There were more enjoyable permutations of eighty-eight notes for them to find."

"Oh my," the senator whispered.

"Now go back to the 1970s again. Remember the *Roots* plagiarism case? And the dozens like it that followed? Around the same time a writer named van Vogt sued the makers of a successful film called *Alien*, for plagiarism of a story forty years later. Two other writers named Bova and Ellison sued a television studio for stealing a series idea. All three collected.

"That ended the legal principle that one does not copyright *ideas* but *arrangements of words*. The number of word-arrangements is finite, but the number of *ideas* is *much* smaller. Certainly, they can be retold in endless ways—*West Side Story* is a brilliant reworking of *Romeo and Juliet*. But it was only possible because *Romeo and Juliet* was in the public domain. Remember too that of the finite number of stories that can be told, a certain number will be *bad stories*.

"As for visual artists—well, once a man demonstrated in the laboratory an ability to distinguish between eighty-one distinct shades of colour accurately. I think that's an upper limit. There is a maximum amount of information that the eye is capable of absorbing, and much of that will be the equivalent of noise—"

"But . . . but . . ." This man was reputed never to have hesitated in any way under any circumstances. "But there'll always be change . . . there'll always be new discoveries, new horizons, new social attitudes, to infuse art with new—"

"Not as fast as artists breed. Do you know about the great split in literature at the beginning of the twentieth century? The mainstream essentially abandoned the Novel of Ideas after Henry James, and turned its collective attention to the Novel of Character. They had sucked that dry by mid-century, and they're still chewing on the pulp today. Meanwhile a small group of writers, desperate for something new to write about, for a new story to tell, invented a new genre called science fiction. They mined the future for ideas. The infinite future—like the infinite coal and oil and copper they had then too. In less than a century they had mined it out; there hasn't been a genuinely original idea in science fiction in over thirty years. Fantasy has always been touted as the 'literature of infinite possibility'—but there is even a theoretical upper limit to the 'meaningfully impossible,' and we are fast reaching it."

"We can create new art forms," he said.

"People have been trying to create new art forms for a long time, sir. Almost all fell by the wayside. People just didn't like them."

"We'll *learn* to like them. Damn it, we'll have to."

"And they'll help, for a while. More new art forms have been born in the last two centuries than in the previous million years—though none in the last fifteen years. Scent-symphonies, tactile sculpture, kinetic sculpture, zero-gravity dance—they're all rich new fields, and they are generating mountains of new copyrights. Mountains of finite size. The ultimate bottleneck is this: that *we have only five senses with which to apprehend art, and that is a finite number*. Can I have some water, please?''

''Of course.'' The old man appeared to have regained his usual control, but the glass which emerged from the arm of her chair contained apple juice. She ignored this and continued.

''But that's not what I'm afraid of, Senator. The theoretical heat-death of artistic expression is something we may never really approach in fact. Long before that point, the game will collapse.''

She paused to gather her thoughts, sipped her juice. A part of her mind noted that it harmonized with the recurrent cinnamon motif of Bulachevski's scent-symphony, which was still in progress.

''Artists have been deluding themselves for centuries with the notion that they create. In fact they do nothing of the sort. They discover. Inherent in the nature of reality are a number of combinations of musical tones that will be perceived as pleasing by a human central nervous system. For millennia we have been discovering them, implicit in the universe—and telling ourselves that we 'created' them. To create implies infinite possibility, to discover implies finite possibility. As a species I think we will react poorly to having our noses rubbed in the fact that we are discoverers and not creators.''

She stopped speaking and sat very straight. Unaccountably her feet hurt. She closed her eyes, and continued speaking.

''My husband wrote a song for me, on the occasion of our fortieth wedding anniversary. It was our love in music, unique and special and intimate, the most beautiful melody I ever heard in my life. It made him so happy to have written it. Of his last ten compositions he had burned five for being derivative, and the others had all failed copyright clearance. But this was fresh, special—he joked that my love for him had inspired him. The next day he submitted it for clearance, and learned that it had been a popular air during his early childhood, and had already been unsuccessfully submitted fourteen times since its original registration. A week later he burned all his manuscripts and working tapes and killed himself.''

She was silent for a long time, and the senator did not speak.

'' 'Ars longa, vita brevis est,' '' she said at last. "There's been comfort of a kind in that for thousands of years. But art is long, not infinite. 'The Magic goes away.' One day we will *use it up*—unless we can learn to recycle it like any other finite resource.'' Her voice gained strength. "Senator, that bill has to fail, if I have to take you on to do it. Perhaps I can't win—but I'm going to fight you! A copyright must not be allowed to last more than fifty years—after which it should be flushed from the memory banks of the Copyright Office. We need selective voluntary amnesia if Discoverers of Art are to continue to work without psychic damage. Facts should be remembered—but dreams?'' She shivered. ''. . . Dreams should be forgotten when we wake. Or one day we will find ourselves unable to sleep. Given eight billion artists with effective working lifetimes in excess of a century, we can no longer allow individuals to own their discoveries in perpetuity. We must do it the way the human race did it for a million years—by forgetting, and rediscovering. Because one day the infinite number of monkeys will have nothing else to write *except* the complete works of Shakespeare. And they would probably rather not *know* that when it happens.''

Now she was finished, nothing more to say. So was the scent-symphony, whose last motif was fading slowly from the air. No clock ticked, no artifact hummed. The stillness was complete, for perhaps half a minute.

"If you live long enough," the senator said slowly at last, "there is nothing new under the sun." He shifted in his great chair. "If you're lucky, you die sooner than that. I haven't heard a new dirty joke in fifty years." He seemed to sit up straight in his chair. "I will kill S.4217896."

She stiffened in shock. After a time, she slumped slightly and resumed breathing. So many emotions fought for ascendancy that she barely had time to recognize them as they went by. She could not speak.

"Furthermore," he went on, "I will not tell anyone why I'm doing it. It will begin the end of my career in public life, which I did not ever plan to leave, but you have convinced me that I must. I am both . . . glad, and—" His face tightened with pain— "and *bitterly* sorry that you told me why I must."

"So am I, sir," she said softly, almost inaudibly.

He looked at her sharply. "Some kinds of fight, you can't feel good even if you win them. Only two kinds of people take on fights like that: fools, and remarkable people. I think you are a remarkable person, Mrs. Martin."

She stood, knocking over her juice. "I wish to God I were a fool," she cried, feeling her control begin to crack at last.

"Dorothy!" he thundered.

She flinched as if he had struck her. "Sir?" she said automatically.

"Do *not* go to pieces! That is an order. You're wound up too tight; the pieces might not go back together again."

"So what?" she asked bitterly.

He was using the full power of his voice now, the voice which had stopped at least one war. "So how many friends do you think a man my age has *got,* damn it? Do you think minds like yours are common? We *share* this business now, and that makes us friends. You are the first person to come out of that elevator and really surprise me in a quarter of a century. And soon, when the word gets around that I've broken faith, people will stop coming out of the elevator. You think like me, and I can't afford to lose you." He smiled, and the smile seemed to melt decades from his face. "Hang on, Dorothy," he said, "and we will comfort each other in our terrible knowledge. All right?"

For several moments she concentrated exclusively on her breathing, slowing and regularizing it. Then, tentatively, she probed at her emotions.

"Why," she said wonderingly, "it *is* better . . . shared."

"Anything is."

She looked at him then, and tried to smile and finally succeeded. "Thank you, Senator."

He returned her smile as he wiped all recordings of their conversation. "Call me Bob."

"Yes, Robert."

Half an Oaf

When the upper half of an extremely fat man materialized before him over the pool table in the living room, Spud nearly swallowed his Adam's apple. But then he saw that the man was a stranger, and relaxed.

Spud wasn't allowed to use the pool table when his mother was home. Mrs. Flynn had been raised on a steady diet of B-movies, and firmly believed that a widow woman who raised a boy by herself in Brooklyn stood a better than even chance of watching her son grow into Jimmy Cagney. Such prophecies, of course, are virtually always self-fulfilling. She could not get the damned pool table out the living room door—God knew how the apartment's previous tenant had gotten it in—but she was determined not to allow her son to develop an interest in a game that could only lead him to the pool hall, the saloon, the getaway car, the insufficiently fortified hideout and the morgue more or less in that order. So she flatly forbade him to go near the pool table even before they moved in. Clearly, playing pool must be a lot of fun, and so at age twelve Spud was regularly losing his lunch money in a neighbourhood pool hall whose savouriness can be inferred from the fact that they let him in.

But whenever his mother went out to get loaded, which was frequently these days, Spud always took his personal cue and bag of balls from their hiding place and set 'em up in the living room. He didn't intend to keep getting hustled for lunch money *all* his life, and his piano teacher, a nun with a literally incredible goiter, had succeeded in convincing him that practice was the only way to master anything. (She had not, unfortunately, succeeded in convincing him to practice the piano.) He was working on a hopelessly impractical triple-cushion shot when the fat man—or rather, half of the fat man—appeared before him, rattling him so much that he sank the shot.

He failed to notice. For a heart-stopping moment he had thought it was his mother, reeling up the fire escape in some new apotheosis of intoxication, hours off schedule. When he saw that it was not, he let out a relieved breath and waited to see if the truncated stranger would die.

The $\frac{\text{fat man}}{2}$ did not die. Neither did he drop the four inches to the surface of the pool table. What he did was stare vacantly around him, scratching his ribs and nodding. He appeared satisfied with something, and he patted the red plastic belt which formed his lower perimeter contentedly, adjusting a derby with his other hand. His face was round, bland and stupid, and he wore a shirt of particularly villainous green.

After a time Spud got tired of being ignored—twelve-year-olds in Brooklyn are nowhere near as respectful of their elders as they are where you come from—and spoke up.

"Transporter malfunction, huh?" he asked with a hint of derision.

"Eh?" said the fat man, noticing Spud for the first time. "Whassat, kid?"

"You're from the *Enterprise*, right?"

"Never heard of it. I'm from Canarsie. What's this about a malfunction?"

Spud pointed.

"So my fly's open, big deal . . ." the $\frac{\text{fat man}}{2}$ let go of his derby and reached down absently to adjust matters, and his thick knuckles rebounded from the green felt tabletop, sinking the seven-ball. He glanced down in surprise, uttered an exclamation, and began cursing with a fluency that inspired Spud's admiration. His pudgy face reddened, taking on the appearance of an enormously swollen cherry pepper, and he struck at the plastic belt with the air of a man who, having petted the nice kitty, has been enthusiastically clawed.

". . . slut-ruttin' gimp-frimpin' turtle-tuppin' clone of a week-old dog turd," he finished, and paused for breath. "I shoulda had my head examined. I shoulda never listened ta that hag-shagger, I *knew* it. 'Practically new,' he says. 'A steal,' he says. Well, it's still got a week left on the warranty, and I'll . . ."

Spud rapped the butt-end of his cue on the floor, and the stranger broke off, noticing him again. "If you're not from the *Enterprise*," Spud asked reasonably, "where are you from? I mean, how did you get here?"

"Time machine," scowled the fat man, gesturing angrily at the belt. "I'm from the future."

"Looks like half of you is still there." Spud grinned.

"Who ast you? What am I, blind? Go on, laugh—I'll kick you in . . . I mean, I'll punch ya face. Bug-huggin' salesman with his big discount, I'll sue his socks off."

The pool hall had taught Spud how to placate enraged elders, and somehow he was beginning to like his hemispheric visitor. "Look, it won't do you any good to get mad at me. *I* didn't sell you a Jap time machine."

"Jap? I wish it was. This duck-fucker's made in Hoboken. Look, get me offa this pool table, will ya? I mean, it feels screwy to look down and see three balls." He held out his hand.

Spud transferred the cue to his left hand, grabbed the pudgy fingers, and tugged. When nothing happened, he tugged harder. The $\frac{\text{fat man}}{2}$ moved slightly. Spud sighed, circled the pool table, climbed onto its surface on his knees, braced his feet against the cushion, and heaved from behind. The half-torso moved forward reluctantly, like a piano on ancient casters. Eventually it was clear of the table, still the same distance from the floor.

"Thanks, kid . . . look, what's your name?"

"Spud Flynn."

"Pleased to meetcha, Spud. I'm Joe Koziack. Listen, are your parents home?"

"My mother's out. I got no father."

"Oh, a clone, huh? Well, that's a break anyway. I'd hate to try and talk my way out of this one with a grownup. No offense. Look, are we in Brooklyn? I gotta get to Manhattan right away."

"Yeah, we're in Brooklyn. But I can't push you to Manhattan—you weigh a ton."

Joe's face fell as he considered this. "How the hell am I gonna get there, then?"

"Beats me. Why don't you walk?"

Joe snorted. "With no legs?"

"You got legs," Spud said. "They just ain't here."

Joe began to reply, then shut up and looked thoughtful. "Might work at that," he decided at last. "I sure an' hell

don't understand how this time-travel stuff works, and it
feels like I still got legs. I'll try it." He squared his
shoulders, looked down and then quickly back up, and
tried a step.

His upper torso moved forward two feet.

"I'll be damned," he said happily. "It works."

He took a few more steps, said, "OUCH, DAMMIT,"
and grabbed at the empty air below him, leaning forward.
"Bashed my cop-toppin' knee," he snarled.

"On what?"

Joe looked puzzled. "I guess on the wall back home in
2007," he decided. "I can't seem to go forward any
further."

Spud got behind him and pushed again, and Joe moved
forward a few feet more. "Jesus, that feels weird," Joe
exclaimed. "My legs're still against the wall, but I still
feel attached to them."

"That's as far as I go," Spud panted. "You're too
heavy."

"How come? There's only half as much of me."

"So what's that—a hundred and fifty pounds?"

"Huh. I guess you're right. But I gotta think of *something*.
I *gotta* get to Manhattan."

"Why?" Spud asked.

"To get to a garage," Joe explained impatiently. "The
guys that make these time-belts, they got repair stations set
up all the way down the temporal line in case one gets
wrecked up or you kill the batteries. The nearest dealership's in Manhattan, and the repairs're free till the warranty runs out. But how am I gonna get there?"

"Why don't you use the belt to go back home?" asked
Spud, scratching his curly head.

"Sure, and find out I left my lungs and one kidney back
here? I could maybe leave my heart in San Francisco, but
my kidney in Brooklyn? Nuts—this belt stays switched off

till I get to the complaint department.'' He frowned might-ily. ''But how?''

''I got it,'' Spud cried. ''Close your eyes. Now try to remember the room you started in, and which way you were facing. Now, where's the door?''

''Uh . . . that way,'' said Joe, pointing. He shuffled sideways, swore as he felt an invisible door-knob catch him in the groin, and stopped. ''Now how the hell do I open the door with no hands?'' he grumbled. ''Oh, crap.'' His torso dropped suddenly, ending up on its back on the floor, propped up on splayed elbows. The derby remained fixed on his head. His face contorted and sweat sprang out on his forehead. ''Shoes . . . too slop-toppin' . . . slip-pery,'' he gasped. ''Can't get . . . a decent grip.'' He relaxed slightly, gritted his teeth, and said, ''There. One shoe. Oh Christ, the second one's always the hardest. Unnh. Got it. Now I gotcha, you son of a foreman.'' After a bit more exertion he spread his fingers on the floor, slid himself backward, and appeared to push his torso from the floor with one hand. Spud watched with interest.

''That was pretty neat,'' the boy remarked. ''From un-derneath, you look like a cross-section of a person.''

''Go on.''

''You had lasagna for supper.''

Joe paled a little. ''Christ, I hope I don't start leaking. Well, anyhow, thanks for everything, kid—I'll be seein' ya.''

''Say, hold on,'' Spud called as Joe's upper body began to float from the living room. ''How're you gonna keep from bumping into things all the way to Manhattan? I mean, it's ten miles, easy, from here to the bridge. You could get run over or something. *Either* half.''

Joe froze, and thought that one over. He was silent for a long time.

''Maybe I got an angle,'' he said at last. He backed

up slightly. "There. I feel the doorway with my heels. Now you move me a couple of feet, okay?" Spud complied.

"Terrific! I can still feel the doorway. When I walk, my legs back home move too. When I stand still and you move me, the legs stay put. So we can do it after all."

" 'We' my foot," Spud objected. "You haven't been paying attention. I told you—I can't push you to New York."

"Look, Spud," Joe said, a sudden look of cunning on his pudding face, "how'd you like to be rich?"

Spud looked skeptical. "Hey, Joe, I watch TV—I read sf—I've heard this one before. I don't know anything about the stock market thirty years ago, I couldn't even tell you who was President then, and you don't look like a historian to me. What could you tell me to make me rich?"

"I'm a sports nut," Joe said triumphantly. "Tell me what year it is, I'll tell you who's gonna win the World Series, the Rose Bowl, the Stanley Cup. You could clean up."

Spud thought it over. He shot pool with one of the best bookies in the neighbourhood, a gentleman named "Odds" Evenwright. On the other hand, Mom would be home in a couple of hours.

"I'll give you all the help I can," Joe promised. "Just give me a hand now and then."

"Okay," Spud said reluctantly. "But we gotta hurry."

"Fine, Spud, fine. I knew I could count on you. All right, let's give it a try." The $\frac{\text{fat man}}{2}$ closed his eyes, turned right and began to move forward gingerly. "Lemme see if I can remember."

"Wait a minute," said Spud with a touch of contempt. Joe, he decided, was not very bright. "You've gotta get out of *this* room first. You're gonna hit that wall in a minute."

Joe opened his eyes, blinked. "Yeah."

"Hold on. Where your legs are—is that this building, thirty-two years from now? I mean, if it is, how come the doors are in different places and stuff?"

"Nah—I started in a ten-year-old building."

Spud sneered. "Cripes, you're lucky you didn't pop out in midair! Or inside somebody's fireplace. That was dumb— you should have started on the ground out in the open someplace."

Joe reddened. "What makes you think there *is* anyplace out in the open in Brooklyn in 2007, smart-mouth? I checked the Hall of Records and found out there was a building here in 1976, and the floor heights matched. So I took a chance. Now stop needlin' me and help me figure this out."

"I guess," Spud said reluctantly, "I'll have to push you out into the hall, and then you can take it from there, I hope." He dug in his heels and pushed. "Hey, squat a little, will you? Your centre of gravity's too high." Koziack complied, and was gradually boyhandled out into the hall. It was empty.

"Okay," Spud panted at last. "Try walking." Joe moved forward tentatively, then grinned and began to move faster, swinging his heavy arms.

"Say," he said, "this is all right."

"Well, let's get going before somebody comes along and sees you," Spud urged.

"Sure thing," Koziack agreed, quickening his pace. "Wouldn't want aaaaaaAAAAAARGH!!!" His eyes widened for a moment, his arms flailed, and suddenly he dropped to the floor and began to bounce violently up and down, spinning rapidly. Spud jumped away, wondering if

Joe had gone mad or epileptic. At last the $\frac{fat\ man}{2}$ came to rest on his back, cursing feebly, the derby still on his head but quite flattened.

"You okay?" Spud asked tentatively.

Joe lurched upright and began rubbing the back of his head vigorously. "Fell down the mug-pluggin' stairs," he said petulantly.

"Why don't you watch where you're going?"

"How the hell am I supposed to do that?" Joe barked.

"Well, be more careful," Spud said angrily. "You keep makin' noise and somebody's gonna come investigate."

"In *Brooklyn*? Come on! Jesus, my ass hurts."

"Lucky you didn't break a leg," Spud told him. "Let's get going."

"Yeah." Groaning, Joe began to move forward again. The pair reached the elevator without further incident, and Joe pushed the DOWN button. "Wish my own building had elevators," he complained bitterly, still trying to rub the place that hurt. *Migod,* thought Spud, *he literally can't find it with both hands!* He giggled, stopped when he saw Joe glare.

The elevator door slid back. A bearded young man with very long hair emerged, shouldered past the two, started down the hall and then did a triple-take in slow motion. Trembling, he took a plastic baggie of some green substance from his pocket, looked from it to Koziack and back again. "I guess it *is* worth sixty an ounce," he said to himself, and continued on his way.

Oblivious, Spud was waving Joe to follow him into the elevator. The $\frac{fat\ man}{2}$ attempted to comply, bounced off empty air in the doorway.

"Shit," he said.

"Come on, come on," Spud said impatiently.

"I *can't*. My own hallway isn't wide enough. You'll have to push me in."

Spud raised his eyes heavenward. He set the "emergency stop" switch. Immediately alarm bells began to yammer, reverberating through the entire building. Swearing furiously, Spud scrambled past Joe into the hallway and pushed him into the elevator as fast as he could, scurrying in after him. He slapped the controls, the clamour ceased, and the car began to descend.

At once Joe rose to the ceiling, banging his head and flattening the derby entirely. The car's descent slowed. He roared with pain and did a sort of reverse-pushup, lowering his head a few inches. He glared down at Spud. "How . . . many . . . floors?" he grunted, teeth gritting with effort.

Spud glanced at the indicator behind Joe. "Three more," he announced.

"Jesus."

The elevator descended at about three-quarter-normal speed, but eventually it reached the ground floor, and the doors opened on a miraculously empty lobby. Joe dropped his hands with a sigh of relief—and remained a few inches below the ceiling, too high to get out the door.

"Oh, for the luvva—what do I do now?" he groaned. Spud shrugged helplessly. As they pondered, the doors slid closed and the car, in answer to some distant summons, began to rise rapidly. Joe dropped like an anvil, let out a howl as he struck the floor. "I'll sue," he gibbered, "I'll sue the bastard! Oh my kidneys! Oh my gut!"

"Oh my achin' back," Spud finished. "Now someone'll see us—I mean, you. Suppose they aren't stoned?" Joe was too involved in the novel sensation of internal bruising; it was up to Spud to think of something. He frowned—then smiled. Snatching the mashed derby from Joe's hand, he pushed the crown back out and placed the hat, upside-down, on the floor in front of Joe.

The door slid back at the third floor: a rotund matron with a face like an overripe grapefruit stepped into the car and then stopped short, wide-eyed. She went white, and then suddenly red with embarrassment.

"Oh, you poor man," she said sympathetically, averting her eyes, and dropped a five-dollar bill in the derby. "I never supported that war myself." She turned around and faced forward, pushing the button marked "L."

Barely in time, Spud leaped onto Joe's shoulders and threw up his hands. They hit the ceiling together with a muffled thud, clamping their teeth to avoid exclaiming. The stout lady kept up a running monologue about a cousin of hers who had also left in Vietnam some part of his anatomy which she was reluctant to name, muffling the sounds the two did make, and she left the elevator at the ground floor without looking back. "Good luck," she called over a brawny shoulder, and was gone.

Spud made a convulsive effort, heaved Joe a few feet down from the ceiling, and leaped from his shoulders toward the closing door. He landed on his belly, and the door closed on his hand, springing open again at once. It closed on his hand twice more before he had enough breath back to scream at Joe, who shook off his stupor and left the elevator, snatching up his derby and holding the door for Spud to emerge. The boy exited on his knees, cradling his hand and swearing.

Joe helped him up. "Sorry," he said apologetically. "I was afraid I'd step on ya."

"With WHAT?" Spud hollered.

"I *said* I was sorry, Spud. I just got shook up. Thanks for helping me out there. Look, I'll split this finnif with you . . ." A murderous glare from Spud cut him off. The boy held out his hand.

"Fork it over," he said darkly.

"Whaddya mean? She give it to me, didn't she?"

"I'll give it to you," Spud barked. "You say you're gonna make me rich, but all I've got so far is a stiff neck and a mashed hand. Come on, give—you haven't got a pocket to put it in anyway."

"I guess you're right, Spud," Joe decided. "I owe ya for the help. If a grownup saw me and found out about the belt, it'd probably cause a paradox or something, and I'd end up on a one-way trip to the Pleistocene. The temporal cops're pretty tough about that kind of stuff." He handed over the money, and Spud, mollified now, stuffed it into his pants and considered their next move. The lobby was still empty, but that could change at any moment.

"Look," he said finally, ticking off options on his fingers, "we can't take the subway—we'd cause a riot. Likewise the bus, and besides, we haven't got exact change. A Brooklyn cabbie *can't* be startled, but five bucks won't get us to the bridge. And we can't walk. So there's only one thing to do."

"What's that?"

"I'll have to clout a car."

Joe brightened. "I knew you'd think of something, kid. Hey, what do I do in the meantime?"

Spud considered. Between them and the curtained lobby-door, some interior decorator's horribly botched bonsai caught (or, more accurately, bushwhacked) his eye; it rose repulsively from a kind of enormous marble wastebasket filled with vermiculite, a good three feet high.

"Squat behind that," he said, pointing. "If anybody comes in, make out like you're tying your shoelace. If you hear the elevator behind you, go around the other side of it."

Joe nodded. "You know," he said, replacing his derby on his balding pink head, "I just thought. While we was upstairs at your place I shoulda grabbed something to wear that went down to the floor. Dumb. Well, I sure ain't goin' back.''

"It wouldn't do you any good anyway," Spud told him. "The only clothes we got like that are Mom's—you couldn't wear them."

Joe looked puzzled, and then light slowly dawned. "Oh yeah, I remember from my history class. This is a tight-ass era. Men couldn't wear dresses and women couldn't wear pants."

"Women can wear pants," Spud said, confused.

"That's right—I remember now. 'The Twilight of Sexual Inequality,' my teacher called it, the last days when women still oppressed men."

"I think you've got that backwards," Spud corrected.

"I don't *think* so," Joe said dubiously.

"I hope you're better at sports. Look, this is wasting time. Get down behind that cactus and keep your eyes open. I'll be back as soon as I can."

"Okay, Spud. Look, uh . . . Spud?" Joe looked sheepish. "Listen, I really appreciate this. I really do know about sports history. I mean, I'll see that you make out on this."

Spud smiled suddenly. "That's okay, Joe. You're too fat, and you're not very bright, but for some reason I like you. I'll see that you get fixed up." Joe blushed and stammered, and Spud left the lobby.

He pondered on what he had said, as with a small part of his attention, he set about stealing a car. It was funny, he thought as he pushed open an unlocked vent-window and snaked his slender arm inside to open the door—Joe was pretty dumb, all right, and he complained a lot, and he was heavier than a garbage can full of cement—but something about him appealed to Spud. *He's got guts*, the boy decided as he smashed the ignition and shorted the wires. *If I found myself in a strange place with no legs, I bet I'd freak out.* He gunned the engine to warm it up fast and tried to imagine what it must be like for Joe to walk around without being able to see where he was going—or rather, seeing where only part of him was going. The notion unsettled him; he decided that in Joe's place he'd be too terrified to move an inch. *And yet,* he reflected as he eased the car—a battered '59 Buick—from its parking space, *that big goon is going to try and make it all the way into Manhattan. Yeah, he's got guts.*

Or perhaps, it occurred to him as he double-parked in front of the door of his building, Joe simply didn't have the imagination to be afraid. *Well, in that case* somebody's *got to help him,* Spud decided, and headed for the opaquely-curtained front door, leaving the engine running. He had never read *Of Mice and Men,* but he had an intuitive conviction that it was the duty of the bright ones to keep the big dumb ones from getting into scrapes. His mother had often said as much of her late husband.

As he pushed open the door he saw Joe—or rather, what there was to see of Joe—bending over a prostrate young woman, tugging her dress off over her head.

"What the *hell* are you doing, you moron!" he screamed, leaping in through the door and slamming it behind him. "You trying to get us busted?"

Joe straightened, embarrassment on his round face. Since he retained his grip on the long dress, the girl's head and arms rose into the air and then fell with a thud as the dress came free. Joe winced. "I'm sorry, Spud," he pleaded. "I couldn't help it."

"What happened?"

"I couldn't help it. I tried to get behind the thing like you said, but there was a wall in the way—of my legs, I mean. So while I was tryin' ta think what to do this fem come in an' seen me an' just fainted. So I look at her for a

while an' I look at her dress an' I think: Joe, would you
rather people look at you funny, or would you rather be in
the Pleistocene? So I take the dress.'' He held it up; its
hem brushed the floor.

Spud looked down at the girl. She was in her late
twenties, apparently a prostitute, with long blonde hair and
a green headband. She wore only extremely small and
extremely loud floral print panties and a pair of sandals.
Her breasts were enormous, rising and falling as she
breathed. She was out cold. Spud stared for a long time.

"Hey," Joe said sharply. "You're only a kid. What're
you lookin' at?"

"I'm not sure," Spud said slowly, "but I got a feeling
I'll figure it out in a couple of years, and I'll want to
remember."

Joe roared with sudden laughter. "You'll do, kid." He
glanced down. "Kinda wish I had my other half along
myself." He shook his head sadly. "Well, let's get
going."

"Wait a minute, stupid," Spud snapped. "You can't
just leave her there. This is a rough neighbourhood."

"Well, what am I sposta do?" Joe demanded. "I don't
know which apartment is hers."

Spud's forehead wrinkled in thought. The laundry room?
No, old Mrs. Cadwallader always ripped off any clothes
left there. Leave the two of them here and go grab one of
Mom's housecoats? No good: either the girl would awaken
while he was gone or, with Joe's luck, a cop would walk
in. Probably a platoon of cops.

"Look," Joe said happily, "it fits. I thought it would—
she's almost as big on top as I am, an' it looked loose."
The $\frac{fat\ man}{2}$ had seemingly become an integer, albeit in drag.
Draped in paisley, he looked something like a psychedelic
priest and something like Henry the Eighth dressed for
bed. As Anne Boleyn might have done, Spud shuddered.

"Well," he said ironically, "at least you're not so conspicuous now."

"Yeah, that's what I thought," Joe agreed cheerfully. Spud opened his mouth, then closed it again. Time was short—someone might come in at any second. The girl still snored; apparently the bang on the head had combined with her faint to put her deep under. They simply couldn't leave her here.

"We'll have to take her with us," Spud decided.

"Hey," Joe said reproachfully.

"You got a better idea? Come on, we'll put her in the trunk." Grumbling, but unable to come up with a better idea, Joe picked the girl up in his beefy arms, headed for the door—and bounced off thin air, dropping her again.

Failing to find an obscenity he hadn't used yet, Spud sighed. He bent over the girl, got a grip on her, hesitated, got a different grip on her, and hoisted her over his shoulder. Panting and staggering, he got the front door open, peered up and down the street, and reeled awkwardly out to the waiting Buick. It took only a few seconds to smash open the trunk lock, but Spud hadn't realized they made seconds that long. He dumped the girl into the musty trunk with a sigh of relief, folding her like a cot, and looked about for something with which to tie the trunk closed. There was nothing useful in the trunk, nor the car itself, nor in his pockets. He thought of weighing the lid down with the spare tire and fetching something from inside the building, but she was lying on the spare, his arms were weary, and he was still conscious of the urgent need for haste.

Then he did a double-take, looked down at her again. He couldn't use the *sandals*, but . . .

As soon as he had fashioned the floral-print trunk latch (which took him a bit longer than it should have), he hurried back inside and pushed Joe to the car with the last of his strength. "I hope you can drive, Spud," Joe said brightly as they reached the curb. "*I* sure as hell can't."

Instead of replying, Spud got in. Joe lowered himself and sidled into the car, where he floated an eerie few inches from the seat. Spud put it in drive, and pulled away slowly. Joe sank deep in the seat-back, and the car behaved as if it had a wood-stove tied to the rear-bumper, but it moved.

Automobiles turned out to be something with which Joe was familiar in the same sense that Spud was familiar with biplanes, and he was about as comfortable with the reality as Spud would have been in the rear cockpit of a Spad (had Spud's Spad sped). A little bit of the Brooklyn-Queens Expressway was enough to lighten his complexion about two shades past albino. But he adapted quickly enough, and by the time the fifth homicidal psychopath had tried his level best to kill them (that is, within the first mile) he found his voice and said, with a fair imitation of diffidence, "I didn't think they'd decriminalized murder this early."

Spud gaped at him.

"Yeah," Joe said, seeing the boy's puzzlement. "Got to be too many people, an' they just couldn't seem to get a war going. That's why I put my life savings into this here cut-rate time-belt, to escape. I lost my job, so I became . . . Eligible. Just my luck I gotta get a lemon. Last time *I'll* ever buy hot merchandise."

Spud stared in astonishment, glanced back barely in time to foil the sixth potential assassin. "Won't the cops be after you for escaping?"

"Oh, you're welcome to escape, if you can. And if you can afford time-travel, you can become a previous administration's problem, so they're glad to see you go. You can only go backward into the past or return to when you started, you know—the future's impossible to get to.''

"How's that?" Spud asked curiously. Time-travel always worked both ways on television.

"Damifino. Somethin' about the machine can recycle reality but it can't create it—whatever that means."

Spud thought awhile, absently dodging a junkie in a panel truck. "So it's sort of open season on your legs back in 2007, huh?"

"I guess," said Joe uneasily. "Be difficult to identify 'em as mine, though. The pictures they print in the daily Eligibles column are always head shots, and they sure can't fingerprint me. I guess I'm okay."

"Hey," Spud said, slapping his forehead and the horn in a single smooth motion (scaring onto the shoulder a little old lady in a new Lincoln Continental who had just pulled onto the highway in front of them at five miles per hour), "it just dawned on me: what the hell *is* going on back in your time? I mean, there's a pair of legs wandering around in crazy circles, falling down stairs, right now they're probably standing still on a sidewalk or something . . ."

"Sitting," Joe interrupted.

". . . sitting on a sidewalk. So what's going on? Are you causing a riot back there or what?"

"I don't think so," Joe said, scratching his chin. "I left about three in the morning."

"Why then?"

"Well, I . . . I didn't want my wife to know I was goin'. I didn't tell her about the belt."

Spud started to nod—he wouldn't have told his mother. Then he frowned sharply. "You mean you left your wife back there to get killed? You . . ."

"No, kid, no!" Joe flung up his hands. "It ain't like you think. I was gonna come back here into the past and

make a bundle on the Series, and then go back to the same
moment I left and buy another belt for Alice. Honest, I
love my wife, dammit!''

Spud thought. "How much do you need?"

"For a good belt, made in Japan? Twenty grand, your
money. Which is the same in ours, in numbers, only we
call 'em Rockefellers instead of dollars.''

Spud whistled a descending arpeggio. "How'd you expect to win that kind of money? That takes a big stake, and
you said you sunk your savings in the belt.''

"Yeah," Koziack smiled, "but they terminate your
life-insurance when you go Eligible, and I got five thousand Rockies from that. I even remembered to change it to
dollars,'' he added proudly. "It's right . . .'' His face
darkened.

". . . here in your pocket,'' Spud finished. "Terrific.''
His eyes widened. "Hey, wait—you're in trouble!''

"Huh?"

"Your legs are back in 2007, sitting on the sidewalk,
right? So they're *creating reality*. Get it? They're making
future—you *can't* go back to the moment you left 'cause
time is going on after it already. So if you don't get back
soon, the sun'll come up and some blood-thirsty nut'll kill
your wife.''

Joe blanched. "Oh Jesus God,'' he breathed. "I think
you're right.'' He glanced at a passing sign, which read,
MANHATTAN—10 MILES. "Does this thing go any
. . . ulp . . . faster?''

The car leaped forward.

To his credit, Joe kept his eyes bravely open as Spud
yanked the car in and out of high-speed traffic, snaking
through holes that hadn't appeared to be there and doing
unspeakable things to the Buick's transmission. But Joe
was almost—almost—grateful when the sound of an ulu-

lating siren became audible over the snarling horns and screaming brakes.

Spud blanced in the mirror, located the whirling gumball machine in the rear-view mirror, and groaned aloud. "Just our luck! The cops—and us with only five bucks between us. Twelve years old, no license, a stolen car, a half a fat guy in a dress—cripes, even fifty bucks'd be cutting it close." Thinking furiously, he pulled over and parked on the grass, beneath a hellishly bright highway light. "Maybe I can go back and talk to them before they see you," he said to Joe, and began to get out.

"Wait, Spud!" Joe said urgently. He snatched a handful of cigarette butts from the ashtray, smeared black grime on Spud's upper lip. "There. Now you look maybe sixteen."

Spud grinned. "You're okay, Joe." He got out.

Twenty feet behind them, Patrolman Vitelli turned to his partner. "Freaks," he said happily. "Kids. Probably clouted the car, no license. Let me have it."

"Don't take a cent less than seventy-five," Patrolman Duffy advised.

"I dunno, Pat. They don't look like they got more than fifty to me."

"Well, all right," Duffy grumbled. "But I want an ounce of whatever they're smokin'. We're running low."

Vitelli nodded and got out of the black and white, one hand on his pistol. Spud met him halfway, and a certain lengthy ritual dialogue was held.

"Five bucks!" Vitelli roared. "You must be outa your mind."

"I wish I was," Spud said fervently. "Honest to God, it's all I got."

"How about your friend?" Vitelli said, and started for the Buick, which sat clearly illuminated in the pool of light beneath the arc-light.

"He's stone broke," Spud said hastily. "I'm takin' him to Bellevue—he thinks he may have leprosy."

Vitelli pulled up short with one hand on the trunk. "You got a license and registration?" he growled.

Spud's heart sank. "I . . ."

Vitelli nodded. "All right, buddy. Let's open the trunk."

Spud's heart bounced off his shoes and rocketed back up, lodging behind his palate. Seeing his reaction, Vitelli looked down at the trunk, noticing for the first time the odd nature of its fastening. He tugged experimentally, flimsy fabric parted, and the trunk lid rose.

Blinking at the light, the blonde hooker sat up stiffly, a muddy treadprint on her . . . person.

The air filled with the sound of screeching brakes.

Vitelli staggered back as if he'd been slapped with a sandbag. He looked from the girl to Spud to the girl to Spud, and his eyes narrowed.

"Oh, boy," he said softly. "Oh boy." He unholstered his gun.

"Look, officer, I can explain," Spud said without the least shred of conviction.

"Hey," said the blonde, clearly dazed.

"Holy shit," said Duffy in the squad car.

"Excuse me," said Joe, getting out of the Buick.

Both cops gasped as they caught sight of him, and Vitelli began to shake his head slowly. Seeing their expressions, the girl raised up onto her knees and peered around the trunk lid, completing the task of converting what had been three lanes of rushing traffic into a goggle-eyed parking lot.

"My dress," she yelped.

Koziack stood beside the Buick a little uncertainly, searching for words in all the likely places. "Oh shit," he said at last, and began to pull the dress over his head, removing the derby. "Pleistocene, here I come."

Vitelli froze. The gun dropped from his nerveless fingers; the hand stayed before him, index finger crooked.

"Tony," came a shaky voice from the squad car, "forget the ounce."

Spud examined the glaze in Vitelli's eyes and bolted for the car. "Come on," he screamed at Joe. The girl barely (I'm sorry, really) managed to jump from the trunk before the car sprang forward like a plane trying to outrun a bullet, lurching off the shoulder in front of a ten-mile traffic pileup that showed no slightest sign of beginning to start up again.

Behind them Vitelli still stood like a statue, imaginary gun still pointing at where Joe had been standing. Tears leaked from his unblinking eyes.

As the girl stared around her with widening eyes, car doors began to open.

Spud was thoroughly spooked, but he relaxed a good deal when the toll-booth attendant at the Brooklyn Bridge failed to show any interest in a twelve-year-old driving a car with the trunk wide open. Joe had the dress folded over where his lap should have been, and the attendant only changed the five and went back to his egg salad sandwich without comment.

"Where are we going?" Spud asked, speaking for the first time since they had left the two policemen and the girl behind.

Joe named a midtown address in the Forties.

"Great. How're we gonna get you from the car into the place?"

Joe chuckled. "Hey, Spud—this may be 1976, but Manhattan is Manhattan. Nobody'll notice a thing."

"Yeah, I guess you're right. What do you figure to do?"

Joe's grin atrophied. "Jeez, I dunno. Get the belt fixed first—I ain't thought about after that."

Spud snorted. "Joe, I think you're a good guy and I'm your pal, but if you didn't have a roof on your mouth, you'd blow your derby off every time you hiccuped. Look, it's simple: you get the belt fixed, you get both halves of you back together, and it's maybe ten o'clock, right?"

"If those goniffs at the dealership don't take too long fixin' the belt," Joe agreed.

"So you give me the insurance money, and use the belt to go a few months ahead. By that time, with the Series and the Bowl games and maybe a little Olympics action, we can split, say, fifty grand. You take your half and take the time-belt back to the moment your legs left 2007, at 10:01. You buy your wife a time-belt first thing in the morning and you're both safe."

"Sounds great," Joe said a little slowly, "but . . . uh . . ."

Spud glanced at him irritably. "What's wrong with it?" he demanded.

"I don't want you should be offended, Spud. I mean, you're obviously a tough, smart little guy, but . . ."

"Spit it out!"

"Spud, there is no way in the world a twelve-year-old kid is gonna take fifty grand from the bookies and keep it." Joe shrugged apologetically. "I'm sorry, but you know I'm right."

Spud grimaced and banged the wheel with his fist. "I'll go to a *lot* of bookies," he began.

"Spud, Spud, you get into that bracket, at your age, the word has just gotta spread. You *know* that."

The boy jammed on the brakes for a traffic light and swore. "Dammit, you're right."

Joe slumped sadly in his seat. "And I can't do it

myself. If I get caught bettin' on sports events of the past myself, it's the Pleistocene for me.''

Spud stared, astounded. ''Then how did you figure to accomplish *anything*?''

''Well . . .'' Joe looked embarrassed. ''I guess I thought I'd find some guy I could trust. I didn't think he'd be . . . so young.''

''A grownup you can *trust*? Joe, you really are a moron.''

''Well, I didn't have no choice, frag it. Besides, it might still work. How much do you think you *could* score, say, on one big event like the Series, if you hustled all the books you could get to?''

Twenty thousand, Spud thought, but he said nothing.

Joe had been right: the sight of half a fat man being dragged across the sidewalk by a twelve-year-old with ashes on his upper lip aroused no reaction at all in midtown Manhattan on a Friday night. One out-of-towner on his way to the theatre blinked a few times, but his attention was distracted almost immediately by a midget in a gorilla suit, wearing a sandwich sign advertising an off-off-off-Broadway play about bestiality. Spud and Joe reached their destination without commotion, a glass door in a group of six by which one entered various sections of a single building, like a thief seeking the correct route to the Sarcophagus Room of Tut's Tomb. The one they chose was labeled, ''Breadbody & McTwee, Importers,'' and opened on a tall stairway. Spud left Joe at the foot of the stairs and went to fetch assistance. Shortly he came back down with a moronic-looking pimply teen-ager in dirty green coveralls, ''Dinny'' written in red lace on his breast pocket.

''Be goddamn,'' Dinny said with what Joe felt was excessive amusement. ''Never seen anything like it. I thought this kid was nuts. Come on, let's go.'' Chuckling to himself, he helped Spud haul Joe upstairs to the shop. They brought him into a smallish room filled with oscilloscopes, signal generators, computer terminals, assorted unidentifiable hardware, tools, spare parts, beer cans, as-yet unpublished issues of *Playboy* and *Analog,* overflowing ashtrays, a muted radio, and a cheap desk piled with carbon copies of God only knew what. Dinny sat on a cigarette-scarred stool, still chuckling, and pulled down a reference book from an overhead shelf. He chewed gum and picked at his pimples as he thumbed through it, as though to demonstrate that he could do all three at once. It was clearly his showpiece. At last he looked up, shreds of gum decorating his grin, and nodded to Joe.

"If it's what I t'ink it is," he pronounced, "I c'n fix it. Got yer warranty papers?"

Joe nodded briefly, retrieved them from a compartment in the time-belt and handed them over. "How long will it take?"

"Take it easy," Dinny said unresponsively, and began studying the papers like an orangutan inspecting the Magna Carta. Joe curbed his impatience with a visible effort and rummaged in a nearby ashtray, selecting the longest butt he could find.

"Joe," Spud whispered, "how come that goof is the only one here?"

"Whaddya expect at nine thirty on a Friday night, the regional manager?" Joe whispered back savagely.

"I hope he knows what he's doing."

"Me too, but I can't wait for somebody better, dammit. Alice is in danger, and my legs've been using up my time for me back there. Besides, I've had to piss for the last hour-and-a-half."

Spud nodded grimly and selected a butt of his own. They smoked for what seemed like an interminable time in silence broken only by the rustling of paper and the sound of Dinny's pimples popping.

"Awright," the mechanic said at last, "the warranty's still good. Lucky you didn't come ta me a week from now."

"The speed you're goin', maybe I have," Joe snapped. "Come on, come on, will ya? Get me my legs back—I ain't got all night."

"Take it easy," Dinny said with infuriating glee. "You'll get your legs back. Just relax. Come on over inna light." Moving with sadistic slowness, he acquired a device that seemed something like a hand-held fluoroscope with a six-inch screen, and began running it around the belt. He stopped, gazed at the screen for a full ten seconds, and sucked his teeth.

"Sorry, mister," he drawled, straightening up and grinning. "I can't help you."

"What the hell are you talkin' about?" Joe roared.

"Somebody tampered with this belt, tried to jinx the override cutout so they could visit some Interdicted Period— probably wanted to see the Crucifixion or some other event that a vested-interest group got declared Off-Limits. I bet that's why it don't work right. It takes a specialist to work on one of these, you know." He smiled proudly, pleased with the last sentence.

"So you can't fix it?" Koziack groaned.

"Maybe yes, maybe no, but I ain't gonna try 'less I see some cash. That belt's been tampered with," Dinny said, relishing the moment. "The warranty's void."

Joe howled like a gutshot buffalo, and stepped forward. His meaty right fist traveled six inches from his shoulder, caught Dinny full in the mouth and dropped him in his tracks, popping the mechanic's upper lip and three pimples. "I'd stomp on ya if I could, ya smart-ass mugger-hugger," Joe roared down at the unconscious Dinny. "Think you're funny!"

"Easy, Joe," Spud yelled. "Don't get excited. We gotta *do* something."

"What the hell *can* we do?" Joe cried despairingly. "That crumb is the only mechanic in a hundred miles— we'll never get to the next one in time, and we haven't got a prayer anyway with four dollars and change. Crummy pap-lapper, I oughta . . . oh *damn* it." He began to cry.

"Hey, Joe," Spud protested, flustered beyond measure at seeing a sober grownup cry, "come on, take it easy. Come on now, cut it out." Joe, his face in his hands, shook his head and kept on sobbing.

Spud thought furiously, and suddenly a light dawned and he was filled with a strange prescience, a déjà vu kind of certainty that startled him with its intensity. He wasted no time examining it. Stepping close to Joe, he bent at the waist, swung from the hip, and kicked the belt as hard as he could, squarely on the spot Dinny had last examined. A sob became a startled yell—and Joe's fat legs appeared beneath him, growing downward from the belt like tubers.

"What the hell did you kick me for?" Joe demanded, glaring indignantly at Spud. "What'd I do to you?"

Spud pointed.

Joe looked down. "Wa-HOO!!" he shouted gleefully. "You *did* it, Spud, I got my legs back! Oh, Spud, baby, you're beautiful, *I got my legs back!*" He began to caper around the room in a spontaneous improvised goat-dance, knocking equipment crashing in all directions, and Spud danced with him, laughing and whooping and for the first time in this story looking his age. Together they careened like an improbable vaudeville team, the big fat man and the moustached midget, howling like fools.

At last they subsided, and Joe sat down to catch his breath. "Woo-ee," he panted, "what a break. Hey, Spud,

I really gotta thank you, honest to God. Look, I been thinkin'—you can't make enough from the bookies for both of us without stickin' your neck way out. So the hell with that, see? I'll give you the Series winner like I promised, but you keep all the dough. I'll figure out some other way to get the scratch—with the belt workin' again it shouldn't be too hard.''

Spud laughed and shook his head. "Thanks, Joe," he said. "That's really nice of you, and I appreciate it—but 'figuring out' isn't exactly your strong suit. Besides, I've been doing some thinking too. If I won fifty bucks shooting pool, that'd make me happy—I'd be proud, I'd've earned it. But to make twenty thousand on a fixed game with no gamble at all—that's no kick. You need the money—you take it, just like we planned. I'll see the bookies tonight.''

"But you earned it, kid," Joe said in bewilderment. "You went through a lotta work to get me here, and you fixed the belt.''

"That's all right," Spud insisted. "I don't want money—but there's one thing you *can* do for me.''

"Anything," Joe agreed. "As soon as I take a piss.''

Three hours later, having ditched the car and visited the home of "Odds" Evenwright, where he placed a large bet on a certain ball-club, Spud arrived home to find precisely what he had expected:

His mother, awesomely drunk and madder than hell, sitting next to the pool table on which his personal cue and balls still rested, waiting for him to come home.

"Hi, Mom," he said cheerfully as he entered the living room, and braced himself. With a cry of alcoholic fury, Mrs. Flynn lurched from her chair and began to close on him.

Then she pulled up short, realizing belatedly that her

son was accompanied by a stranger. For a moment, old reflex manners nearly took hold, but the drink was upon her and her Irish was up. "Are you the tramp who's been teachin' my Clarence to shoot pool, you tramp?" she screeched, shaking her fist and very nearly capsizing with the effort. "You fat bum, are you the one'sh been corrupting my boy?"

"Not me," Joe said politely, and disappeared.

"They ran out of pink elephants," he explained earnestly, reappearing three feet to the left and vanishing again.

"So I came instead," he went on from six feet to the right.

"Which is anyway novel," he finished from behind her, disappeared one last time and reappeared with his nose an inch from hers. Her eyes crossed, kept on crossing, and she went down like a felled tree, landing with the boneless grace of the totally stoned.

Spud giggled, and it was not an unsympathetic giggle. "Thanks, Joe," he said, slapping the $\frac{\text{fat man}}{1}$ on the back. "You've done me a big favour."

"Glad I could help, kid," Joe said, putting his own arm around the boy. "It must be tough to have a juicer for an old lady."

"Don't worry, Joe," Spud said, feeling that same unexplainable certainty he had felt at the time-belt repair shop. "Somehow I've got a feeling Mom has taken her last drink."

Joe nodded happily. "I'll be back after the Series," he said, "and we can always try a second treatment."

"Okay, but we won't have to. Now get out of here and get back to your wife—it's late."

Joe nodded again. "Sure thing, Spud." He stuck out his hand. "Thanks for everything, pal—I couldn't have made it without you. See you in a couple o' weeks and then, who knows—Alice an' I might just decide this era's the one we want to settle down in.''

''Not if you're smart,'' Spud said wryly.

''Well, in that case, maybe I'll be seein' ya again sometime,'' Joe pointed out. He reached down, making an adjustment on the time-belt, waved good-bye and vanished.

Or nearly. A pair of fat legs still stood in the living room, topped by the time-belt. As Spud stared, one of the legs stamped its feet in frustration and fury.

Sighing, Spud moved forward to kick the damned thing again.

High Infidelity

Ruby hung at the teetering edge of orgasm for as long as she could bear it, mewing with pleasure and with joy. Then control and consciousness spun away together: she clenched his hair with both hands, yanked in opposite directions, and went thundering over the edge. Her triumphant cry drowned out his triumphant growl; she heard neither. When the sweet explosion had subsided, she lay marinating in the afterglow, faintly surprised as always to be still alive. Her fingers toyed aimlessly with the curly hair they had just been yanking. The tongue at her clitoris gave one last, lazy lick, and a shudder rippled up her body. I am, she thought vaguely, a very lucky woman.

After a suitable time her husband lifted his head and smiled fondly up at her. "Who was I this time?" he asked.

"Sam Hamill," she said happily. "And you were terrific."

"My dear, your taste is as good as your taste is good," Paul Meade said.

She smiled. "Damn right. I married you, didn't I?"

"Was I in this one?"

"Watching from the doorway. Even bigger and harder than usual."

He climbed up her body. "Really?" She reached down to guide him into her, and he was even bigger and harder than usual. They both grinned at that, and gasped together as he slid inside. "I'll bet my eyes were the size of floppy disks."

"The old-fashioned big ones," she agreed. "Who can I be for you now?"

"Anonymous grateful groupie," he murmured in her ear, beginning to move his hips. "The Process saved your child's life, and you're thanking me as emphatically as you can."

If Ruby Meade had an insecurity, this was it. She knew that Paul got such offers—his work and his achievement made it inevitable—and she supposed that they must be uniquely hard to turn down. But she had trusted her husband utterly and implicitly for more than two decades now. "Oh, *doctor*," she said in an altered voice, and locked her legs around his familiar back. "Anything you want, doctor, any way you want me." She suggested some ways in which he might want her, and his tempo increased with each suggestion, and soon she no longer had the breath to speak. Automatically he covered both her ears, the way she liked him to, with his left cheek and his left hand, and dropped into third gear. When he was very close, he lifted his head up as he always did, replacing his cheek with his right hand, and murmured "Give me your tongue," and as always she gave him all the tongue she had, and he sucked it into his mouth with something just short of too much force as he galloped to completion. He roared as his sperm sprayed into her, and with the ease of long practice she brought her legs down under his and pointed her toes so that his last strokes could bring her off too.

I am, Ruby thought vaguely sometime later, an *especially* lucky woman.

Paul rolled off with his usual care and reached for his cigarettes. " 'They say,' " he sang softly, puffing one alight, " 'Ruby you're like a dream, not always what you seem . . .' "

"I love you too, baby."

They shared a warm smile, and then he pulled his eyes away. "I have to go to Zurich tomorrow," he said. "Be gone about a week, maybe a week and a half. They called while you were working."

"A *week*—?" she began, and caught herself.

"I know," he said, misunderstanding. "It's a long time. But it can't be helped. It seems they tried The Process over there with a donor *of the opposite sex*. Rather important official, and they didn't dare wait for another donor. I want to check it out—I expect it to be fascinating."

I am, Ruby thought, going to kill him.

"Besides," he said, "think how thirsty I'll be for you when I get home. And how thirsty you'll be for me."

"Yes," she said, her voice convincing, "that'll be nice."

"I'll be moving around a lot," he said, "but if you need to get hold of me in an emergency, just get in touch with Sam. He'll know where I am day to day."

"Okay," she said, thinking briefly that it would serve him right if she did. Get in touch with Sam. Paul's tendency toward automatic punning had, over the years, rubbed off on her. She was ashamed of the rogue thought at once, but her disappointment remained.

* * *

She examined that disappointment the next morning, over a cup of caff, after she had kissed him good-bye and sent him on his way.

It was not the trip itself she minded. He had been away for longer periods before, and would be again; the bio-physicist whose work had made brain-transplant a simple and convenient procedure would always be in demand, and he refused as many invitations as he possibly could. Nor did she envy him the trip; one of the reasons she had become a writer was that she *liked* squatting in her own cave, alone with her thoughts; most strange places and strange people made her uneasy. She was not truly jealous of his groupies either, not seriously—she knew that she would get the full benefit of whatever erotic charge he got from them. (Oh, anyone could be tempted beyond their ability to withstand . . . but she knew from long experience that Paul was wise enough and honest enough with himself not to get into such situations. He was much more likely to be mugged than seduced, and he had never been mugged.) Besides, she got propositions of her own in her fan mail.

No, it was the timing of the trip that gave her this terrible hollow-stomach feeling.

He had forgotten.

How *could* he forget? Next Monday, the eighteenth of July, 1999, was not only her forty-fifth birthday, but their twentieth anniversary.

To be sure, he had been busier this last year, since the news of his brain-stem matching process had become public knowledge, than ever before in their lives. His grasp on minutiae had begun to slip; he tended to be absent-minded at times now. Nonetheless, *he should have remembered*.

She finished her caff and looked at his going-away present. As was their custom when he went on a trip, they had given each other erotic videotapes; ''a little something to keep you company," was the ritual phrase. The one she had given him was a homemade job, featuring her in a nurse's uniform (at least at the outset), since she knew that nurses figured prominently in his fantasy life. Paul and Ruby had made a few erotic tapes together—most couples did nowadays—but somehow, from a vestige of old-fashioned shyness, perhaps, she had never made a solo tape for him until now. She had intended it for an anniversary present, one of several she had hidden away, and she resented a little not getting to see his reactions as he premièred it. But there had been no time to slip out to the store and pick up something else before his semiballistic had lifted for Zurich.

In fact, she had secretly hoped that he would express surprise at her having a present on hand for an unexpected trip, thereby forcing her to explain. But he truly was getting absent-minded, for he had simply thanked her for the gift and put it into his luggage.

She unwrapped his gift now. It was a thoughtful selection; from the still on the box-cover she could see that it starred an actress she liked, a woman who had the same general build, colouration, and hairstyle as Ruby, and generally seemed to share an interest in multiple partners. She would probably enjoy the tape—would probably *have* enjoyed it, rather, if it had been given to her on July eighteenth. Somehow that made it worse.

She tossed the tape into the back of a drawer, poured more caff, and went into her office to forget her resentment in work. Working on a novel always cheered her when she was down; her characters' problems always seemed so much more immediate and urgent than her own.

He'll remember, she thought just before sinking entirely into the warm glow of creation. Sometime between now and next Monday he'll see a calendar, or something will jog his memory, and boy will he be contrite when he calls! Why, he might even cancel and come right home.

But he did not call that night, or Friday night, or Saturday night, and by Sunday she had stopped believing that he would.

So she thought of calling him. But if she told him, reminded him of the date, she would spoil his trip. And if she didn't, she would hurt even more when she hung up. Besides, to contact Paul she would have to go through Sam Hamill, and if she called Sam he would want to come over and chat—Sam was a lonely divorcé—and a wise instinct told her not to spend time with a single man, about whom she had frequently fantasized, at a time when she was mad as hell at her absent husband. It was wisdom of the kind that had kept Paul and Ruby's marriage alive for twenty years.

So she took refuge in logic. My husband is a good and kind and considerate man who has dedicated himself to making me happy since 1979. He is as good and as successful in his profession as I am in mine. He is trustworthy and responsible. He is a gifted lover and a valued friend, and surely I cannot be so irrational as to stack up against all that something as trivial as a single memory-lapse, and I'm going to kill the son of a bitch if he hasn't called me in ten seconds, I swear I will.

Unfortunately, she finished her novel that afternoon.

Late that night she selected one of her favourite tapes, an "old reliable" that starred the actress who vaguely resembled her, and popped it into the deck. But halfway to her orgasm the tape reminded her of Paul's going-away gift, which reminded her of her gift to him and the warm glow in which it had been recorded, the happy expectation of sharing it with him on their anniversary. Suddenly, and for Ruby unusually, orgasm was unattainable. Shortly she gave up, popped the tape, and cried herself to sleep.

And of course the next day was Monday. She woke sad and stiff and horny in equal proportions, and her house had never seemed emptier. Three times before lunch she was strongly tempted to call him, once coming so close as to put on make-up preparatory to getting his number from Sam. But she could not. She thought of rereading the new book to see if it was any good, but knew she should give it a week to seep out of her short-term memory before tackling it. At four in the afternoon the phone rang and she ran the length of the house . . . to find that the call was from their son Tom in Luna City. He wanted to wish them both a happy anniversary and her a happy birthday, and he expressed great tactless surprise that Paul was away from home on this day of days. She loved Tom dearly, but he was no diplomat, and although she kept a cheerful mien through the conversation, she hung up in black depression. It had occurred to her briefly to have *Tom* call Paul, but it was not fair to involve the boy, and besides, he could not really afford a second interplanetary call. But an opportunity just out of reach is even worse than no opportunity at all.

Finally she decided that horniness was churning up her emotions unnecessarily. What she wanted, of course, was Paul, his lips and fingers and penis. She reckoned that the closest available substitute was to masturbate to the new tape he had given her. But her subconscious recalled her failure of the night before; she found herself taking the slidewalk to a pharmacy for a tube of Jumpstarts. It was a particularly hot day; the sun baked thoughts and feelings from her brain, and she was grateful to get back indoors again.

Ruby had never taken libido-enhancers in her life before, had never expected to need to. But she was in a

go-to-hell mood, she was forty-five and alone on her
anniversary, and she was determined to have herself a
good time if it killed her. She took two Jumpstarts from
the tube and washed them down with vodka. Then she got
the new tape and took it into the bedroom, whistling
softly. She stripped quickly. As she broke open the seal on
the tape box, the drug smacked her, suddenly and hard: the
hollow feeling in her stomach moved downward about a
third of a metre, and she felt herself smiling a smile that
Paul was going to regret having missed. She slid the tape
home into the slot, acutely conscious of the sexual meta-
phor therein, and rummaged in her night table for her
favourite vibrator, the one that strapped to her pubis and
left both hands free. As she finished putting it on, she
started to the window to polarize it. But when she was
halfway there the TV screen lit up with the tape's teaser,
and she stopped in her tracks. Her first impulse was to
laugh—when Paul heard about this, he would just die!
—which sparked her second impulse, to burst into tears,
but both of these were washed away in an elapsed time of
about half a second by her third impulse, which was to
switch on the vibrator and jump into bed. No, she corrected just in time, the other way round!

The actor who shared the screen with her doppelganger
was an unknown. Not only had she never seen him before,
the tape's producers had not seen fit to use his face on the
cover. Paul could not have known. But the resemblance
that the star bore to Ruby was nothing compared to the
resemblance that this rookie bore to Sam Hamill.

Jumpstart is a time-release drug. It keeps the user on a
rising crest of excitement for anywhere from a half hour to
an hour before it permits climax. The tape was perhaps
twenty minutes along, in the midst of an especially delicious scenario, when Ruby thought she heard a noise
outside her bedroom window. She cried out and tore her

eyes from the screen, and was not sure whether or not she caught a flicker of a head pulling away from view. At once she put the tape on pause and darkened the screen, her pulse hammering in her ears, and decided she should grab a robe and then phone the police. No, dammit, the other way round! Occasionally, the MD plates on the car in the garage attracted a junkie. She shut down the vibrator to hear better.

The front door chimed.

Awash in adrenalin, she grabbed her robe, got the family pistol and went to the door. She activated the camera—and this time she did burst out laughing. Standing on her doorstep, looking not in the least like a junkie or a man who had just been peering in a lady's bedroom window, was Sam.

Either the drug is making me hear things, she decided, or Sam scared him away. She safetied the pistol and put it aside, and activated the door mike. "Hi, Sam. What's up?"

"Hi, Ruby. Nothing much. Paul asked me to look in on you while he was away."

He did, did he? she thought, and without thinking about what she was doing she shrugged on the robe and let him in.

She had forgotten what she must look and smell like. As she cleared the door he raised his eyebrows and said, "Oh, I—uh, I hope I'm not . . . disturbing you."

She blushed and then recovered. "Not at all, Sam, really. What are you drinking?"

"Anything cold would be wonderful," he said gratefully. "I've been walking for hours. God, it's hot out there. Look, do you suppose I could use your shower before we get talking?"

"Of course. You know where it is. Wups—half a minute."

She went quickly to the bedroom, shut the door behind her, popped the tape and put it and its box under the bed. After a second's hesitation she took off the vibrator and put that under the bed too. Then she adjusted the air unit to sweep the musk from the room, opened the door, and told him to come ahead. She was dimly aware that she was on dangerous ground. But she heard herself say, "I'll bring you that drink," as he disappeared into the master bathroom.

She was back with the drink nearly at once. She saw her hand reach for the bathroom doorknob, and forced it to knock instead. "Here's a knock for you," she punned, and he reached out for the drink. "Thanks, Ruby." She glimpsed a third of his bare upper torso and kept her face straight with a great effort until the door had closed again. Then she stood there, wrestling with her thoughts, until she heard the shower start up. The urge to go through that door was nearly overwhelming.

Well, she thought, there's only one way to defuse this. She went to her bed and stretched out on it. She switched the TV to the movie channel with the sound suppressed. I'm perfectly safe until the water stops, she thought, and when it does I just turn the sound up and pull the robe over me. Between my hair-trigger and this damned drug, there should be plenty of time. Reassured, she parted the robe and began to masturbate furiously. Just a door away, she thought wildly, that's the closest I've been to really cheating since I wrecked my first marriage.

The bathroom door opened and he emerged, dripping wet, the shower still roaring behind him.

They both froze in shock. She could see each individual water droplet on his body with total clarity, could see her tiny reflection in half a hundred of them, dancing with reflected TV light. His hair was still mostly dry. His erection was rampant. There was a mole just below his left ribs. She knew she would never forget the sight of him as long as she lived. "Was there something you wanted?" she heard herself say.

It took him two tries to get his voice working. "I won't lie to you, Ruby. I was looking for your laundry hamper."

Her weirdness quotient had been exceeded long since. "My laundry hamper."

"I was jerking off in the shower, and suddenly I wanted something that smelled like you. I've wanted you for a long time, Ruby—you know that."

His penis twitched with his pulse. It had a different curve than Paul's. She spread her legs wide, and framed her vagina with her fingers. "Do you think this will smell enough like me, Sam?"

He came to her at once.

In the midst of it all, she momentarily regained enough rationality to be stunned at how good it was. One of the things that had helped her overcome the infrequent temptations of the last twenty years had been the awareness that on a purely physical level, no brief encounter with a stranger could ever be as satisfying as what she got from a husband who had devoted himself to a study of her body, of her likes and dislikes and her unique personal erogenous zones. Why, the logic went, risk all that for a seven-second spasm that was bound to be inferior? As Paul liked to say, familiarity breeds content.

She had failed, she now saw, to allow for the possibility of telepathy. Or rather, for the possibility that telepathy might come to pass between two people who had not spent years working on it. Sam seemed to sense her desires almost before she did, or else miraculously had precisely dovetailing desires of his own. Nor was he catering to her; there was a delicious selfishness in the way he plundered her.

She revelled in the *newness* of him, glorified in the discovery of hair where she was not accustomed to finding any, of bones and muscles knit together in unfamiliar ways, of an unmistakably differently shaped penis, a mouth that tasted different. She had always known that variety was sweet, but in the more than two decades since she had foresworn it she had not thought she missed it. Now it enraptured her. And there was an extra fillip to her joy, for she had only had two other Caucasians in her life, and one of those a woman, and the straight hair snarled in her fingers now was a sweet mystery. For the first time in her life she came with her legs up in the air, and clawed deep tracks in his back without knowing it.

When she could see and hear and think again, she realized that he was still in her, still hard, still thrusting. All at once she was horrified at herself and what she had done. It was in her mind to expel him and roll away, to stop short at least of that one final symbolic infidelity, the acceptance of someone else's sperm. She wanted to do so very much. But she could not do it to Sam—poor, dear Sam, who had not asked to be involved in her problems, and had gone too far to stop now. She saw that she must, for her honour, do her very best to bring him off, and then send him home and never never never be alone with him again.

Which gave it all a sort of bittersweet poignance that, after a short time, was startlingly erotic—she felt herself being caught up again in the passion she was dutifully trying to fake. His knowing hands caressed her flanks, came up to knead her breasts against his chest, slid up her throat to her hair. Her breath came in noisy gulps, and she knew she was getting close again. His hands left her hair then and curled over both her ears, a split second after he murmured "Give me your tongue," and automatically she did and as he sucked it hard between his lips and came like gangbusters her eyes opened wide as they could go and looked into his from a distance of a few centimetres. His eyes were sparkling. She clutched at the top of his head and felt where the scalp flap had been resutured, and as his hands came away from her ears and went down to push her legs out straight beneath him, she heard him whisper into her open mouth, "Happy Annibirthary, darling—Sam said to give you his best," and her heart—there is no other way to say it—came.

Antinomy

The first awakening was just awful.

She was naked and terribly cold. She appeared to be in a plastic coffin, from whose walls grew wrinkled plastic arms with plastic hands that did things to her. Most of the things hurt dreadfully. *But I don't have nightmares like this*, she thought wildly. She tried to say it aloud, and it came out, "A."

Even allowing for the sound-deadening coffin walls, the voice sounded distant. "Christ, she's awake already."

Eyes appeared over hers, through a transparent panel she had failed to see since it had showed only a ceiling the same colour as the coffin's interior. The face was masked and capped in white, the eyes pouched in wrinkles. *Marcus Welby. Now it makes enough sense. Now I'll believe it. I* don't *have nightmares like this.*

"I believe you're right." The voice was professionally detached. A plastic hand selected something that lay by her side, pressed it to her arm. "There."

Thank you, Doctor. If my brain doesn't want to remember what you're operating on me for, I don't much suppose it'll want to record the operation itself. Bye.

She slept.

The second awakening was better.

She was astonished not to hurt. She had expected to hurt, somewhere, although she had also expected to be too dopey to pay it any mind. Neither condition obtained.

She was definitely in a hospital, although some of the gadgetry seemed absurdly ultramodern. *This certainly isn't Bellevue,* she mused. *I must have contracted something fancy. How long has it been since I went to bed "last night"?*

Her hands were folded across her belly; her right hand held something hard. It turned out to be a traditional nurse-call buzzer—save that it was cordless. Lifting her arm to examine it had told her how terribly weak she was, but she thumbed the button easily—it was not spring loaded. "*Nice* hospital," she said aloud, and her voice sounded too high. *Something with my throat? Or my ears? Or my . . . brain?*

The buzzer might be improved, but the other end of the process had not changed appreciably; no one appeared for a while. She awarded her attention to the window beside her, no contest in a hospital room, and what she saw through it startled her profoundly.

She *was* in Bellevue, after all, rather high up in the new tower; the rooftops below her across the street and the river beyond them told her that. But she absorbed the datum almost unconsciously, much more startled by the policeman who was flying above those rooftops, a few hundred feet away, in an oversize garbage can.

Yep, my brain. The operation was a failure, but the patient lived.

For a ghastly moment there was a great abyss within her,

into which she must surely fall. But her mind had more strength than her body. She willed the abyss to disappear, and it did. *I may be insane, but I'm not going to go nuts over it,* she thought, and giggled. She decided the giggle was a healthy sign, and did it again, realizing her error when she found she could not stop.

It was mercifully shorter than such episodes usually are; she simply lost the strength to giggle. The room swam for a while, then, but lucidity returned rather rapidly.

Let's see. Time travel, huh? That means . . .

The door opened to admit—not a nurse—but a young man of about twenty-five, five years her junior. He was tall and somehow self-effacing. His clothes and appearance did not strike her as conservative, but she decided they probably were—for this era. He did not look like a man who would preen more than convention required. He wore a sidearm, but his hand was nowhere near the grip.

"What year is this, anyway?" she asked as he opened his mouth, and he closed it. He began to look elated and opened his mouth again, and she said, "And what did I die of?" and he closed it again. He was silent then for a moment, and when he had worked it out she could see that the elation was gone.

But in its place was a subtler, more personal pleasure. "I congratulate you on the speed of your uptake," he said pleasantly. "You've just saved me most of twenty minutes of hard work."

"The hell you say. I can deduce what *happened*, all right, but that saves you twenty seconds, max. 'How' and 'why' are going to take just as long as you expected. And don't forget 'when.' " Her voice still seemed too high, though less so.

"How about 'who'? I'm Bill McLaughlin."

"I'm Marie Antoinette, *what the hell year is it?*" The italics cost her the last of her energy; as he replied "1998," his voice faded and the phosphor dots of her vision began to enlarge and drift apart. She was too bemused by his answer to be annoyed.

Something happened to her arm again, and picture and sound returned with even greater clarity. "Forgive me, Ms. Harding. The first thing I'm supposed to do is give you the stimulant. But then the first thing you're supposed to do is be semiconscious."

"And we've dispensed with the second thing," she said, her voice normal again now, "which is telling me that I've been a corpsicle for ten years. So tell me why, and why I don't *remember* any of it. As far as I know I went to sleep last night and woke up here, with a brief interlude inside something that must have been a defroster."

"I thought you *had* remembered, from your first question. I hoped you had, Ms. Harding. You'd have been the first . . . never mind—your next question made it plain that you don't. Very briefly, ten years ago you discovered that you had leukemia . . ."

"Myelocytic or lymphocytic?"

"Neither. Acute."

She paled. "No wonder I've suppressed the memory."

"You haven't. Let me finish. Acute Luke was the diagnosis, a new rogue variant with a bitch's bastard of a prognosis. In a little under sixteen weeks they tried corticosteroids, L-aspiraginase, cytosine arabinoside, massive irradiation, and mercrystate crystals, with no more success than they'd expected, which was none and negatory. They told you that the new bone-marrow transplant idea showed great promise, but it might be a few years. And so you elected to become a corpsicle. You took another few weeks arranging your affairs and then went to a Cold Sleep Centre and had yourself frozen."

"*Alive?*"

"They had just announced the big breakthrough. A

week of drugs and a high-helium atmosphere and you can defrost a living person instead of preserved meat. You got in on the ground floor.''

''And the catch?''

''The process scrubs the top six months to a year off your memory.''

''Why?''

''I've been throwing around terminology to demonstrate how thoroughly I've read your file. But I'm not a doctor. I don't understand the alleged 'explanation' they gave me, and I dare say you won't either.''

''Okay.'' She forgot the matter, instantly and forever. ''If you're not a doctor, who are you, Mr. McLaughlin?''

''Bill. I'm an Orientator. The phrase won't be familiar to you—''

''—but I can figure it out, Bill. Unless things have slowed down considerably since I was alive, ten years is a hell of a jump. You're going to teach me how to dress and speak and recognize the ladies' room.''

''And hopefully to stay alive.''

''For how long? Did they fix it?''

''Yes. A spinal implant, right after you were thawed. It released a white-cell antagonist into your blood-stream, and it's triggered by a white-cell surplus. The antagonist favours rogue cells.''

''Slick. I always liked feedback control. Is it foolproof?''

''Is anything? Oh, you'll need a new implant every five years, and you'll have to take a week of chemotherapy here to make sure the implant isn't rejected before we can let you go. But the worst side-effect we know of is partial hair-loss. You're fixed, Ms. Harding.''

She relaxed all over, for the first time since the start of the conversation. With the relaxation came a dreamy feeling, and she knew she had been subtly drugged, and was pleased that she had resisted it, quite unconsciously, for as long as had been necessary. She disliked don't-worry drugs; she preferred to worry if she had a mind to.

"Virginia. Not Ms. Harding. And I'm pleased with the Orientator I drew, Bill. It will take you awhile to get to the nut, but you haven't said a single inane thing yet, which under the circumstances makes you a remarkable person."

"I like to think so, Virginia. By the way, you'll doubtless be pleased to know that your fortune has come through the last ten years intact. In fact, it's actually grown considerably."

"There goes your no-hitter."

"Beg pardon?"

"Two stupid statements in one breath. First, of *course* my fortune has grown. A fortune the size of mine can't *help* but grow—which is one of the major faults of our economic system. What could be sillier than a goose that insists on burying you in golden eggs? Which leads to number two: I'm anything but pleased. I was hoping against hope that I was broke."

His face worked briefly, ending in a puzzled frown. "You're probably right on the first count, but I think the second is ignorance rather than stupidity. I've never been rich." His tone was almost wistful.

"Count your blessings. And be grateful you can count that high."

He looked dubious. "I suppose I'll have to take your word for it."

"When do I start getting hungry?"

"Tomorrow. You can walk now, if you don't overdo it, and in about an hour you'll be required to sleep."

"Well, let's go."

"Where to?"

"Eh? *Outside*, Bill. Or the nearest balcony or solarium. I haven't had a breath of fresh air in ten years."

"The solarium it is."

As he was helping her into a robe and slippers the door chimed and opened again, admitting a man in the time-honoured white garb of a medical man on duty, save that the stethoscope around his neck was cordless as the call-buzzer had been. The pickup was doubtless in his breast pocket, and she was willing to bet that it was warm to the skin.

The newcomer appeared to be a few years older than she, a pleasant-looking man with grey-ribbed temples and plain features. She recognized the wrinkled eyes and knew he was the doctor who had peered into her plastic coffin.

McLaughlin said, "Hello, Dr. Higgins. Virginia Harding, Dr. Thomas Higgins, Bellevue's Director of Cryonics."

Higgins met her eyes squarely and bowed. "Ms. Harding. I'm pleased to see you up and about."

Still has the same detached voice. Stuffy man. "You did a good job on me, Dr. Higgins."

"Except for a moment of premature consciousness, yes, I did. But the machines say you weren't harmed psychologically, and I'm inclined to believe them."

"They're right. I'm some tough."

"I know. That's why I brought you up to Level One Awareness in a half-day instead of a week. I knew your subconscious would fret less."

Discriminating machines, she thought. *I don't know that I like that.*

"Doctor," McLaughlin cut in, "I hate to cut you off, but Ms. Harding has asked for fresh air, and—"

"—and has less than an hour of consciousness left today. I understand. Don't let me keep you."

"Thank you, Doctor," Virginia Harding said. "I'd like to speak further with you tomorrow, if you're free."

He almost frowned, caught himself. "Later in the week, perhaps. Enjoy your walk."

"I shall. Oh, how I shall. Thank you again."

"Thank Hoskins and Parvati. They did the implant."

"I will, tomorrow. Good-bye, Doctor."

She left with McLaughlin, and as soon as the door had closed behind them, Higgins went to the window and slammed his fist into it squarely, shattering the shatter-proof glass and two knuckles. Shards dropped thirty long stories, and he did not hear them land.

McLaughlin entered the office and closed the door.

Higgins's office was not spare or austere. The furnishings were many and comfortable, and in fact the entire room had a lived-in air which hinted that Higgins's apartment might well be spare and austere. Shelves of books covered two walls; most looked medical and all looked used. The predominant colour of the room was black—not at all a fashionable colour—but in no single instance was the black morbid, any more than is the night sky. It gave a special vividness to the flowers on the desk, which were the red of rubies, and to the profusion of hand-tended plants which sat beneath the broad east window (now opaqued) in a riotous splash of many colours for which our language has only the single word "green." It put crisper outlines on anything that moved in the office, brought both visitors and owner into sharper relief.

But the owner was not making use of this sharpening of perception at the moment. He was staring fixedly down at his desk; precisely, in fact, at the empty place where a man will put a picture of his wife and family if he has them. He could not have seen McLaughlin if he tried; his eyes were blinded with tears. Had McLaughlin not seen them, he might have thought the other to be in an autohyp-notic trance or a warm creative fog, neither of which states were unusual enough to call for comment.

Since he did see the tears, he did not back silently out of

the office. "Tom." There was no response. "Tom," he
said again, a little louder, and then "TOM!"

"Yes?" Higgins said evenly, sounding like a man talking on an intercom. His gaze remained fixed, but the
deep-set wrinkles around it relaxed a bit.

"She's asleep."

Higgins nodded. He took a bottle from an open drawer
and swallowed long. He didn't have to uncap it first, and
there weren't many swallows that size left. He set it,
clumsily, on the desk.

"For God's sake, Tom," McLaughlin said half-angrily.
"You remind me of Monsieur Rick in *Casablanca*. Want
me to play 'As Times Goes By' now?"

Higgins looked up for the first time, and smiled
beatifically. "You might," he said, voice steady. " 'You
must remember this . . . as times goes by.' " He smiled
again. "I often wonder." He looked down again, obviously forgetting McLaughlin's existence.

Self-pity in this man shocked McLaughlin, and cheerful
self-pity disturbed him profoundly. "Jesus," he said harshly.
"That bad?" Higgins did not hear. He saw Higgins's hand
then, with its half-glove of bandage, and sucked air through
his teeth. He called Higgins's name again, elicited no
reaction at all.

He sighed, drew his gun and put a slug into the ceiling.
The roar filled the office, trapped by sound-proofing. Higgins started violently, becoming fully aware just as his
own gun cleared the holster. He seemed quite sober.

"Now that I've got your attention," McLaughlin said
dryly, "would you care to tell me about it?"

"No." Higgins grimaced. "Yes and no. I don't suppose
I have much choice. She didn't remember a thing." His
voice changed for the last sentence; it was very nearly a
question.

"No, she didn't."

"None of them have yet. Almost a hundred awakenings, and not one remembers anything that happened more than ten to twelve months before they were put to sleep. And still somehow I hoped . . . I had hope . . ."

McLaughlin's voice was firm. "When you gave me her file, you said 'used to know her,' and that you didn't want to go near her 'to avoid upsetting her.' You asked me to give her special attention, to take the best possible care of her, and you threw in some flattery about me being your best Orientator. Then you come barging into her room on no pretext at all, chat aimlessly, break your hand and get drunk. So you loved her. And you loved her in the last year."

"I diagnosed her leukemia," Higgins said emotionlessly. "It's hard to miss upper abdomen swelling and lymph node swelling in the groin when you're making love, but I managed for weeks. It was after she had the tooth pulled and it wouldn't stop bleeding that . . ." He trailed off.

"She loved you too."

"Yes." Higgins's voice was bleak, hollow.

"Bleeding Christ, Tom," McLaughlin burst out. "Couldn't you have waited to . . ." He broke off, thinking bitterly that Virginia Harding had given him too much credit.

"We tried to. We knew that every day we waited decreased her chances of surviving cryology, but we tried. She insisted that we try. Then the crisis came . . . oh damn it, Bill, *damn* it."

McLaughlin was glad to hear the profanity—it was the first sign of steam blowing off. "Well, she's alive and healthy now."

"Yes. I've been thanking God for that for three months now, ever since Hoskins and Parvati announced the unequivocal success of spinal implants. I've thanked God over ten thousand times, and I don't think He believed me once. I don't think *I* believed me once. Now doesn't that make me a selfish son of a bitch?''

McLaughlin grinned. ''Head of Department and you live like a monk, because you're selfish. For years, every dime you make disappears down a hole somewhere, and everybody wonders why you're so friendly with Hoskins & Parvati, who aren't even in your own *department*, and only now, as I'm figuring out where the money's been going, do I realize what a truly selfish son of a bitch you are, Higgins.''

Higgins smiled horribly. ''We talked about it a lot, that last month. I wanted to be frozen too, for as long as they had to freeze her.''

''What would that have accomplished? Then neither of you would have remembered.''

''But we'd have entered and left freeze at the *same time,* and come out of it with sets of memories that ran nearly to the day we met. We'd effectively be precisely the people who fell in love once before; we could have left notes for ourselves and the rest would've been inevitable. But she wouldn't hear of it. She pointed out that the period in question could be any fraction of forever, with no warranty. I insisted, and got quite histrionic about it. Finally she brought up our age difference.''

''I wondered about the chronology.''

''She was thirty, I was twenty-five. Your age. It was something we kidded about, but it stung a bit when we did. So she asked me to wait five years, and then if I still wanted to be frozen, fine. In those five years I clawed my way up to head of section here, because I wanted to do everything I could to ensure her survival. And in the fifth year they thought her type of leukemia might be curable with marrow transplants, so I hung around for the two years it took to be sure they were wrong. And in the eighth year Hoskins started looking for a safe white-cell antago-

nist, and again I had to stay room temperature to finance
him, because nobody else could smell that he was a
genius. When he met Parvati, I knew they'd lick it, and I
told myself that if they needed me, that meant she needed
me. I wasn't wealthy like her—I had to keep working to
keep them both funded properly. So I stayed."

Higgins rubbed his eyes, then made his hands lie very
still before him, left on right. "Now there's a ten-year
span between us, the more pronounced because she hasn't
experienced a single minute of it. Will she love me again
or won't she?" The bandaged right hand escaped from the
left, began to tap on the desk. "For ten years I told myself
I could stand to know the answer to that question. For ten
years it was the last thing I thought before I fell asleep and
the first thing I thought when I woke up. *Will she love me
or won't she?*

"She made me promise that I'd tell her everything when
she was awakened, that I'd tell her how our love had been.
She swore that she'd love me again. I promised, and she
must have known I lied, or suspected it, because she left a
ten-page letter to herself in her file. The day I became
Department Head I burned the fucking thing. I don't want
her to love me because she thinks she should.

"Will she love me or won't she? For ten years I believed I could face the answer. Then it came time to wake
her up, and I lost my nerve. I couldn't stand to know the
answer. I gave her file to you.

"And then I saw her on the monitor, heard her voice
coming out of my desk, and I knew I couldn't stand *not* to
know."

He reached clumsily for the bottle, and knocked it clear
off the desk. Incredibly, it contrived to shatter on the thick
black carpet, staining it a deeper black. He considered
this, while the autovac cleaned up the glass, clacking in
disapproval.

"Do you know a liquor store that delivers?"

"In *this* day and age?" McLaughlin exclaimed, but Higgins was not listening. "Jesus Christ," he said suddenly. "Here." He produced a flask and passed it across the desk.

Higgins looked him in the eye. "Thanks, Bill." He drank.

McLaughlin took a long swallow himself and passed it back. They sat in silence for a while, in a communion and a comradeship as ancient as alcohol, as pain itself. Synthetic leather creaked convincingly as they passed the flask. Their breathing slowed.

If a clock whirs on a deskface and no one is listening, is there really a sound? In a soundproof office with opaqued windows, is it not always night? The two men shared the long night of the present, forsaking past and future, for nearly half an hour, while all around them hundreds upon hundreds worked, wept, smiled, dozed, watched television, screamed, were visited by relatives and friends, smoked, ate, died.

At last McLaughlin sighed and studied his hands. "When I was a grad student," he said to them, "I did a hitch on an Amerind reservation in New Mexico. Got friendly with an old man named Wanoma, face like a map of the desert. Grandfather-grandson relationship—close in that culture. He let me see his own grandfather's bones. He taught me how to pray. One night the son of a nephew, a boy he'd had hopes for, got alone-drunk and fell off a motorcycle. Broke his neck. I heard about it and went to see Wanoma that night. We sat under the moon—it was a harvest moon—and watched a fire until it was ashes. Just after the last coal went dark, Wanoma lifted his head and cried out in Zuni. He cried out, 'Ai-yah, my heart is full of sorrow.' "

McLaughlin glanced up at his boss and took a swallow. "You know, it's impossible for a white man to say those

words and not sound silly. Or theatrical. It's a simple
statement of a genuine universal, and there's no way for a
white man to say it. I've tried two or three times since.
You can't say it in English.''

Higgins smiled painfully and nodded.

''I cried out too,'' McLaughlin went on, ''after Wanoma
did. The English of it was, 'Ai-yah, my brother's heart is
full of sorrow. His heart is my heart.' Happens I haven't
ever tried to say that since, but you can see it sounds
hokey too.''

Higgins's smile became less pained, and his eyes lost
some of their squint. ''Thanks, Bill.''

''What'll you do?''

The smile remained. ''Whatever I must. I believe I'll
take the tour with you day after tomorrow. You can use
the extra gun.''

The Orientator went poker-faced. ''Are you up to it,
Tom? You've got to be fair to her, you know.''

''I know. Today's world is pretty crazy. She's got a
right to integrate herself back into it without tripping over
past karma. She'll never know. I'll have control on Thursday, Bill. Partly thanks to you. But you do know why I
selected you for her Orientator, don't you?''

''No. I don't think I do.''

''I thought you'd at least have suspected. Personality
Profiles are a delightful magic. Perhaps if we ever develop
a science of psychology we'll understand why we get
results out of them. According to the computer, your PP
matches almost precisely to my own—of ten years ago.
Probably why we get along so well.''

''I don't follow.''

''Is love a matter of happy accident or a matter of
psychological inevitability? Was what 'Ginia and I had
fated in the stars, or was it a chance of jigsawing of
personality traits? Will the woman she was ten years ago

love the man I've become? Or the kind of man I was then? Or some third kind?''

"Oh, fine," McLaughlin said, getting angry. "So I'm your competition."

"Aha," Higgins pounced. "You do feel something for her."

"I . . ." McLaughlin got red.

"You're my competition," Higgins said steadily. "And, as you have said, you are my brother. Would you like another drink?''

McLaughlin opened his mouth, then closed it. He rose and left in great haste, and when he had gained the hallway he cannoned into a young nurse with red hair and improbably grey eyes. He mumbled apology and continued on his way, failing to notice her. He did not know Deborah Manning.

Behind him, Higgins passed out.

Throughout the intervening next day Higgins was conscious of eyes on him. He was conscious of little enough else as he sleepwalked through his duties. The immense hospital complex seemed to have been packed full of grey Jello, very near to setting. He ploughed doggedly through it, making noises with his mouth, making decisions, making marks on pieces of paper, discharging his responsibilities with the least part of his mind. But he was conscious of the eyes.

A hospital grapevine is like no other on earth. If you want a message heard by every employee, it is quicker to tell two nurses and an intern than it would be to assemble the staff and make an announcement. Certainly McLaughlin had said nothing, even to his hypothetical closest friend; he knew that any closest friend has at least one *other* closest friend. But at least three OR personnel knew that the Old Man had wakened one personally the other day.

And a janitor knew that the Old Man was in the habit of dropping by the vaults once a week or so just after the start of the graveyard shift, to check on the nonexistent progress of a corpsicle named Harding. And the OR team and the janitor worked within the same (admittedly huge) wing, albeit on different floors. So did the clerk-typist in whose purview were Virginia Harding's files, and she was engaged to the anesthetist. Within twenty-four hours, the entire hospital staff and a majority of the patients had added two and two.

(Virginia Harding, of course, heard nary a word, got not so much as a hint. A hospital staff may spill Mercurochrome. It often spills blood. But it never spills beans.)

Eyes watched Higgins all day. And so perhaps it was natural that eyes watched him in his dreams that night. But they did not make him afraid or uneasy. Eyes that watch oneself continuously become, after a time, like a second ego, freeing the first from the burden of introspection. They almost comforted him. They helped.

I have been many places, touched many lives since I touched hers, he thought as he shaved the next morning, *and been changed by them. Will she love me or won't she?*

There were an endless three more hours of work to be taken care of that morning, and then at last the Jello dispersed, his vision cleared and she was before him, dressed for the street, chatting with McLaughlin. There were greetings, explanations of some sort were made for his presence in the party, and they left the room, to solve the mouse's maze of corridors that led to the street and the city outside.

It was a warm fall day. The streets were unusually crowded, with people and cars, but he knew they would not seem so to Virginia. The sky seemed unusually overcast, the air particularly muggy, but he knew it would seem otherwise to her. The faces of the pedestrians they passed seemed to him markedly cheerful and optimistic, and he felt that this was a judgement with which she *would* agree. This was not a new pattern of thought for him. For over five years now, since the world she knew had changed enough for him to perceive, he had been accustomed to observe that world in the light of what she would think of it. Having an unconscious standard of comparison, he had marked the changes of the last decade more acutely than his contemporaries, more acutely perhaps than even McLaughlin, whose interest was only professional.

Too, knowing her better than McLaughlin, he was better able to anticipate the questions she would ask. A policeman went overhead in a floater bucket, and McLaughlin began to describe the effects that force-fields were beginning to exert on her transportation holdings and other financial interests. Higgins cut him off before she could, and described the effects single-person flight was having on social and sexual customs, winning a smile from her and a thoughtful look from the Orientator. When McLaughlin began listing some of the unfamiliar gadgetry she could expect to see, Higgins interrupted with a brief sketch of the current state of America's spiritual renaissance. When McLaughlin gave her a personal wrist-phone, Higgins showed her how to set it to refuse calls.

McLaughlin had, of course, already told her a good deal about Civil War Two and the virtual annihilation of the American black, and had been surprised at how little surprised she was. But when, now, he made a passing reference to the unparalleled savagery of the conflict, Higgins saw a chance to make points by partly explaining that bloodiness with a paraphrase of a speech Virginia herself had made ten years before, on the folly of an urban-renewal package concept which had sited low-income housing immediately around urban and suburban transportation hubs. "Built-in disaster," she agreed approvingly, and did not feel obliged to mention that the same thought had occurred to her a decade ago. Higgins permitted himself to be encouraged.

But about that time, as they were approaching one of the new downtown parks, Higgins noticed the expression on McLaughlin's face, and somehow recognized it as one he had seen before—from the inside.

At once he was ashamed of the fatuous pleasure he had been taking in outmanoeuvring the younger man. It was a cheap triumph, achieved through unfair advantage. Higgins decided sourly that he would never have forced this "duel with his younger self" unless he had been just this smugly sure of the outcome, and his self-esteem dropped sharply. He shut his mouth and resolved to let McLaughlin lead the conversation.

It immediately took a turning he could not have followed if he tried.

As the trio entered the park, they passed a group of teen-agers. Higgins paid them no mind—he had long since reached the age when adolescents, especially in groups, regarded him as an alien life form, and he was nearly ready to agree with them. But he noticed Virginia Harding noticing them, and followed her gaze.

The group was talking in loud voices, the incomprehensible gibberish of the young. There was nothing Higgins could see about them that Harding ought to find striking. They were dressed no differently than any one of a hundred teen-agers she had passed on the walk so far, were quite nondescript. Well, now that he looked closer, he saw rather higher-than-average intelligence in most of the faces. Honour-student types, down to the carefully cultivated look of aged cynicism. That *was* rather at variance with the raucousness of their voices, but Higgins still failed to see what held Harding's interest.

"What on earth are they saying?" she asked, watching them over her shoulder as they passed.

Higgins strained, heard only nonsense. He saw McLaughlin grinning.

"They're Goofing," the Orientator said.

"Beg pardon?"

"Goofing. The very latest in sophisticated humour."

Harding still looked curious.

"It sort of grew out of the old Firesign Theater of the seventies. Their kind of comedy laid the ground-work for the immortal Spiwack, and he created Goofing, or as he called it, speaking with spooned tongue. It's a kind of double-talk, except that it's designed to actually convey information, more or less in spite of itself. The idea is to *almost* make sense, to get across as much of your point as possible without ever saying anything comprehensible."

Higgins snorted, afraid.

"I'm not sure I understand," Harding said.

"Well, for instance, if Spiwack wanted to publicly libel, say, the president, he'd Goof. Uh . . ." McLaughlin twisted his voice into a fair imitation of a broken-down prizefighter striving to sound authoritative. "That guy there, see, in my youth we would of referred to him as a man with a tissue-paper asshole. What you call a kinda guy that sucks blueberries through a straw, see? A guy like what would whistle at a doorknob, you know what I mean? He ain't got all his toes."

Harding began to giggle. Higgins began sweating, all over.

"I'm tellin' ya, the biggest plum *he's* got is the one under his ear, see what I'm sayin'? If whiskers was pickles, he'd have a goat. First sign of saddlebags an' he'll be under his pants. If I was you I'd keep my finger out of *his* nose, an' you can forget I said so. Good night."

Harding was laughing out loud now. "That's marvellous!'' A spasm shook her. "That's the most . . . *con-spicuous* thing I've ever baked." McLaughlin began to laugh. "I've never been so identified in all my shoes." They were both laughing together now, and Higgins had about four seconds in which to grab his wrist-phone behind his back and dial his own code, before they could notice him standing there and realize they had left him behind and become politely apologetic, and he just made it, but even so he had time in which to reflect that a shared belly-laugh can be as intimate as making love. *It may even be a prerequisite,* he thought, and then his phone was humming its A-major chord.

The business of unclipping the earphone and fiddling with the gain gave him all the time he needed to devise an emergency that would require his return, and he marvelled at his lightning cleverness that balked at producing a joke. He really tried, as he spoke with his nonexistent caller, prolonging the conversation with grunts to give himself time. When he was ready he switched off, and in his best W.C. Fields voice said, "It appears that one of my clients has contracted farfalonis of the blowhole," and to his absolute horror they both said "Huh?" together and then got it, and in that moment he hated McLaughlin more than he had ever hated anything, even the cancer that had come sipping her blood a decade before. *Keep your face straight,* he commanded himself savagely. *She's looking at you.*

And McLaughlin rescued the moment, in that split second before Higgins's control would have cracked, doing his prizefighter imitation. "Aw Jeez, Tom, that's hard cider. If it ain't one thing, it's two things. Go ahead; we'll keep your shoes warm."

Higgins nodded. "Hello, Virginia."

"Gesundheit, Doctor," she said, regarding him oddly.

He turned on his heel to go, and saw the tallest of the group of teen-agers fold at the waist, take four rapid steps backward and fall with the boneless sprawl of the totally drunk. *But drunks don't spurt red from their bellies*, Higgins thought dizzily, just as the flat *crack* reached his ears.

Mucker!

Eyes report: a middle-aged black man with three days' growth of beard, a hundred metres away and twenty metres up in a stolen floater bucket with blood on its surface. Firing a police rifle of extremely heavy calibre with snipersights. Clearly crazed with grief or stoned out of control, he is not making use of the sights, but firing from the hip. His forehead and cheek are bloody and one eye is ruined: some policeman sold his floater dearly.

Memory reports: It has been sixteen weeks since the Treaty of Philadelphia officially "ended" C.W. II. Nevertheless, known-dead statistics are still filtering slowly back to next-of-kin; the envelope in his breast pocket looks like a government form letter.

Ears report: Two more shots have been fired. Despite eyes' report, his accuracy is hellish—each shot hit someone. Neither of them is Virginia.

Nose reports: All three (?) wounded have blown all sphincters. Death, too, has its own smell, as does blood. The other one: is that fear?

Hand reports: Gun located, clearing holster . . . now. Safety off, barrel coming up fast.

WHITE OUT!

The slug smashed into Higgins's side and spun him completely around twice before slamming him to earth beside the path. His brain continued to record all sensory reports, so in a sense he was conscious; but he would not audit these memories for days, so in a sense he was unconscious too. His head was placed so that he could see Virginia Harding, in a sideways crouch, extend her gun and fire with extreme care. McLaughlin stood tall before her, firing rapidly from the hip, and her shot took his right earlobe off. He screamed and dropped to one knee.

She ignored him and raced to Higgins's side. "It looks all right, Tom," she lied convincingly. She was efficiently taking his pulse as she fumbled with his clothing. "Get an ambulance," she barked at someone out of vision. Whoever it was apparently failed to understand the archaism, for she amended it to "A doctor, dammit. *Now,*" and the whip of command was in her voice. As she turned back to Higgins, McLaughlin came up with a handkerchief pressed to his ear.

"You got him," he said weakly.

"I know," she said, and finished unbuttoning Higgins's shirt. Then, *"What the hell did you get in my way for?"*

"I . . . I," he stammered, taken aback. "I was trying to protect *you.*"

"From a rifle like *that?*" she blazed. "If you got between one of those slugs and me all you'd do is tumble it for me. Blasting away from the hip like a cowboy . . ."

"I was trying to spoil his aim," McLaughlin said stiffly.

"You bloody idiot, you can't scare a kamikaze! The only thing to do was drop him, fast."

"I'm sorry."

"I nearly blew your damn head off."

McLaughlin began an angry retort, but about then even Higgins's delayed action consciousness faded. The last sensation he retained was that of her hands gently touching his face. That made it a fine memory-sequence, all in all, and when he reviewed it later on he only regretted not having been there at the time.

All things considered, McLaughlin was rather lucky. It took him only three days of rather classical confusion to face his problem, conceive of several solutions, select the least drastic, and persuade a pretty nurse to help him put it into effect. But it was after they had gone to his apartment and gone to bed that he really got lucky; his penis flatly refused to erect.

He of course did not, at that time, think of this as a stroke of luck. He did not know Deborah Manning. He in fact literally did not know her last name. She had simply walked past at the right moment, a vaguely-remembered face framed in red hair, grey eyes improbable enough to stick in the mind. In a mood of go-to-hell desperation he had baldly propositioned her, as though this were still the promiscuous seventies, and he had been surprised when she accepted. He did not know Debbie Manning.

In normal circumstances he would have considered his disfunction trivial, done the gentlemanly thing and tried again in the morning. In the shape he was in it nearly cracked him. Even so, he tried to be chivalrous, but she pulled him up next to her with a gentle firmness and looked closely at him. He had the odd, inexplicable feeling that she had been . . . *prepared* for this eventuality.

He seldom watched people's eyes closely—popular opinion and literary convention to the contrary, he found people's mouths much more expressive of the spirit within. But something about her eyes held his. Perhaps it was that they were not trying to. They were staring only for information, for a deeper understanding . . . he realized with a start that they were looking at his mouth. For a moment he started to *look* back, took in clean high cheeks and soft lips, was beginning to genuinely notice her for the first time when she said "Does she know?" with just the right mixture of tenderness and distance to open him up like a clam.

"No," he blurted, his pain once again demanding his attention.

"Well, you'll just have to tell her then," she said earnestly, and he began to cry.

"I can't," he sobbed, "I *can't*."

She took the word at face value. Her face saddened. She hugged him closer, and her shoulder blades were warm under his hands. "That *is* terrible. What is her name, and how did it come about?"

It no more occurred to him to question the ethics of telling her than it had occurred to him to wonder by what sorcery she had identified his brand of pain in the first place, or to wonder why she chose to involve herself in it. Head tucked in the hollow between her neck and shoulder, legs wrapped in hers, he told her everything in his heart. She spoke only to prompt him, keeping her *self* from his attention, and yet somehow what he told her held more honesty and truth than what he had been telling himself.

"He's been in the hospital for three days," he concluded, "and she's been to visit him twice a day—and she's begged off our Orientation Walks every damn day. She leaves word with the charge nurse."

"You've tried to see her anyway? After work?"

"No. I can read print."

"Can't you read the print on your own heart? You don't seem like a quitter to me, Bill."

"Dammit," he raged, "I don't *want* to love her, I've tried *not* to love her, and I can't get her out of my head."

She made the softest of snorting sounds. "You will be given a billion dollars if in the next ten seconds you do *not* think of a green horse." Pause. "You know better than that."

"Well, how do you get someone out of your head, then?"

"Why do you want to?"

"Why? Because . . ." he stumbled. "Well, this sounds silly in words, but . . . I haven't got the right to her. I mean, Tom has put literally his whole life into her for ten years now. He's not just my boss—he's my friend, and if he wants her that bad he ought to have her.''

"She's an object, then? A prize? He shot more tin ducks, he wins her?''

"Of course not. I mean he ought to have his *chance* with her, a fair chance, without tripping over the image of himself as a young stud. He's *earned* it. Dammit, I . . . this sounds like ego, but I'm unfair competition. What man can compete with his younger self?''

"Any man who has grown as he aged,'' she said with certainty.

He pulled back—just far enough to be able to see her face. "What do you mean?'' He sounded almost petulant.

She brushed hair from her face, freed some that was trapped between their bodies. "Why did Dr. Higgins rope you into this in the first place?''

He opened his mouth and nothing came out.

"He may not know,'' she said, "but his subconscious does. Yours does too, or you wouldn't be so damfool guilty.''

"What are you talking about?''

"If you *are* unfair competition, he does not deserve her, and I don't care how many years he's dedicated to her sacred memory. Make up your mind: are you crying because you can't have her or because you could?'' Her voice softened suddenly—took on a tone which only his subconscious associated with that of a father confessor from his Catholic youth. "Do you honestly believe in your heart of hearts that you could take her away from him if you tried?''

Those words could certainly have held sting, but they did not somehow. The silence stretched, and her face and gaze held a boundless compassion that told him that he must give her an answer, and that it must be the truth.

"I don't know,'' he cried, and began to scramble from

the bed. But her soft hands had a grip like iron—and there was nowhere for him to go. He sat on the side of the bed, and she moved to sit beside him. With the same phenomenal strength, she took his chin and turned his face to see hers. At the sight of it he was thunderstruck. Her face seemed to glow with a light of its own, to be somehow *larger* than it was, and with softer edges than flesh can have. Her neck muscles were bars of tension and her face and lips were utterly slack; her eyes were twin tractor beams of incredible strength locked on his soul, on his attention.

"Then you have to find out, don't you?" she said in the most natural voice in the world.

And she sat and watched his face go through several distinct changes, and after a time she said "Don't you?" again very softly.

"Tom is my friend," he whispered bleakly.

She released his eyes, got up and started getting dressed. He felt vaguely that he should stop her, but he could not assemble the volition. As she dressed, she spoke for the first time of herself. "All my life people have brought problems to me," she said distantly. "I don't know why. Sometimes I think I attract pain. They tell me their story as though I had some wisdom to give them, and along about the time they're restating the problem for the third time they tell me what they want to hear; and I always wait a few more paragraphs and then repeat it back to them. And they light right up and go away praising my name. I've gotten used to it."

What do I want to hear? he asked himself, and honestly did not know.

"One man, though . . . once a man came to me who had been engaged to a woman for six years, all through school. They had gotten as far as selecting the wallpaper for the house. And one day she told him she felt a Vocation. God had called her to be a nun." Debbie pulled red hair out from under her collar and swept it back with both hands, glancing at the mirror over a nearby bureau. "He was a devout Catholic himself. By his own rules, *he couldn't even be sad*. He was supposed to rejoice." She rubbed at a lipstick smear near the base of her throat. "There's a word for that, and I'm amazed at how few people know it, because it's the word for the sharpest tragedy a human can feel. 'Antinomy.' It means, 'contradiction between two propositions which seem equally urgent and necessary.' " She retrieved her purse, took out a pack of Reefer and selected one. "I didn't know what in hell's name to tell that man," she said reflectively, and put the joint back in the pack.

Suddenly she turned and confronted him. "I still don't, Bill. *I* don't know which one of you Virginia would pick in a fair contest, and I don't know what it would do to Dr. Higgins if he *were* to lose her to you. A torch that burns for ten years must be awfully hot." She shuddered. "It might just have burned him to a crisp already.

"But you, on the other hand: I would say that you could get over her, more or less completely, in six months. Eight at the outside. If that's what you decide, I'll come back for you in . . . oh, a few weeks. You'll be ready for me then." She smiled gently, and reached out to touch his cheek. "Of course . . . if you do that . . . you'll never know, will you?" And she was gone.

Five minutes later he jumped up and said, "Hey wait!" and then felt very foolish indeed.

Virginia Harding took off her headphones, switched off the stereo, and sighed irritably. Ponty's bow had just been starting to really smoke, but the flood of visual imagery it evoked had been so intolerably rich that involuntarily she had opened her eyes—and seen the clock on the far wall. The relaxation period she had allowed herself was over.

Here I sit, she thought, *a major medical miracle, not a week out of the icebox and I'm buried in work. God, I hate money.*

She could, of course, have done almost literally anything she chose; had she requested it, the president of the hospital's board of directors would happily have dropped whatever he was doing and come to stand by her bedside and turn pages for her. But such freedom was too crushing for her to be anything but responsible with it.

Only the poor can afford to goof off. I can't even spare the time for a walk with Bill. Dammit, I still owe him an apology too. She would have enjoyed nothing more than to spend a pleasant hour with the handsome young Orientator, learning how to get along in polite society. But business traditionally came before pleasure, and she had more pressing duties. A fortune such as hers represented the life energy of many many people; as long as it persisted in *being* hers, she meant to take personal responsibility for it. It had been out of her direct control for over a decade, and the very world of finance in which its power inhered had changed markedly in the interim. She was trying to absorb a decade at once—and determined to waste no time. A powered desk with computer-bank inputs had been installed in her hospital room, and the table to the left of it held literally hundreds of microfloppy disks, arranged by general heading in eight caddies and chronologically within them. The table on the right held the half-carton she had managed to review over the last five days. She had required three one-hour lectures by an earnest, aged specialist-synthesist to understand even that much. She had *expected* to encounter startling degrees and kinds of change, but this was incredible.

Another hour and a half on the Delanier-Garcia Act,

she decided, *half an hour of exercise, lunch and those damnable pills, snatch ten minutes to visit Tom and then let the damned medicos poke and prod and test me for the rest of the afternoon. Supper if I've the stomach for any, see Tom again, then back to work. With any luck I'll have 1987 down by the time I fall asleep. God's teeth.*

She was already on her feet, her robe belted and slippers on. She activated the intercom and ordered coffee, crossed the room and sat down at the desk, which began to hum slightly. She lit its monitor screen, put the Silent Steno on standby and was rummaging in the nearest caddy for her next disk when a happy thought struck her. Perhaps the last disk in the box would turn out to be a summary. She pulled it out and fed it to the desk, and by God it was—it appeared to be an excellent and thorough summary at that. *Do you suppose,* she asked herself, *that the last disk in the last box would be a complete overview? Would Charlesworthy & Cavanaugh be that thoughtful? Worth a try. God, I need some shortcuts.* She selected that disk and popped the other, setting it aside for later.

The door chimed and opened, admitting one of her nurses—the one whose taste in eyeshadow was abominable. He held a glass that appeared to contain milk and lemon juice half and half with rust flakes stirred in. From across the room it smelled bad.

"I'm sorry," she said gravely. "Even in a hospital you can't tell me that's a cup of coffee."

"Corpuscle paint, Ms. Harding," he said cheerfully. "Doctor's orders."

"Kindly tell the doctor that I would be obliged if he would insert his thumb, rectally, to the extent of the first joint, pick himself up and hold himself at arm's length until I drink that stuff. Advise him to put on an overcoat first, because hell's going to freeze over in the meantime. And speaking of hell, where *in* it is my coffee?"

"I'm sorry, Ms. Harding. No coffee. Stains the paint—you don't want tacky corpuscles."

"*Dammit . . .*"

"Come on, drink it. It doesn't taste as bad as it smells. Quite."

"Couldn't I take it intravenously or something? Oh Christ, give it to me." She drained it in a single gulp and shivered, beating her fists on her desk in revulsion. "God. God. God. Damn. Can't I just have my leukemia back?"

His face sobered. "Ms. Harding—look, it's none of my business, but if I was you, I'd be a little more grateful. You give those lab boys a hard time. You've come back literally from death's door. Why don't you be patient while we make sure it's locked behind you?"

She sat perfectly still for five seconds, and then saw from his face that he thought he had just booted his job out the window. "Oh Manuel, I'm sorry. I'm not angry. I'm . . . astounded. You're right, I haven't been very gracious about it all. It's just that, from my point of view, as far as *I* remember, I never *had* leukemia. I guess I resent the doctors for trying to tell me that I ever was that close to dying. I'll try and be a better patient." She made a face. "But God, that stuff tastes ghastly."

He smiled and turned to go, but she called him back. "Would you leave word for Bill McLaughlin that I won't be able to see him until tomorrow after all?"

"He didn't come in today," the nurse said. "But I'll leave word." He left, holding the glass between thumb and forefinger.

She turned back to her desk and booted the new disk, but did not open it. Instead she chewed her lip and fretted. *I wonder if I was as blasé last time. When they told me I had it. Are those memories gone because I want them to be?*

She knew perfectly well that they were not. But anything that reminded her of those missing six months upset her. She could not reasonably regret the bargain she had made, but almost she did. Theft of her memories struck her as the most damnable invasion of privacy, made her very flesh crawl, and it did not help to reflect that it had been done with her knowledge and consent. From her point of view it had *not*; it had been authorized by another person who had once occupied this body, now deceased, by suicide. A life shackled to great wealth had taught her that her memories were the *only* things uniquely hers, and she mourned them, good, bad, or indifferent. Mourned them more than she missed the ten years spent in freeze: she had not *experienced* those.

She had tried repeatedly to pin down exactly what was the last thing she could remember before waking up in the plastic coffin, and had found the task maddeningly difficult. There were half a dozen candidates for last-remembered-day in her memory, none of them conveniently cross-referenced with time and date, and at least one or two of those appeared to be false memories, cryonic dreams. She had the feeling that if she had tried immediately upon awakening, she would have remembered, as you can sometimes remember last night's dream if you try at once. But she had been her usual efficient self, throwing all her energies into adapting to the new situation.

Dammit, I want those memories back! I know I swapped six months for a lifetime, but at that rate it'll be five months and twenty-five days before I'm even breaking even. I think I'd even settle for a record of some kind—if only I'd had the sense to start a diary!

She grimaced in disgust at the lack of foresight of the dead Virginia Harding, and opened the data-disk with an angry gesture. And then she dropped her jaw and said, "Jesus Christ in a floater bucket!"

The screen read, "PERSONAL DIARY OF VIRGINIA HARDING."

If you have never experienced major surgery, you are probably unfamiliar with the effects of three days of morphine followed by a day of Demerol. Rather similar results might be obtained by taking a massive dose of LSD-25 while hopelessly drunk. Part of the consciousness is fragmented . . . and part expanded. Time-sense and durational perception go all to hell, as do coordination, motor skills, and concentration—and yet often the patient, turning inward, makes a quantum leap toward a new plateau of self-understanding and insight. Everything seems suddenly clear: structures of lies crumble, hypocrisies are stripped naked, and years' worth of comfortable rationalizations collapse like cardboard kettles, splashing boiling water everywhere. Perhaps the mind reacts to major shock by reassessing, with ruthless honesty, everything that has brought it there. Even Saint Paul must have been close to something when he found himself on the ground beside his horse, and Higgins had the advantage of being colossally stoned.

While someone ran an absurd stop-start, variable-speed movie in front of his eyes, comprised of doctors and nurses and I.V. bottles and bedpans and blessed pricks on the arm, his mind's eye looked upon himself and pronounced him a fool. His stupidity seemed so massive, so transparent in retrospect that he was filled with neither dismay nor despair, but only with wonder.

My God, it's so obvious! *How could I have had my eyes so tightly shut? Choking up like that when they started to Goof, for Christ's sake—do I need a neon sign? I used to have a sense of humour—if there was anything Ginny and I had in common it was a gift for repartee—and after ten years of "selfless dedication" to Ginny and leukemia and keeping the money coming that's exactly what I haven't got anymore and I damned well know it. I've shriveled up like a raisin, an ingrown toenail of a man.*

I've been a zombie for ten mortal years, telling myself that neurotic monomania was a Great And Tragic Love, trying to cry loud enough to get what I wanted. The only friend I made in those whole ten years was Bill, and I didn't hesitate to use him when I found out our PPs matched. I knew bloody well that I'd grown smaller instead of bigger since she loved me, and he was the perfect excuse for my ego. Play games with his head to avoid overhauling my own. I was going to lose, I knew I was going to lose, and then I was going to accidentally "let slip" the truth to her, and spend the next ten years bathing in someone else's pity than my own. What an incredible, impossible, histrionic fool I've been, like a neurotic child saying, "Well, if you won't give me the candy I'll just smash my hand with a hammer."

If only I hadn't needed her so much when I met her. Oh. I must find some way to set this right, as quickly as possible!

His eyes clicked into focus, and Virginia Harding was sitting by his bedside in a soft brown robe, smiling warmly. He felt his eyes widen.

"Dilated to see you," he blurted and giggled.

Her smile disappeared. "Eh?"

"Pardon me. Demerol was first synthesized to wean Hitler off morphine; consequently, I'm Germanic-depressive these days." *See? The ability is still there. Dormant, atrophied, but still there.*

The smile returned. "I see you're feeling better."

"How would you know?"

It vanished again. "What are you talking about?"

"I know you're probably quite busy, but I expected a visit before this." *Light, jovial—keep it up, boy.*

"Tom Higgins, I have been here twice a day ever since you got out of OR."

"What?"

"You have conversed with me, lucidly and at length, told me funny stories and discussed contemporary politics with great insight, as far as I can tell. You don't remember."

"Not a bit of it." He shook his head groggily. *What did I say? What did I tell her?* "That's incredible. That's just incredible. You've been here . . ."

"Six times. This is the seventh."

"My God. I wonder where *I* was. This is appalling."

"Tom, you may not understand me, but I know precisely how you feel."

"Eh?" *That made you jump.* "Oh yes, your missing six months." *Suppose sometime in my last three days we had agreed to love each other forever—would that still be binding now?* "God, what an odd sensation."

"Yes, it is," she agreed, and something in her voice made him glance sharply at her. She flushed and got up from her bedside chair, began to pace around the room. "It might not be so bad if the memories just stayed *completely* gone . . ."

"What do you mean?"

She appeared not to hear the urgency in his voice. "Well, it's nothing I can pin down. I . . . I just started wondering. Wondering why I kept visiting you so regularly. I mean, I like you—but I've been so damned busy I haven't had time to scratch, I've been missing sleep and missing meals, and every time visiting hours opened up I stole ten minutes to come and see you. At first I chalked it off to a not unreasonable feeling that I was in your debt—not just because you defrosted me without spoiling anything, but because you got shot trying to protect me too. There was a rock outcropping right next to you that would have made peachy cover."

"I . . . I . . ." he sputtered.

"That felt right," she went on doggedly, "but not entirely. I felt . . . I *feel* something else for you, something I don't understand. Sometimes when I look at you, there's . . . there's a feeling something like déjà vu, a vague feeling that there's something between us that I don't know. I know it's crazy—you'd surely have told me by now—but did I ever know you? Before?"

There it is, tied up in pink ribbon on a silver salver. You're a damned fool if you don't reach out and take it. In a few days she'll be out of this mausoleum and back with her friends and acquaintances. Some meddling bastard will tell her sooner or later—do it now, while there's still a chance. You can pull it off: you've seen your error—now that you've got her down off the damn pedestal you can give her a mature love, you can grow tall enough to be a good man for her, you can do it right this time.

All you've got to do is grow ten years' worth overnight.

"Ms. Harding, to the best of my knowledge I never saw you before this week." *And that's the damn truth.*

She stopped pacing, and her shoulders squared. "I told you it was crazy. I guess I didn't want to admit that all those memories were completely gone. I'll just have to get used to it I suppose."

"I imagine so." *We both will.* "Ms. Harding?"

"Yes?"

"Whatever the reasons, I do appreciate your coming to see me, and I'm sorry I don't recall the other visits, but right at the moment my wound is giving me merry hell. Could you come back again, another time? And ask them to send in someone with another shot?"

He failed to notice the eagerness with which she agreed. When she had gone and the door had closed behind her, he lowered his face into his hands and wept.

*   *   *

Her desk possessed a destruct unit for the incineration of confidential reports, and she found that it accepted unerasable disks. She was just closing the lid when the door chimed and McLaughlin came in, looking a bit haggard. "I hope I'm not intruding," he said.

"Not at all, come in," she said automatically. She pushed the *burn* button, felt the brief burst of heat, and took her hand away. "Come on in, Bill, I'm glad you came."

"They gave me your message, but I . . ." He appeared to be searching for words.

"No, really, I changed my plans. Are you on call tonight, Bill? Or otherwise occupied?"

He looked startled. "No."

"I intended to spend the night reading these damned reports, but all of a sudden I feel an overwhelming urge to get stinking drunk with someone—no." She caught herself and looked closely at him, seemed to see him as though for the first time. "No, by God, to get stinking drunk with *you*. Are you willing?"

He hesitated for a long time.

"I'll go out and get a bottle," he said at last.

"There's one in the closet. Bourbon okay?"

Higgins was about cried out when his own door chimed. Even so, he nearly decided to feign sleep, but at the last moment he sighed, wiped his face with his sleeves, and called out, "Come in."

The door opened to admit a young nurse with high cheeks, soft lips, vivid red hair, and improbably grey eyes.

"Hello, nurse," he said. He did not know her either. "I'm afraid I need something for pain."

"I know," she said softly, and moved closer.

In the Olden Days

George Maugham returned home from work much later than usual, and in a sour frame of mind. He was tired and knew that he had missed an excellent home-cooked meal, and things had not gone well at work despite his extra hours of labour. His face, as he came through the door, held that expression that would cause his wife to become especially understanding.

"Light on in the kids' window," he said crankily as he hung his coat by the door and removed his boots. "It's late."

Luanna Maugham truly was an extraordinary woman. With only a minimal use of her face and the suggestion of a shrug and the single word "Grandpa," she managed to convey amusement and irony and compassion and tolerant acceptance, and thereby begin diffusing his potential grumpiness. He felt the last of it bleed from him as she put into his hands a cup of dark sweetness which he knew perfectly well would turn out to be precisely drinking temperature. He understood how much she did for him.

But he still felt that he should follow up the issue of their children's bedtime. "I wish he wouldn't keep them up so late," he said, pitching his voice to signal his altered motivation.

"Well," she said, "they can sleep in tomorrow morning— no school. And he does tell fairy tales *so* well, dear."

"It's not the fairy tales I mind," he said, faintly surprised to feel a little of his irritation returning. "I just hope he's not filling their heads with all that other garbage." He sipped from his cup, which was indeed the right temperature. "All those hairy old stories of his. About the Good Old Days When Men Were Men and Women Knew Their Place." He shook his head. Yes, he was losing his good humour again.

"Why do his stories bother you so?" she asked gently. "Honestly, they seem pretty harmless to me."

"I think all that old stuff depresses them. Nightmares and that sort of thing. Confuses them. Boring, too, the same old stuff over and over again."

Mrs. Maugham did *not* point out that their two children never had nightmares, or permitted themselves to be bored. She made, in fact, no response at all, and after a sufficient pause, he shook his head and continued speaking, more hesitantly. "I mean . . . there's something about it I can't . . ." He glanced down at his cup, and perhaps he found there the words he wanted. He sipped them. "Here it is: if the Good Old Days were so good, then I and my generation were fools for allowing things to change—then the world that *we* made is inferior—and I don't think it is. I mean, every generation of kids grows up convinced that their parents are idiots who've buggered everything up, don't they, and I certainly don't want or need *my* father encouraging the kids to feel that way." He wiped his lip with the heel of his hand. "I've worked hard, all my life, to make this a better world than the one I was born into, and . . . and it is, Lu, it *is*."

She took his face in her hands, kissed him, and bathed him in her very best smile. "Of course it is," she lied.

"And that," Grandpa was saying just then, with the warm glow of the storyteller who knows he has wowed 'em again, "is the story of how Princess Julie rescued the young blacksmith Jason from the Dark Tower, and together they slew the King of the Dolts." He bowed his head and began rolling his final cigarette of the night.

The applause was, considering the size of the house, gratifying. "That was really neat, Grandpa," Julie said enthusiastically, and little Jason clapped his hands and echoed, "Really neat!"

"Now, tomorrow night," he said, and paused to lick his cigarette paper, "I'll tell you what happened *next*."

"Oh God, yes," Julie said, smacking her forehead, "the Slime Monster, I forgot, he's still loose."

"The Slime Monster!" Jason cried. "But that's my favourite *part*! Grampa tell *now*."

"Oh yes, please, Grampa," Julie seconded. In point of fact, she was not really all that crazy about the Slime Monster—he was pretty yucky—but now he represented that most precious commodity any child can know: a few minutes more of after-bedtime awakeness.

But the old man had been braced for this. "Not a chance, munchkins. Way past your bedtimes, and your folks'll—"

A chorus of protests rained about his head.

"Can it," he said, in the tone that meant he was serious, and the storm chopped off short. He was mildly pleased by this small reflection of his authority, and he blinked, and when his eyes opened Julie was holding out the candle to light his cigarette for him, and little Jason was inexpertly but enthusiastically trying to massage the right knee which, he knew (and occasionally remembered), gave Grandpa trouble a lot, because of something that Jason understood was called "our fright us." How, the old man wondered mildly, do they manage an instant one-eighty without even shifting gears?

"You can tell us tomorrow, Grampa," Julie assured him, with the massive nonchalance that only a six-year-old girl can lift, "I don't matter about it." She put down the candle and got him an ashtray.

"Yeah," Jason picked up his cue. "Who cares about a dumb old Slime Monster?" He then attempted to look as if that last sentence were sincere, and failed; Julie gave him a dirty look for overplaying his hand.

Little con artists, Grandpa thought fondly, there's hope for the race yet. He waited for the pitch, enjoying the knee-massage.

"I'll make you a deal, Grampa," Julie said.

"A deal?"

"If I can ask you a question you can't answer, you have to tell about the Olden Days for ten minutes."

He appeared to think about it while he smoked. "Seven minutes." There was no timepiece in the room.

"Nine," Julie said at once.

"Eight."

"Eight and a half."

"Done."

The old man did not expect to lose. He was expecting some kind of trick question, but he felt that he had heard most, perhaps all, of the classic conundrums over the course of his years, and he figured he could cobble up a trick answer to whatever Julie had up her sleeve. And she sideswiped him.

"You know that poem, 'Roses are red, violets are blue'?" she asked.

"Which one? There are hundreds."

"That's what I mean," she said, springing the trap. "I know a millyum of 'em. Roses are red, violets are blue—"

"—outhouse is smelly and so are you," Jason interrupted loudly, and broke up.

She glared at her younger brother and pursed her lips. "Don't be such a child," she said gravely, and nearly caught Grandpa smiling. "So that's my question."

"What?"

"Why do they always say that?"

"You mean, 'Roses are red, violets—?'"

"When they're *not*."

"Not what?"

She looked up at the ceiling as though inviting God to bear witness to the impossibility of communicating with grownups. "*Blue*," she said.

The old man's jaw dropped.

"Violets are *violet*," she amplified.

He was thunderstruck. She was absolutely right, and all at once he could not imagine why the question had not occurred to him decades earlier. "I'll be damned. You win, Princess. I have no idea how that one got started. You've got me dead to rights."

"Oh boy," Jason crowed, releasing Grandpa's knee at once and returning to his bed. "You kids nowadays," he prompted as Julie crawled in beside him.

Grandpa accepted the inevitable.

"You kids nowadays don't know nothing about nothing," he said. "Now in the Olden Days . . ."

Grinning triumphantly, Julie fluffed up her pillow and stretched out on the pallet, pulling her blanket delicately up over her small legs, just to the knees. Jason pulled his own blanket to his chin, uncaring that this bared his feet, and stared at the ceiling.

". . . in the Olden Days it wasn't like it is these days. Men were men in them days, and women knew their place in the world. This world has been going straight to hell since I was a boy, children, and you can dip me if it looks like getting any better. Things you kids take for granted nowadays, why, in the Olden Days we'd have laughed at the thought. Sometimes we did.

"F'rinstance, this business of gettin' up at six in the goddam morning and havin' a goddam potato pancake for breakfast, an' then walkin' twenty goddam kilometres to the goddam little red schoolhouse—in the Olden Days there wasn't *none* of that crap. We got up at eight like civilized children, and walked twenty goddam metres to where a *bus* come and hauled us the whole five klicks to a school the likes of which a child like you'll never see, more's the pity."

"Tell about the bus," Jason ordered.

"It was big enough for sixty kids to play in, and it was warm in the winter, sometimes *too* warm, and God Himself drove it, and it smelled wonderful and just the same every day. And when it took you home after school, there was none of this nonsense of grabbing some refried beans and goin' off to haul rock and brush for the goddam road crew for fifty cents a week, I'll tell you that. Why, if a feller had tried to hire me when I was your age, at a good salary, mind you, they'd have locked him up for *exploiting* me! No sir, we'd come home after a hard day of learning, and we'd play ball or watch TV or read a book, whatever we felt like—ah Christ, we lived like kings and we never even knew it!

"You, Julie, you'll have children before you're sixteen, and a good wife and mother you'll be—but in the Olden Days you might have been an executive, or a doctor, or a dancer. Jason, you'll grow up to be a good farmer—if they don't hang you—but if you'd been born when I was, you could have made movies in Thailand, or flown airliners to Paris, or picked rocks off the goddam face of the Moon and brought 'em home. And before any of that, you both could have had something you're never going to know—a mysterious, terrible, wonderful thing called adolescence.

"But my generation, and your father and mother's, we threw it all away, because it wasn't perfect. The best I can explain it is that they all voted themselves a free lunch, democratic as hell, and then tried to duck out when the cheque arrived. They spent every dime they had, and all of your money besides, and they *still* had to wash some dishes. There was two packs of idiots, you see. On one side you had rich sons of bitches, excuse my language, and they were arrogant. Couldn't be bothered to build a nuclear power plant to specs or a car that worked, couldn't be bothered to hide their contempt. Why, do you know that banks actually used to set out, for the use of their customers, pens that didn't work—and then chain them in place to prevent their theft? Worse than that, they were the dumbest aristocrats in the history of man. They couldn't be bothered to take care of their own peasants. I mean, if you want a horse to break his back for you, do you feed him, or take all his hay to make yourself pillows and mattresses?

"And then on the other side you had sincere, well-meanin' folks who were even dumber than the rich. Between the anti-teckers and the no-nukers and the stop-fusion people and the small-is-beautiful types and the appropriate-technology folks and the back-to-the-landers they managed to pull the plug, to throw away the whole goddam solar system. The car might have got us all to a gas station, running on fumes and momentum—but now that they shut the engine down there ain't enough gas left to get it started again . . .

"They let the space program die—they let all of high tech society die, because it wasn't perfect—and now the planet just hasn't got the metals or the power or the technology to bring it back; we're damn lucky to feed ourselves. Now there really *is* Only One Earth—and it never was big enough . . ."

The old man's cigarette was too short to keep smoking. He pinched it out between two fingers, salvaged the unburnt tobacco, and began to take up his tale again. Then he saw that the children were both fast asleep. He let his breath out, covered them, and blew out the candle. He thought about going downstairs to ask his son-in-law how things had gone in the fields, whether the crop had been saved . . . but the stairs were hard on the old man's our fright us, and he really did not want to risk hearing bad news just now. Instead he went to the window and watched the moon, lonely now for several decades, and after a time he cried. For the children, who could never never hope that one day their grandchildren might have the stars . . .

Chronic Offender

In respectful memory of Damon Runyon,
Who knows no other tense than the present,
And sometimes the future.

You will think that when a guy sees eighty summers on Broadway, he sees it all, and until recently so will I. It is a long time since I see something that surprises me very much, and in fact the last time I remember being surprised is when the Giants take the wind for L.A. But when I come home a couple of nights after my eightieth birthday, along about four bells in the morning, and find a ghost watching my TV, I am surprised no little, and in fact more than somewhat.

At first I do not figure him for a ghost. What I figure him for is a hophead, what they call nowadays a junkie, and most guys will figure this proposition for a cinch, at that. I decide that my play is to go out again, and have a cup of coffee, and come back when he is finished, or maybe even ask the gendarmes to come back *before* he is finished. But Astaire will never hoof again and neither will I, because I have not even managed to get her into reverse when this character hauls out a short John Roscoe and says like this:

"Stand and deliver."

This is when I figure him for a ghost, because I recognize the words he uses, and then his voice, and finally his face, and who is it but Harry the Horse.

Now, Harry the Horse is never a guy I am apt to hang around with, as he is a very tough guy, who will shoot you as soon as look at you, and maybe even sooner. Furthermore he is many years dead at this time, and I figure the chances are good that the climate where he is lately is hot enough to make him irritable. In fact, I am wishing more with every passing moment to go have this cup of coffee, but I cannot see any price at all on arguing with a John Roscoe, especially such a John Roscoe as is being piloted by Harry the Horse, or even his ghost. So I up with my mitts and say as follows:

"Don't shoot, Harry."

Well, it turns out that nobody is more surprised than Harry when *he* recognizes *me*. I cannot figure this, since I always understand that ghosts know who they are haunting, but then again I never hear of a ghost packing a John Roscoe, at that. In fact, I start to wonder if maybe Harry the Horse is not a hallucination, and I am gone daffy.

You have to understand that Harry the Horse looks not a day older than when I see him last, which is going back about fifty years. Furthermore his suit is the kind they do not make for fifty years, except it looks no older than is customary on Harry when I know him, and likewise his hair is greased up like only some of the spics and smokes still do anymore, and in fact he looks in every respect like he does when I last see him, except that he is not smiling and not laying down and does not seem to have several .45 calibre holes in him. In fact, he looks pretty good, except for his forehead being wrinkled up a little like something is on his mind.

"Well," he says, "it is certainly good to see you, even if you do become an ugly old geezer. I will never think to guzzle your joint if I know it is you. If fact, I will not guzzle your joint, even though this causes me some inconvenience, because," he says, "you have always been aces with me. So now you must help me pick some other joint to guzzle."

Now, I hear of ghosts that like to scare a guy out of his pants, although personally I never meet one, but I never hear that they are interested in the contents of the pants pockets. Even if they are the ghost of Harry the Horse. "Harry," I say, "what would a guy such as yourself be doing working the second storey?"

"Well," Harry the Horse says, "that is a long story. But if I do not tell the story to someone soon I think I will go crazy, and in fact you are just the guy to tell it to, because you remember the way things used to be in 1930."

"Harry," I say, "I have nothing better to do than to hear your story."

And Harry the Horse nods, and says to me like this:

One day me and Spanish John and Little Isadore all happen to be in the sneezer together, on account of a small misunderstanding about the colour of some money we are spending, and I wish to say in passing that this beef is a total crock, as we steal that money fair and square from a bank on Third Avenue, and can we help it if things are so bad that banks are starting to pass out funny money? But anyway there we are in the sneezer, so naturally we call Judge Goldfobber to get us out. As you know, Judge Goldfobber is by no means a judge, and never is a judge, and in my line it is a hundred-to-one against him ever being a judge, but he is a lawyer by trade, and he is better than Houdini at getting citizens out of the sneezer, and in fact when it comes to getting out of the sneezer Goldfobber is usually cheaper than buying a real judge, at that.

So we call him and he comes right down and springs us, and then he takes us back uptown to his office and pours us a couple of shots of scotch, and furthermore it is scotch he gets from Dave the Dude, and you know that Dave the Dude handles only the very best merchandise. So we knock them back and then Goldfobber says like this: "Boys, when I spring a guy for bad paper it is my firm policy never to accept my fee in cash. None of you has any gold or securities, so I propose to take it out in trade."

"Judge," I say, "you are always a good employer, and in fact it seems to me that every time you put a little job our way, we will come away with a few bobs for our trouble. Furthermore you are a right gee, because you put down several potatoes to bail us out, and you must know that you have no more chance of seeing us show up in court than Hoover has of seeing another vote. So we are happy to entertain your proposition."

"Well," he says, "it is not exactly a job you can be proud of."

"How do you mean?" Little Isadore asks.

"For one thing, it involves chilling a guy, and an old guy besides, and furthermore he is one of those guys who is so brilliant that he is like a baby. It is not exactly sporting."

"Judge," Spanish John says to him, "I and my friends are suffering greatly from the unemployment situation, because if nobody is working and making money, there is nobody for us to rob, and if there is nobody for us to rob, we are reduced to robbing banks, and you see how that works out. I do not speak for my friends, but I myself will be happy to chill somebody just on general principles, and if it is an old guy that does not shoot back, why, so much the better."

"It involves work," Judge Goldfobber says.

"How do you mean 'work'?"

"Physical exertion. Manual labor. You will have to carry something very much like a phone booth, and which weighs maybe twice as much as a phone booth, down three flights of stairs and deliver it to my place out on the Island."

"Judge," I say, greatly horrified, "we are eternally grateful for what you do for us. But to do manual labour in satisfaction of a debt is perilously close to honest work, and that is more grateful than I, for one, wish to be. However," I say as he starts to frown, "not only am I grateful, but I just remember that you know where Isadore and me bury Boat-Race Benny three years ago, so we will accept your job."

So he gives us an address up in Harlem, and that night we borrow a truck somebody is not using to go up there.

The job goes down as easy as a doll's drawers, or maybe even easier. The building is a big fancy joint, with a doorman and everything, but the lock on the back door does not give Little Isadore any difficulty, and neither does the lock on the apartment door of the old geezer. The name on his door is "Doctor Philbert Twitchell," so we figure him for a sawbones, except it turns out he is not that kind of doctor, but the professor kind.

Anyway, we stick him up in his bed, and we scare him so bad we nearly save ourselves the trouble of croaking him. We tell him to show us the phone booth, and toots wheat, and he just blinks at us. This Doc Twitchell is about a million years old and bald as an eight ball, and I wish to say I never see another guy like him for blinking.

In fact I remember thinking that he will be a handy guy to have around on a hot day, since he keeps a pretty good breeze going, except of course that by the time the next hot day comes around he will not be blinking so good, and is apt to smell bad, besides.

About the time I haul the hammer back on my Roscoe he gives up blinking and gets up and puts on a bathrobe that looks like it belongs to Jack Johnson, and he takes us to the phone booth. It is in a big room way in back of his apartment, and the room is a kind of a lavatory, like in this movie I see when I am ten years old called *Frankenstein*, which I hear they are going to remake as a talkie. Anyway there is all kinds of machines and gadgets and gizmos, and a wire the size of a shotgun barrel taped along the floor from the wall to the bottom of this phone booth. It is the size and shape of a phone booth, but it does not really look much like one, and in fact it makes me think of a stand-up coffin, except for all the wires and things hanging off of it. There is no door in it, so I can see the thing is empty, and it occurs to me that it will make a fair coffin, at that, since we can carry the Doc downstairs in it and save an extra trip.

"Okay," I say. "This is a cinch. Spanish John, you go down and get the dolly out of the back of the truck. Little Isadore, you go along and wait for him at the door, keep lookout whilst I croak the Doc here." At this the Doc starts in blinking a mile a minute. He starts to say something, and then he thinks better of it and waits until Spanish John and Little Isadore are gone, and then he starts talking even faster than he is blinking, which is pretty fast talking indeed. He talks kind of tony, with lots of big fancy words, but I give you the gist:

"Goldfobber the mouthpiece sends you guys to see me, am I right?"

I admit this, and start putting the silencer on my John Roscoe.

"Would you consider double-crossing Goldfobber?"

"Certainly. What is your proposition?"

"You mean Goldfobber does not tell you?" he says, very surprised.

"Tell me what?"

"This thing you call a phone booth is a time machine."

"You mean like a big clock? Where is the hands?"

"No, no," he says, real excited. "A machine for travelling in time."

"In time for what?"

"No, *through* time! My machine can take you into next week, or next year, or the year after that. It is the only one in the world."

"Well, I never hear of such a machine, at that."

"Of course not," he says. "You and me and that thief Goldfobber are the only three people in the world that know about it."

"Okay," I tell him. "So get to the part about why I should double-cross Goldfobber."

"Don't you see?" he says, blinking away. "You can travel to tomorrow night, read the stock market quotations, and then come back to today and buy everything that is going to go up."

"I do not know too many guys in the stock racket," I tell him, "and furthermore I hear it is a chancy proposition. But if I understand you, I can go to tomorrow night and read the racing results, and then come back and bet on all the winning ponies?" I am commencing to get excited.

"Exactly," he says, jumping up and down a little. "Likewise the World Series, and the football, and the elections, and—the sky is the limit."

By now I am figuring the angles, and I am more excited than somewhat. This is a machine such as a guy could get very rich with, and I am a guy such as likes the idea of being very rich. "Does it work backwards? Can I go back to yesterday, or last week?"

"Hell, no!" he says, or anyway that is what the things he says come down to. "Oh, it can be done," he says, "but I never have the guts to do it, and in fact only a dope will try it. Why—" His voice gets real quiet and solemn, like a funeral. "—you might make a pair of ducks."

I can make no sense of this, but he says it like it is something to be very, very afraid of, and I figure he ought to know. But I decide it does not matter, because I figure going to tomorrow is plenty good enough for me. I point my Roscoe at the Doc. "Prove to me that this machine does like you say."

"Give me your watch," he says, and I do so. "See?" he says. "It is just now exactly five minutes to midnight, am I right?" I look at the watch and he is perfectly right. He puts the watch on the floor of the phone booth. "How long do you figure it is before your associate comes back with the dolly?"

"Well," I tell him, "figuring he has a pint in his pants pocket, and he knows we are in no special hurry, maybe it takes him another five minutes."

"Okay," he says. "So I set the machine for two minutes." He fiddles with some dials and things on the outside of the phone booth, and pushes a button. The light goes way down, like when a guy gets it at Sing Sing, and even before it comes back up I see that the phone booth isn't there anymore. The big wire ends in a plug; the socket for it is gone. It scares me so much I almost scrag the Doc by accident—and now that I think of it, it is a better thing all the way around if I do, at that—but the slug misses him clean. Since I have the silencer on, it is six-to-one that Little Isadore never even hears the shot.

Then I just watch the Doc blink for two minutes, and

finally—pop!—the phone booth is back again. My watch is still in it, and the watch is still ticking, but it says that it is still five minutes of midnight. The machine works.

"Say," I tell the Doc, "this is okay. Can you set this thing to go and then come right back again?"

"Certainly," he says. "Watch." He fiddles with it again, and this time when he pushes the button the light and the phone booth both kind of . . . flicker, like a movie. "See?" he says. "It just goes into tomorrow, stays there an hour, and comes right back to the instant it leaves."

My head hurts when I try to think about this. "Okay," I said, "here is what you do. You set that thing to take me into the future. I want to see what the world looks like when the Depression is over, so you better send me a long way. Say, fifty years—they ought to have the country back on its feet by then. Have the phone booth go to 1980, stay there for a whole day, and then come right back to here. You can do this?"

"It's a cinch," he says, blinking up a storm, and he does like I say. "There. Just push the button and off she goes."

"Can't I make it work from inside?"

"Certainly," he says, and shows me another button on the inside. "I am planning to experiment with people," he says, "instead of just objects and wop pigs, when you boys guzzle my joint. In fact I will do it already, except I decide I should patent the phone booth first, and I bring the idea to that gonif Goldfobber, which I now regret."

(Actually he does not call it a phone booth, any more than he uses any of the regular words I am putting in his mouth. What he calls it is—give me a minute—a Chronic Lodge Misplacer, I think he says.)

"What happens to the wop pigs?" I ask him, beginning to get a little nervous.

"Not a thing," he says. "They come back perfectly copacetic and in the pink, and in fact there they are now." And he points, and sure enough over in the corner is a bunch of cages full of little wop pigs, and I am relieved to see that they look happy, and there are no empty cages. "Well," he says, "what do you say? I make you rich and you do not make me dead; you cannot get a better deal than that."

"Sure I can," I say, and his eyelids commence to flutter so fast I can feel the breeze a clear six feet away. The right eye seems to blink faster than the left, so that is the eye I shoot him in. Then I go out and scrag Little Isadore, and I meet Spanish John on the landing where he is communing with his pint and scrag him too, and then I put him on the dolly and carry him upstairs and stretch him out next to Little Isadore. It make me no little sad to see them lying there, because they are my friends a long time, but I cannot help but think how fortunate it is that it is me Doc Twitchell tells his secret to, because otherwise I will be laying there stiff and one of my friends will be standing around feeling sad, and I do not wish a friend of mine to have this sorrow.

Then I go back to the phone booth.

I figure the deal for a cinch. I will go to 1980, and I will go to the Public Library. They got books in there that are records of all the pony-races ever run, and naturally I knew where they keep these books since I often have recourse to them in the course of business. I will burgle the joint and heist such books as relate to races from 1930 to 1980, which certainly cannot take me more than a day, and then I will come back to 1930 and find out what it is like to be a millionaire.

So I step into the phone booth and push the button.

All of a sudden it is very dark, and the lights do not come back up, so I figure I maybe blow a fuse, or some such. I step out of the phone booth and light a match, and I almost drop it. The whole room is completely different. Mostly what it is, is empty. The Doc's body is gone, and so are all the gizmos and gadgets and such, and even the cages full of little wop pigs.

The match goes out, and I think about it, and now I think about it, of course it figures that a joint does not look the same after fifty years, and especially not if you croak the guy who owns it. It does not seem like *any*body owns this joint for a long time, and I figure that for a piece of luck, all things considered.

Until I light the second match and notice the other thing that is missing.

The big wire.

Well, hell, I say to myself, of course it will not still be around after fifty years. So while I am out guzzling the track records I will guzzle a bunch of big wire from a wire place, and a plug as well . . .

Except the light switch does not work when I try it, and it looks like there is no electric in the apartment now, because I keep finding little home-made candles in all the rooms, all burned down. There is nothing else in the joint but junk, and there is no water in the crapper or the faucets, and I commence to get the idea that this building is abandoned. So now I must get the electric turned back on, as well as heist the track records and the wire. Except I do not see how I will get the electric turned on, as I do not happen to be holding any potatoes at the moment, and in fact what I am is broke. To heist potatoes and track records and wire and get the electric turned on, all in one day, is a pretty full day, even for a tough guy such as myself.

But if this is what I must do to be the richest guy in the world, then I will take a crack at it. So I leave, and you know what? Harlem is all full of smokes these days. Oh, you hear about this? Yeah, I guess you will at that. Anyway, not only is Harlem all over smokes, but these are very hostile smokes, such as I never see before. I run into one on the landing, and I show him the equalizer to clear him out of my way, and what does he do but say something about my ma and then haul out an equalizer of his own. It is only good fortune that I escape the shame of being croaked by a smoke, and this shakes me up no little. I pass some other smokes in the street outside, and they all act unfriendly too. One of them tries to tell me I am a Hunkie, which I cannot figure until I see he wears black cheaters and probably is blind. Except he is by no means blind, because he outs with a shiv as long as my foot and tries to put a couple new vents in my suit, and I am forced to break his face.

This brings a whole bunch of smokes, all hollering and carrying on in smoke, and some in spic, and I decide I will leave Harlem for the time being. I run pretty good and build up a good lead, but then I blow it when I decide to steal a heap. I get it hot-wired okay but the shift is all funny and I cannot find the clutch anyplace. So I leave the heap just before these ten dozen yelling smokes catch up, and a few blocks later I find a taxi waiting at a red light and jump in. The jockey starts to give me a hard time, but I show him the Roscoe and tell him to take me where the white people live, and toots wheat, so he shuts up and drives, without putting on the meter even. I try to see how he drives with no clutch, but I cannot see his feet, and besides he never seems to use the shift at all.

While he drives the short I look around. Harlem does not seem to be a class neighbourhood anymore, naturally, what with all the smokes living in it, and in fact it is nothing but a dump. Doc Twitchell's building is by no means the only one abandoned. But when we get downtown I see that things are not much better there. Oh, there are some awful fancy big new buildings here and there, but there are also a great many buildings just as broken down as the ones up in Harlem. I see many more winos and rumdums and hopheads on the street than I remember, and furthermore there is garbage all over the place in big piles. So I tell the jockey to pull up and buy a paper, and what do you know? I do not go far enough forward in time, because it seems the Depression is still going on, and nobody is looking to see it get any better. I cannot figure this, because I ask the jockey and he tells me the president after Hoover is a Democrat, and furthermore who is it but the governor of New York, Frank Roosevelt. So I guess you never know.

It just keeps getting worse. I have the jockey take me to the Library, only the Library is not where I left it, and in fact it is a whole new building altogether. I can see that even if I get into this joint, I cannot find where they now keep the track records in the dark, and I have no flashlight, so there is nothing for it but to do a daylight heist in the morning. And it figures I cannot get the electric turned on or the wire until sun-up, either. So I figure all I can do now is scare up some potatoes for operating expenses. Only I decide to scare up a drink first, as I am all of a sudden very very thirsty. So I take the jockey's potatoes and tell him to take me to Lindy's. Only he never hears of Lindy's or of Good-Time Charlie's, or the Bohemian Club, or any other deadfall I name, not even the Stork Club. So I tell him I wish a drink, and he hauls me off and brings me to this place all full of bright lights and guys wearing dolls' clothes, and where they wish two bobs for a drink of scotch which is nothing but a shot. In fact, it is in my mind to shoot the jockey for this, except for some reason he is gone when I come out, even though I tell him to wait.

I walk a couple of blocks, figuring to guzzle a few

pedestrians, but my luck is terrible, as half of them are broke and the other half shoot back, and one of them actually has the brass to pick my pocket while I am shaking him down and take the rest of the jockey's potatoes, so now I am broke again.

It goes like that all night. I can tell you all manner of stories, like what happens when I go over to Central Park to get a little shut-eye, and what a dump Times Square turns into, but you probably hear all this already and besides I see that you are tired, so I will make a long story short.

So when the Library opens up the next day, I go in and ask this old doll about the track records, and she says they do not have these books anymore. She says they have the information I wish but it is not in books anymore. I know this will sound nutty, but I make her say it twice, very slow: the information is on her crow film. So I ask her to give me some of her crow film, and she does, and what is it but a little tiny thing like a roll of caps, or maybe like a little reel for a movie that is two minutes long, and for all I know nowadays crows do watch such films in this town. She puts it in a machine and it makes words on a screen, like a newsreel, only it does not move unless you make it. I have her get the crow film with the right horse records on it, and I watch how she works it until I figure I can do it myself. So now I must steal not only the drawer full of crow film but the machine to read it, and I am not sure it will fit in the phone booth with me.

But I figure I will cross that bridge when I get to Brooklyn, and I thank the old doll and watch where she puts the drawer full of crow film back, and I go try to price the wire I need. You will not think there can be more than one kind of wire as big around as a shotgun barrel, but it turns out there are several dozen such kinds, and I do not know which kind I want. But I figure I will come back that night after closing and borrow a dozen kinds and try them all.

Then I shake down a necktie salesman for some change and call the electrics, and they tell me that to turn on the electric in that building, for even one night, they have to have a security deposit of no less than two hundred potatoes. This two yards must be in cash, and furthermore there are fire inspectors to be greased, and so forth, and it will take at least a week.

By this time I am commencing to get somewhat discouraged, and in fact I am downright unhappy. That night I go back up to Harlem, with some trivial difficulty, and I sit in that phone booth from eleven-thirty to twelve-thirty, just in case it will still go home without the electric, and it does not. I figure the Doc slips it to me pretty good, and in fact it is a dirty shame I cannot croak him twice, or even three times.

So I figure I am stuck here, and am not apt to become a rich guy after all, and in fact it is time to do a little second-storey work and build up my poke. So I bust your joint, and I wish to know how come, if the Depression is still around, movies get so cheap that you can show talkies in your own joint, with colours yet, and furthermore you can leave them running while you take the air. Also where is the projector?

When Harry the Horse finishes telling me this story, and I finish telling him about television, I get out the old nosepaint and we have a few, and in fact we have more than a few, although Harry the Horse says he once makes better booze in a trash can, and as a matter of fact I know this to be true. A little while after the bottle is empty an idea comes to me, and I say to Harry the Horse like this:

"Harry, you are welcome to stay at my joint as long as you wish, naturally, because you are always aces with me.

But if you still wish to go back to 1930 and be a rich guy, I think I can fix it.''

"It is too late," he says. "The Doc sets the phone booth to go home after twenty-four hours, and it does not, so I am stuck here even if I get the electric and the wire and the crow film machine, which I figure is about a twenty-to-one shot.''

"Harry," I tell him, "you will naturally not know this, but nowadays almost all the clocks in this man's town are on electric, and if you pull out the plug, the clock *stops*. So I figure if we plug the phone booth back in, twenty-four hours after *that* it goes home, with you inside, and maybe also this crow film machine.''

Harry thinks this over, and starts to cheer up. "This appeals to me no little," he says, "with or without the crow film machine. I like 1930 better.''

I decide maybe Harry the Horse is not so dumb, at that.

"But can you fix the rest?" he asks.

"I think I can.''

So I call up my friend Toomey the electrician, who everybody calls Socket. He is a little agitated at being woke up at five bells in the morning, but I tell him there is a couple of guys here that wish to sell a dozen lids of Hawaiian pot for thirty bobs a lid, and he says, "On my way," and hangs up.

Harry the Horse wishes this translated. "Well," I explain, "Prohibition is over since a little after I see you last—''

Harry is greatly surprised to hear this. "What do the coppers do for a living?''

"Well, there is this pot, which is nothing but muggles, only it is now as illegal as booze used to be. And right now in this man's town there are maybe six million citizens as are apt to pay sixty bobs for an ounce of this muggles, and thirty is a very good price.''

Harry the Horse shakes his head at this, and just then the bell rings and it is none other than Socket, all out of breath. He is a young guy, but a very good electrician, and in fact he wires my joint for me when I get the air condition, and for a young guy he knows the way things are. He is very aggravated when he finds that there is no Hawaiian muggles, and in fact he turns and starts to leave. But when he puts his hand out to the doorknob he finds a shiv pinning his sleeve to the door so that he cannot reach the knob, and when he looks around he sees Harry the Horse deciding where to put the next one, so Socket realizes he does not wish to reach the knob after all, and says as much.

So we explain the story to Socket, which uses up my last bottle of sauce, and he says he is willing to look the proposition over. When we hit the street I wonder how we are going to get up to Harlem, because I am not anxious to take the subway. But right off we find a hack who is so thoughtless as to park where he cannot make a quick getaway, so when Harry the Horse sticks his John Roscoe in the window of the short there is nothing the jockey can do except get out and give us his short. A few blocks away we change plates, and then we pick up Socket's tools and electric stuff from his joint and head up Broadway at a hell of a clip, and we are in Harlem in no time, or maybe less.

We get into the building with no trouble, and Socket even manages to cop a lid of Mexican muggles from a little skinny smoke we find in the lobby, before we chase the smoke out. Socket puffs up on this muggles while he checks out the electric room in the basement, and he likes what he sees in the electric room. "I can power this building for a few days," he tells us. "Alarms will go off downtown, and sooner or later an inspector comes to see what the hell, but with the red tape and all, it has to be a good two or three days before he gets here." He goes ahead and does this, and then he takes a light bulb out of his pouch and puts it in the wall, and it works. He puts away his flashlight and pokes around the basement, and what does he find but a real old hunk of wire, as big around as a shotgun barrel and in every respect such as Harry the Horse describes it, except for the cobwebs. In fact, Socket says he figures it is the original wire, which is tossed down in the basement and forgotten by whoever rents Doc Twitchell's apartment after he croaks. This is water on the wheel of Harry the Horse, who now begins to think maybe his luck is back with him, and to like Socket besides. Harry is very anxious for this to work, because a few minutes before he is obliged to plug a rat the size of a Doberman, and Harry the Horse is thoroughly disgusted with 1980 for letting rats into a class neighbourhood like Harlem, smokes or no smokes.

So we go up to the third floor and there is the phone booth, just like Harry the Horse describes it except that there is a hophead sleeping in it. We chase the hophead out and Socket sets the wire back up the way it is supposed to be, and plugs it in. Right away the phone booth starts to hum, and Harry the Horse gets a great big smile on his pan.

Socket puts a light bulb in the ceiling and turns it on, and then he looks the phone booth over. "I cannot figure much of this," he says, "but this part here has to be the delay timer. If you want to go back right now you just twist this back to zero—"

"Not yet," Harry the Horse says. "It is nice to know I do not have to wait twenty-four hours, but I am not yet ready. I must go guzzle the crow film and the machine."

All of a sudden Harry the Horse frowns, like he sees a fly in the ointment. I begin to see the same fly too, and so does Socket, because he speaks up and says like this:

"Harry, I know what you are thinking. You do not wish to leave us here while you go rob my crow film—"

"What do you mean, your crow film?" Harry asks angrily. "It is my crow film."

"Of course," Socket says real quick. "The point is, you are afraid if you leave us behind with the machine, it may not be here when you get back, or us either for that matter, and I am honest enough to admit that this is at least a ten-to-one shot. If you are as honest, you will admit that what you think you will do about this is scrag us both. Is this not so?"

"I like your style, kid," Harry the Horse says to him, "but I will admit that this seems like the good thing to do."

"I thank you for your honesty," Socket says. "You will understand that I am altogether opposed to this proposition, on general principles. So here is my thought: how about if I come with you while you swipe the crow film machine, and generally be of assistance (for it is sure to be heavy), and meanwhile our mutual friend here," meaning me, "will keep watch over the phone booth and keep the junkies out of it. He is not apt to take the lam with it, on account of he is an old geezer who cannot cut it in 1930 without a joint or a job, and besides if he does you will surely scrag me and I am his friend."

"This sounds jake to me," Harry the Horse decides, so off they go together, hurrying a bit because it is a little past six bells in the morning and the sun will be up soon. They come back in about an hour with a drawer full of crow film and the machine for it, and while Harry the Horse checks to make sure the machine fits in the phone booth, Socket looks over the phone booth some more. "I think I begin to figure this out," he says.

"Frankly," Harry the Horse says, "and I hope you will

not be offended, I am not so sure. You say if I twist this little dingus here I go right back where I start, right?''

"Right to the moment you leave," Socket agrees.

"I am reluctant," Harry the Horse says, "to tamper with the way Doc Twitchell leaves the machine, and then test the result with my personal body. It is more than half a day until the phone booth is supposed to go back—suppose I get there a half day early?"

"That is impossible," Socket tells him. "That would be a pair of ducks."

Harry the Horse frowns. "That is exactly what I mean. I wish to have no truck whatsoever with these ducks, as Doc Twitchell tells me they are bad medicine."

By this time I am tired of hanging around in Harlem with Harry the Horse, and I do not care a fig if he does get a pair of ducks, or even a pair of goats or chickens. "Harry," I say, "my good friend Socket knows all about this science jazz. He reads all the rocket ship stuff and you can rely on him. It is a piece of cake."

Maybe I say it too enthusiastic, because Harry frowns even more. "If it is so safe," he says to me, "why do you not be the one who tries it out? In fact," he says, "I think this is a terrific idea."

Now, this horrifies me no little, and in fact more than somewhat, but I am not about to let on to Harry the Horse that I am horrified, or he is apt to figure I care more about myself than him, and become insulted. So I swallow and head for the phone booth.

"As soon as you get there and see that everything is copacetic," Harry tells me, "you push the button again. It is still set the same way, so it should bring you right back here. Do not monkey with it."

"Wait!" Socket yells, and this seems like a terrific idea to me. "Listen, Harry," he says, "I figure this gizmo will take him back to the very instant he leaves, or maybe a split second after. But if he then pushes the button again right away, it brings him forward the same amount of time as before—and he arrives a second after you do, a day and a half ago. Except that there is already a phone booth here, and nowhere for his to *go*, so there is a big explosion.''

My blood pressure now goes up into the paint cards. Harry thinks about this, and I can see it is a strain for him. ''So how do we do this?''

''Well,'' Socket says, ''I think I get the hang of this phone booth, and if I am right this dial here is for years, and this one is for days, and this one is hours, and so on. See, the years one is on fifty, and the rest are in neutral.''

''So?''

''So all he has to do when he gets back to 1930 is move the days dial forward one notch, and the hours dial ahead seven notches, and the minutes, say thirty to be on the safe side, and he arrives here about fifteen minutes from now.''

Harry the Horse looks at me. ''Do you get that?'' he says.

''Yeah,'' I tell him, a little distracted because something just occurs to me.

''Listen,'' Socket says to me, ''for the love of Pete do not fail to set the delay timer again before you push the button to come back here. Anything over five minutes is probably fine. Otherwise as soon as you get here you slingshot right back to 1930 again.''

''Got you,'' I say, and he turns the delay gizmo back to zero.

All of a sudden the lights get dim like a brown-out, and when they come back up again Harry the Horse and Socket are nowhere to be seen. What is to be seen is a lot of gadgets and gizmos and little wop pigs and an old dead guy I know is Doc Twitchell.

I will be damned, I say to myself, it works.

Perhaps I should do like I promise Harry the Horse and

go right back. If I do not arrive back at the right time he is apt to get angry and scrag my young friend Socket. But I figure I can reset the dials to any time I want, and if it does not work out right it is Socket's fault for giving me the bum steer.

And besides, I cannot help myself.

I go into the livingroom and get some subway tokens and a couple of bobs from Little Isadore's pants pocket, and I take the A train down to Broadway.

Broadway is just beginning to jump when I get there, on account of it is just past midnight, and I wish to tell you it looks *swell*. The guys and dolls are all out taking the air, and I see faces I do not see for a long long time. I see Lance McGowan, and Dream Street Rose, and Bookie Bob, and Miss Missouri Martin, and Dave the Dude with Miss Billy Perry on his arm, and Regret the Horseplayer, and Nicely-Nicely Jones, and the Lemon Drop Kid, and Waldo Winchester the newspaper scribe, and all kinds of people. I see Joe the Joker give Frankie Ferocious a hot-foot while Frankie is taking a shine from a little smoke. I see Rusty Charlie punch a draft horse square in the kisser and stretch it in the street. I buy an apple from Madame La Gimp. I find the current location of Nathan Detroit's permanent floating crap game, and lose a few bobs. I stick my noodle into Lindy's, and I watch a couple of dolls take it off at the Stork Club, the way dolls used to take it off, and I even have a drink at Good-Time Charlie's, even though Good-Time Charlie naturally does not recognize me and serves me the same liquor he serves his customers. You know something? It is the best booze I taste in fifty years.

I see people and places and things that I say good-bye to a long time ago, and it feels so good that after a while I haul off and bust out crying.

Somehow I never seem to bump into myself—my thirty-year-old self—while I am walking around, and I guess this is just as well, at that. After a while I decide that I am awake a long time for a guy my age, so I walk over to Central Park and take a snooze near the pond. When I wake up it is just coming on daylight, and I am hungry and there is very little of Little Isadore's dough left, so I take the A train back up to Harlem and sneak in the back door of Doc Twitchell's building again. When I get back to the phone booth it is just about half past seven bells, so I set the dial ahead one day and no hours and no minutes, and then I set the delay thing and push the button.

The lights go down and up and there are Harry the Horse and Socket again. Socket looks very glad to see me, and for that matter so does Harry the Horse. "It works great," I tell them, and step out.

"This is good news," Harry says, "because I am commencing to get impatient. Socket, I am sorry I do not trust you. Both of you are right gees, and you both assist me more than somewhat, and I tell you what I will do. When I get back home and become a rich guy, I will put half of the first million I make into a suitcase, and I will bring the suitcase to the First National Bank downtown and tell them to surrender it to you guys in fifty years, and you can go right down there today and get it. How is that for gratitude?"

Socket's face gets all twisted up funny for a minute, like he wants to say something and does not want to say it, all at the same time. "Harry," I say, "do you ever come back yourself?"

"Naw," he says. "This stuff gives me the willies, and 1980 you can keep. As soon as I get back home I shoot up this phone booth until it does not work anymore. I have all I need to be a rich guy, and if anybody else gets ahold of the phone booth, maybe it gets around and they start not having horse races anymore or something. So this is good-bye." He puts the crow film machine and the drawer full of crow films in the booth, and steps in with them.

"Well, Harry," I say, "I wish to thank you for your generosity. Half a million bobs is pretty good wages for a electric guy and a dago pig. Enjoy your riches and good-bye."

He has Socket move the delay gizmo back to zero, and the lights go down and up again, and that is the last I ever see of Harry the Horse, any way you look at it.

"Socket," I start to say, "I hope you do not think for a minute that there is any half a million clams waiting at the bank for us—"

"I *know* there is not," he says, and he shows me a little teeny light bulb the size of a peanut. "I do not like the way this mug talks about plugging people such as yourself and me, so while he and I are guzzling the crow film machine I decide it will be a great gag if I take this bulb out when he is not looking, and sure enough he never knows any different. I regret this later when he speaks of a million iron men, but I cannot think of a tactful way to bring the matter up, and he still has the gat, so I let it ride. Without this bulb," he says, "Harry the Horse cannot read the crow film, and they do not make this bulb fifty years ago."

Well, at this I am so surprised that I never get around to telling Socket Toomey why it is that *I* am so certain there are no half a million potatoes waiting for us at the First National Bank. And perhaps I even feel a little guilty, too, considering that Harry the Horse gives me the seven happiest hours of my life.

Because before I get on the A train to go back up to Harlem, fifty years ago, I call up Judge Goldfobber at his place out on the Island; and I tell him that the reason Harry the Horse and Spanish John and Little Isadore are late bringing the phone booth is because they are planning to double-cross him and keep it for themselves. Who Judge Goldfobber thinks I am, and why I am calling him, is anybody's guess—but I know he believes me, and furthermore makes very good time in from the Island, because I can remember back almost fifty years ago to when I am in the bleachers the day a real judge gives Judge Goldfobber the hot squat, on account of his personal revolver matches up with six slugs they dig out of Harry the Horse.

No Renewal

Douglas Bent Jr. sits in his kitchen, waiting for his tea to heat. It is May twelfth, his birthday, and he has prepared wintergreen tea. Douglas allows himself this extravagance because he knows he will receive no birthday present from anyone but himself. By a trick of Time and timing, he has outlived all his friends, all his relatives. The concept of neighbourliness, too, has predeceased him; not because he has none, but because he has too many.

His may be, for all he knows, the last small farm in Nova Scotia, and it is bordered on three sides by vast mined-out clay pits, gaping concentric cavities whose insides were scraped out and eaten long ago, their husk thrown away to rot. On the remaining perimeter is an apartment-hive, packed with antlike swarms of people. Douglas knows none of them as individuals; at times, he doubts the trick is possible.

Once Douglas's family owned hundreds of acres along what was then called simply the Shore Road; once the

Bent spread ran from the Bay of Fundy itself back over the peak of the great North Mountain, included a sawmill, rushing streams, hundreds of thousands of trees, and acre after acre of pasture and hay and rich farmland; once the Bents were one of the best-known families from Annapolis Royal to Bridgetown, their livestock the envy of the entire Annapolis Valley.

Then the petrochemical industry died of thirst. With it, of course, went the plastics industry. Clay suddenly became an essential substitute—and the Annapolis Valley is mostly clay.

Now the Shore Road is the Fundy Trail, six lanes of high-speed traffic; the Bent spread is fourteen acres on the most inaccessible part of the Mountain; the sawmill has been replaced by the industrial park that ate the clay; the pasture and the streams and the farmland have been disemboweled or paved over; all the Bents save Douglas Jr. are dead or moved to the cities; and perhaps no one now living in the Valley has ever seen a live cow, pig, duck, goat or chicken, let alone eaten them. Agribusiness has destroyed agriculture, and synthoprotein feeds (some of) the world. Douglas grows only what crops replenish themselves, feeds only himself.

He sits waiting for the water to boil, curses for the millionth time the solar-powered electric stove that supplanted the family's woodburner when firewood became impossible to obtain. Electric stoves take too long to heat, call for no tending, perform their task with impersonal callousness. They do not warm a room.

Douglas's gnarled fingers idly sort through the wintergreen he picked this morning, spurn the jar of sugar that stands nearby. All his life Douglas has made wintergreen tea from fresh maple sap, which requires no sweetening. But this spring he journeyed with drill and hammer and tap and bucket to his only remaining maple tree, and found it dead. He has bought maple-flavoured sugar for his birthday tea, but he knows it will not be the same. Then again, next spring he may find no wintergreen.

So *many* old familiar friends have failed to reappear in their season lately—the deer moss has gone wherever the hell the deer went to, crows no longer raid the compost heap, even the lupines have decreased in number and in brilliance. The soil, perhaps made self-conscious by its conspicuous isolation, no longer bursts with life.

Douglas realizes that his own sap no longer runs in the spring, that the walls of his house ring with no voice save his own. If a farm surrounded by wasteland cannot survive, how then shall a man? *It is my birthday,* he thinks, *how old am I today?*

He cannot remember.

He looks up at the ˙goddamelectricclock (the family's two-hundred-year-old cuckoo clock, being wood, did not survive the Panic Winter of '94), reads the date from its face (there are no longer trees to spare for fripperies like paper calendars), sits back with a grunt. *2049, like I thought, but when was I born?*

So many things have changed in Douglas's lifetime, so many of Life's familiar immutable aspects gone forever. The Danielses to the east died childless: their land now holds a sewage treatment plant. On the west the creeping border of Annapolis Royal has eaten the land up, excreting concrete and steel and far too many people as it went. Annapolis is now as choked as New York City was in Douglas's father's day. Economic helplessness has driven Douglas back up the North Mountain, step by inexorable step, and the profits (he winces at the word) that he reaped from selling off his land parcel by parcel (as, in his youth, he bought it from his ancestors) have been eaten away by the rising cost of living. Here, on his last fourteen acres, in the two-story house he built with his own hands and by Jesus *wood*, Douglas Bent Jr. has made his last stand.

He questions his body as his father taught him to do, is told in reply that he has at least ten or twenty more years of life left. *How old am I?* he wonders again, *forty-five? Fifty? More?* He has simply lost track, for the years do not mean what they did. It matters little; though he may have vitality for twenty years more, he has money for no more than five. Less, if the new tax laws penalizing old age are pushed through in Halifax.

The water has begun to boil. Douglas places wintergreen and sugar in the earthenware mug his mother made (back when clay was dug out of the backyard with a shovel), moves the pot from the stove, and pours. His nostrils test the aroma: to his dismay, the fake smells genuine. Sighing from his belly, he moves to the rocking chair by the kitchen window, places the mug on the sill, and sits down to watch another sunset. From here Douglas can see the Bay, when the wind is right and the smoke from the industrial park does not come between. Even then he can no longer see the far shores of New Brunswick, for the air is thicker than when Douglas was a child.

The goddamclock hums, the mug steams. The winds are from the north—a cold night is coming, and tomorrow may be one of the improbable "bay-steamer" days with which Nova Scotia salts its spring. It does not matter to Douglas: his solar heating is far too efficient. His gaze wanders down the access road which leads to the highway; it curves downhill and left and disappears behind the birch and alders and pine that line it for a half mile from the house. If Douglas looks at the road right, he can sometimes convince himself that around the bend are not stripmining shells and brick apartment-hives but arable land, waving grain and the world he once knew. Fields and yaller dogs and grazing goats and spring mud and tractors and barns and goat berries like stockpiles of B-B shot . . .

Douglas's mind wanders a lot these days. It has been a long time since he enjoyed thinking, and so he has lost the habit. It has been a long time since he had anyone with whom to share his thoughts, and so he has lost the inclination. It has been a long time since he understood the world well enough to think about it, and so he has lost the ability.

Douglas sits and rocks and sips his tea, spilling it down the front of his beard and failing to notice. *How old am I?* he thinks for the third time, and summons enough will to try and find out. Rising from the rocker with an effort, he walks on weary wiry legs to the living room, climbs the stairs to the attic, pausing halfway to rest.

My father was sixty-one, he recalls as he sits, wheezing, on the stair, *when he accepted euthanasia. Surely I'm not that old. What keeps me alive?*

He has no answer.

When he reaches the attic, Douglas spends fifteen minutes in locating the ancient trunk in which Bent family records are kept. They are minutes well spent: Douglas is cheered by many of the antiques he must shift to get at the trunk. Here is the potter's wheel his mother worked; there the head of the axe with which he once took off his right big toe; over in the corner a battered peavey from the long-gone sawmill days. They remind him of a childhood when life still made sense, and bring a smile to his grizzled features. It does not stay long.

Opening the trunk presents difficulties—it is locked and Douglas cannot remember where he put the key. He has not seen it for many years, or the trunk for that matter. Finally he gives up, smashes the old lock with the peavey, and levers up the lid (the Bents have always learned leverage as they got old, working efficiently long after strength has gone). It opens with a shriek, hinges protesting their shattered sleep.

The past leaps out at him like the woes of the world from Pandora's Box. On top of the pile is a picture of Douglas's parents, Douglas Sr. and Sarah, smiling on their wedding day, Grandfather Lester behind them near an enormous barn, grazing cattle visible in the background.

Beneath the picture he finds a collection of receipts for paid grain bills, remembers the days when food was cheap enough to feed animals, and there were animals to be fed. Digging deeper, he comes across canceled cheques, insurance policies, tax records, a collection of report cards and letters wrapped in ribbon. Douglas pulls up short at the hand-made rosary he gave his mother for her fifteenth anniversary, and wonders if either of them still believed in God even then. Again, it is hard to remember.

At last he locates his birth certificate. He stands, groaning with the ache in his calves and knees, and threads his way through the crowded attic to the west window, where the light from the setting sun is sufficient to read the fading document. He seats himself on the shell of a television that has not worked since he was a boy, holds the paper close to his face and squints.

"May twelfth, 1999," reads the date at the top.

Why, I'm sixty years old, he tells himself in wonderment. *Sixty. I'll be damned.*

There is something about that number that rings a bell in Douglas's tired old mind, something he can't quite recall about what it means to be sixty years old. He squints at the birth certificate again.

And there on the last line, he sees it, sees what he had almost forgotten, and realizes that he was wrong—he will be getting a birthday present today after all.

For the bottom line of his birth certificate says, simply and blessedly, ". . . expiry date: May twelfth, 2059."

Downstairs, for the first time in years, there is a knock at the door.

Common Sense

The blind man was watching a videotape when the phone chimed. Bemused, he put the tape deck on *pause* and *hold*, fed the phone circuit to the screen. He frowned at what he saw.

"Good day, Captain," he began formally. "What can I—"

"Ranny will you come to the bridge?" the caller interrupted.

The blind man closed his eyes, but nothing went away. He stiffened in his chair, and then slumped.

"That hurt, Jax," he said at last.

"Damn it, would I *ask* if I didn't need to?"

Ran's face changed. "I suppose not. Milk and sugar in mine." He shut off phone and deck and left, handling himself economically in free-fall.

Ran Mushomi concentrated on the people; the bridge itself hurt too much to look at. He already knew Captain

Jaxwen Kartr and Executive Officer Thorm Exton. But he was startled to see another passenger on the bridge, and profoundly startled to recognize him: Old Man Groombridge himself, president and owner of Intersystem Transport Incorporated. Ran's hackles rose.

"What's he doing here?"

"It's my starship," Groombridge said.

"Traveling to Koerner's World," the Captain said, "like you and two hundred other people, Ranny."

"And a damned good thing I happened to be, too," Groombridge added.

"All right, what's this all about?"

"We need your help," the Captain said, tossing him a bulb of coffee with milk and sugar.

Ran laughed. It was an ugly sound.

Groombridge snorted. "I told you it was a waste of time."

"Ranny, *listen*," Captain Kartr said, her voice urgent. "This is important, damn it."

"To a groundhog?" he asked bitterly.

"Look." She activated a screen. It showed a . . . thing, apparently at rest in space.

"Looks like a lumpy testicle."

"Ran—"

"Or a planet with pimples. Wow, they move. How big is it?"

"About two metres in diameter. It's alive. We think it's sentient. And we think it's hurt."

Ran made no visible reaction; the widening of his eyes was of course unseen beneath his goggles.

"We dropped into normal space for mid-course corrections, as usual," Groombridge said, "and it blundered right into our screens."

"How do you know it's alive?"

"It's trying to pull free of the tractor beam right now," the Captain said.

Ran nodded. "And it must be hurt, because it's not succeeding."

"More than that. Kreel tried to make contact with it." Like most ships' medicos, Kreel was a Domanti empath. "He's down in his own sickbay now, sedated, and you know what it takes to sedate a Domanti. That thing *hurts*."

"How do you know it's sentient?"

"We don't, for sure," the Exec said. "Kreel thought so, but . . ."

"So what do you want me for?"

"Advice," the Captain said. "I respect your brains, Ranny."

"Advice on what?"

"How to communicate with the damned thing."

"What's the problem? Your ship's computer can translate *anything*."

"Given enough input, sure. That's the kicker. Ranny, *we don't know what it uses for senses*."

"Oh."

"Maybe we could cure whatever's wrong with it. Maybe not; maybe we could just talk to it until it dies, find out where and how to find its kin. It's a *new species,* Ranny, and interstellar space seems to be its natural habitat. We don't know what fires its metabolism, how it moves, we don't know *anything*."

"The problem," Ran quoted to himself softly, " 'is to get the mule's attention . . .' " He smiled. "I begin to see. A new species could make Intersystem even richer. But every minute you sit here in normal space, you lose millions in schedule penalties—and you dasn't move the thing."

"Correct," Groombridge said unhappily. "We can't take it into n–space with us without bringing it inboard, and we have no way of knowing whether it can survive inside a radiation-opaque hull.''

"Let alone whether it can survive n–space," Ranny agreed. "A pretty problem."

"Hell, yes," Groombridge growled. "Every other sentient race we've ever encountered have been planet-dwellers, with sensory equipment more or less analogous to our own. I never imagined we'd find a space-dweller."

"And if we lose this one, the odds are slightly less than zero that we'll ever find another," Exton put in.

Ran was thinking hard. "Let's see—even a space-dweller would have *some* use for light, visible or otherwise."

"Sure," the Captain agreed. "On a cosmic scale. All we have to do to 'talk' with it is turn a couple of stars on and off. But how does it *reply*?"

"Doesn't it put out anything?"

"Yeah. Constant body temperature about eight degrees Absolute. Electrical potential fluctuates around its surface in what might very well be meaningful patterns. If so, how do *we* reply? *My* electrical potential varies across my surface—but not at will. The computer has to have *dialogue*, even on the 'Me Tarzan—you Jane' level, before it can begin extrapolating language.''

Ran locked his hands behind his head, the free-fall equivalent of chin-on-fist. "Hmm. I'd bet my socks it perceives gravity gradients, but that's no use. You must have tried radio frequencies by now." He squeezed coffee. "What's it made of?"

"Beats us."

"Damnation," Groombridge said. "We assume that others of its race exist. They must have some means of interspecies communication."

"Perhaps," Ran said. "But there's no reason to assume it's anything we've ever encountered. Maybe they communicate through n–space."

"How about—" the multibillionaire began, and then caught himself.

"Mr. Groombridge," Captain Kartr said diplomatically, "believe me, we've tried everything in the electromagnetic spectrum. As far as I know, the damned things converse by witchcraft. We need something else. A breakthrough."

"I've got it," Ran said with absolute confidence, and sipped coffee.

Involuntary muscle reactions sent the other three spinning around the bridge. Groombridge recovered first. "Well? Out with it, man!"

"Will you meet my price?"

Groombridge began to sputter, then regained control. "Name it."

"I want my ticket back."

"Out of the question."

Captain Kartr decided to stick her neck out. "Sir, with all due respect, Ranny's the best skipper you ever had. I was his exec when he lost his optic nerves saving the *Heimdall*. He spent the last eighty-five years getting rich enough to afford a Visual Analog System, and now he's got better vision than *I* have. Nobody deserves a master's ticket more."

Groombridge studied Ran's VAS goggles. The computer built into them, that processed the signals for their camera lenses into a form which his visual cortex could accept, was as expensive as a good starship computer. They did not provide sight as Ran had once known it—it took about ten years to learn to interpret the new data—but that accomplished, they provided a very satisfactory substitute. "I'm familiar with Mr. Mushomi's record and history. I followed his case, and I'm afraid I agree with what the Board decided last week. It simply isn't sensible to have all the command functions of an n–space vessel funneled through a single, potentially fallible system."

"I repeat," Ran said quietly, although there was murder in his heart. He had once been a *starship pilot*. "Meet my price and I can solve your problem. Payment on delivery."

Interstellar executives *hate* to reverse themselves—but Groombridge was not a fool, and the clock was ticking. "All right, damn you," he snarled. "You'll get your ticket and the command of your choice—witnessed, recorded and binding. Now *give*."

"Get me a pressure suit, Jax," Ran said instantly, and laughed, because his superior peripheral vision allowed him to see all three stunned faces at once.

Many hours later the ship was once again under weigh in n–space, and Ran and Jax were celebrating in the Captain's quarters.

"Who would ever have guessed that what the god damned thing needed was water ice?" she said, taking fresh bulbs of Scotch from the cooler and tossing one to Ran.

"Certainly not me. With a metabolism evolved in space, it must take him a long time to get thirsty."

"And even longer to die of it," Jax agreed. "You *earned* your ticket back, Ranny. Nobody else in the Universe could have done it."

"Nonsense," he said cheerfully, and sucked Scotch. "I spent those eighty-five years earning my eyes on Darkside, because my handicap didn't exist there. It's got a permanent, opaque, planet-wide cloud cover. The natives call it 'God's Rectum,' because it's the only place in the Universe where the sun never shines." The Captain giggled. "Quite a few optic-nerve cases go there—they're not different anymore. *Everybody* knows hand-talk on Darkside."

"S'not what I mean. Oh, that speeded things up, sure, which is penalty saved. But we couldn't have done *anything* without your original insight. I still don't see how you could have been so *sure* the thing had tactile sense."

"I wasn't," Ran said complacently. "I was bluffing Groombridge. What did I have to lose if I was wrong?"

Jax stared openmouthed, then roared with laughter. "You son of a bitch, you were *guessing*?"

"Well, it just seemed reasonable to me. I pictured a race of beings evolved in interstellar space, and I just . . . pictured them *touching* a lot. It's lonely out there." He drained his Scotch. "And after that, of course, all we had to do was use our . . ."

Rubber Soul

But I don't believe in this stuff, he thought, enjoying himself hugely. *I said I didn't; weren't you listening?*[1]

He sensed amusement in those around him—Mum, Dad, Stuart, Brian, Mal and the rest[2]—but not in response to his attempt at irony. It was more like the amusement a group of elders might feel toward a young man about to lose his virginity, amusement at his too-well-understood bravado. It was too benevolent to anger him, but it did succeed in irritating him. He determined to do this thing as well as it had ever been done.

Dead easy, he punned.[3] *New and scary and wonderful, that's what I'm good at. Let's go!*

Then the source of the bright green light came that one increment nearer, and he was transfixed.

Oh!

Time stopped, and he began to understand.

And was grabbed by the scruff of the neck and yanked backward. Foot of the line for you, my lad! He howled

149

his protest, but the light began to recede; he felt himself moving backward through the tunnel, slowly at first but with constant acceleration. He clutched at Dad and Mum, but for the second time they slipped through his fingers and were gone. The walls of the tunnel roared past him, the light grew faint, and then all at once he was in interstellar space, and the light was lost among a million billion other pinpoints. A planet was below him, rushing up fast, a familiar blue-green world.

Bloody hell, he thought. *Not again!*

Clouds whipped up past him. He was decelerating, somehow without stress. Landscape came up at him, an immense sprawling farm. He was aimed like a bomb at a large three-story house, but he was decelerating so sharply now that he was not afraid. Sure enough, he reached the roof at the speed of a falling leaf—and sank gracefully through the roof, and the attic, finding himself at rest just below the ceiling of a third-floor room.

Given its rural setting, the room could hardly have been more incongruous. It looked like a very good Intensive Care Unit, with a single client. Two doctors garbed in traditional white gathered around the figure on the bed, adjusting wires and tubes, monitoring terminal readouts, moving with controlled haste.

The room was high-ceilinged; he floated about six feet above the body on the bed. He had always been nearsighted. He squinted down, and recognition came with a shock.

Christ! You're joking! I done *that bit.*

He began to sink downward. He tried to resist, could not. The shaven skull came closer, enveloped him. He gave up and invested the motor centers, intending to use this unwanted body to kick and punch and scream. Too late he saw the trap: the body was full of morphine.

He had time to laugh with genuine appreciation at this last joke on him, and then consciousness faded.

After a measureless time he woke. Nothing hurt; he felt wonderful and lethargic. Nonetheless he knew from experience that he was no longer drugged, at least not heavily. Someone was standing over him, an old man he thought he knew.

"Mister Mac," he said, mildly surprised.[4]

The other shook his head. "Nope. He's dead."

"So am I."

Another deadpan headshake from the old man. "Dirty rumor. We get 'em all the time, you and I."[5]

His eyes widened. The voice was changed, but unmistakable. "Oh, my God—it's *you*!"

"I often wonder."

"But you're *old*."

"So are you, son. Oh, you don't look it, I'll grant you that, but if I told you how old you are you'd laugh yourself spastic, honest. Here, let me lift your bed."

The bed raised him to a half-sitting position, deliciously comfortable. "So you froze me carcass and then brought me back to life?"

The old man nodded. "Me and him." He gestured behind him.

The light was poor, but he could make out a figure seated in darkness on the far side of the room. "Who—?"

The other stood and came forward slowly.

My God, was his first thought. *It's me*! Then he squinted—and chuckled. "What do you know? The family Jules. Hello, son."[6]

"Hello, Dad."

"You're a man grown, I see. It's good to see you. You look good." He ran out of words.

The man addressed began to smile, and burst into tears and fled the room.[7]

He turned back to his older visitor. "Bit of a shock, I expect."

They looked at each other for an awkward moment. There were things that both wanted to say. Neither was quite ready yet.

"Where's Mother?" he asked finally.[8]

"Not here," the old man said. "She didn't want any part of it."

"Really?" He was surprised, not sure whether or not to be hurt.

"She's into reincarnation, I think. This is all blasphemy and witchcraft to her. She cooperated—she gave us permission, and helped us cover up and all. But she doesn't want to hear about it. I don't know if she'll want to see you, even."[9]

He thought about it. "I can understand that. I promised Mother once I'd never haunt her. Only fair. She still makin' music?"

"I don't think so."

There was another awkward silence.

"How's the wife?" he asked.

The old man winced slightly. "Well enough, I hear. She went right back out the window a while back."[10]

"I'm sorry."

"Sorriest thing I've seen all day, son. You comfy?"

"Yeah. How about Sean?"[11]

"He doesn't know about this yet. His mother decided not to burden him with it while he was growing up. But you can see him if you want, in a few days. You'll like him, he's turned out well. He loves you."

A surge of happiness suffused him, settled into a warm glow. To cover it he looked around the room, squinting at the bewildering array of machines and instruments. "This must have set you back a packet."

The old man smiled for the first time. "What's the

good of being a multimillionaire if you can't resurrect the dead once in a while?"

"Aye, I've thought that a few times meself." He was still not ready to speak his heart. "What about the guy that got me?"

"Copped it in the nick. Seems a lot of your best fans were behind bars."[12]

"Why'd he do it?"

"Who knows? Some say he thought he was you, and you were an impostor. Some say he just wanted to be somebody. He said God told him to do it, 'coz you were down on churches and that."[13]

"Oh, Jesus. The silly fucker." He thought for a time. "You know that one I wrote about bein' scared, when I was alone that time?"

"I remember."

"Truest words I ever wrote. God, what a fuckin' prophet! 'Hatred and jealousy, gonna be the death of me.' "[14]

"You had it backward, you know."

"How do you mean?"

"Nobody ever had better reason to hate you than Jules."

He made no reply.

"And nobody ever had better reason to be jealous of you than me."

Again he was speechless.

"But it was him thought it up in time, and me pulled it off. His idea and enthusiasm. My money. Maybe nobody else on Earth could have made that much nicker drop off the books. So you got that backward, about them bein' the *death* of you." He smiled suddenly. "Old Jules. Just doin' what I told him to do, really."

"Makin' it better."

The old man nodded. "He let you under his skin, you see."[15]

"Am I the first one they brought back, then?"

"One of the first half-dozen. That Wilson feller in California got his daughter back.[16] It's not exactly on the National Health."

"And nobody knows but you and Jules? And Mother?"

"Three doctors. My solicitor. A cop in New York used to know, a captain, but he died. And George and Ringo know, they send their best."[17]

He winced. "I was rough on George."[18]

"That you were, son. He forgives you, of course. Nobody else knows in all the wide world."

"Christ, that's a relief. I thought I was due for another turn on the flaming cupcake. Can you imagine if they fuckin' *knew?* It'd be like the last time was *nothing.*"

It was the old man's first real grin, and it melted twenty years or more from his face. "Sometimes when I'm lying awake I get the giggles just thinking about it."

He laughed aloud, noting that it did not hurt to laugh. "Talk about upstaging Jesus!"[19]

They laughed together, the old man and the middle-aged man. When the laugh ended, they discovered to their mutual surprise that they were holding hands. The irony of that struck them both simultaneously.[20] But they were both of them used to irony that might have stunned a normal man, and used to sharing such irony with each other; they did not let go. And so now there was only the last question to be asked.

"Why did you do it, then? Spend all that money and all that time to bring me back?"

"Selfish reasons."

"Right. Did it ever occur to you that you might be calling me back from something important?"

"I reckoned that if I could pull it off, then it was okay for me to do it."

He thought wistfully of the green light . . . but he was, for better or worse, truly alive now. Which was to say that he wanted to stay alive. "Your instincts were always good. Even back in the old scufflin' days."

"I didn't much care, if you want to know the truth of it. You left me in the lurch, you know. It was the end of the dream, you dying, and everybody reckoned I was the one broke us up so it was my fault somehow. I copped it all. My music turned to shit and they stopped comin' to hear it, I don't remember which happened first. It all went sour when you snuffed it, lad. You had to go and break my balls in that last interview . . ."[21]

"That *was* bad karma," he agreed. "Did you call me back to haunt me, then? Do you want me to go on telly and set the record straight or something?"

The grip on his hand tightened.

"I called you back because you're a better song-writer than I am. Because I miss you." The old man did not cry easily. "Because I love you." He broke, and wept unashamedly. "I've always loved you, Johnny. It's shitty without you around."

"Oh, Christ, I love you too." They embraced, clung to each other and wept together for some time.

At last the old man released him and stepped back. "It's a rotten shame we're not gay. We always did make such beautiful music together."

"Only the best fuckin' music in the history of the world."

"We will again. The others are willing. Nobody else would ever know. No tapes, nothing. Just sit around and play."

"You're incorrigible." But he was interested. "Are

you serious? How could you possibly keep a thing like that secret? No bloody way—"

"It's been a *long* time," the old man interrupted. "You taught me, you taught all three of us, a long time ago, how to drop off the face of the earth. Just stop making records and giving interviews. They don't even come 'round on anniversaries anymore. It'll be dead easy."

He was feeling somewhat weary. "How . . . how long has it been?"

"Since you snuffed it? Get this—I told you it'd give you a laugh. It's been two dozen years."

He worked it out, suddenly beginning to giggle. "You mean, I'm . . . ?"

The old man was giggling too. "Yep."

He roared with laughter. "Will you still feed me, then?"

"Aye," the old man said. "And I'll always need you, too."[22]

Slowly he sobered. The laugh had cost him the last of his strength. He felt sleep coming. "Do you really think it'll be good, old friend? Is it gonna be *fun*?"

"As much fun as whatever you've been doing for the last twenty-four years? I dunno. What was it like?"

"I dunno anymore. I can't remember. Oh—Stu was there, and Brian." His voice slurred. "I think it was okay."

"This is going to be okay, too. You'll see. I've given you the middle eight. Last verse was always your specialty."[23]

He nodded, almost asleep now. "You always did believe in scrambled eggs."[24]

The old man watched his sleeping friend for a time. Then he sighed deeply and went to comfort Julian and phone the others.

Concordiat to "Rubber Soul"

In the fall of 1981, I chanced to be in New York City because my wife Jeanne had been invited to perform with the Beverly Brown Dansensemble at the Riverside Dance Festival. On October 9, feeling slightly silly but quite unable to help myself, I took my six-year-old daughter Luanna with me on a pilgrimage of sorts, up Central Park West to Seventy-second Street. To the building called the Dakota. I felt a powerful need to bid "Happy Birthday" to a dead man, who should on that day have turned forty-one.

Perhaps two or three hundred people subject to the same need were already present, gathered around the limo entrance where it had happened. It was curiously difficult to name their mood. Sometimes it felt like subdued good cheer, and sometimes it felt like barely concealed despair. I stood across the street with my daughter and watched and listened to ragged choruses of appropriate songs and tried, without the least success, to name my own mood. What was I doing here?

Suddenly a black limo pulled up in front of me. Its sole passenger was an elderly white-haired dowager who plainly was in a position to buy the Dakota if the fancy had struck her. I thought of *old* money, perhaps royalty. She powered down her window and addressed a group of us standing more or less together. "What is going on?" she asked quite politely.

The man standing next to me pointed across the street at the Dakota, and said simply, "It's his birthday."

She followed his pointing finger, and she must have taken his meaning instantly, because at once she burst explosively into tears. "Drive on," she mumbled, dabbing at her eyes with a fifty-dollar hankie, and the limo pulled away.

That universally loved he was.

So it seems to me that my story "Rubber Soul" should need no concordiat, that its protagonist was/is a genuinely universal culture hero, that its internal references and allusions require no explanation for most of you—else I should not have offered it for sale.

But my esteemed editors take the not unreasonable position that while most of you will get most of the references, it is unlikely that any of you will get *all* of them; wherefore they have requested this concordiat. I bow to their superior wisdom, and their superior bargaining position. You, however, must feel free to skip this section and go on to the next story if it suits you.

1) I intended this as a reference to the song "God" on the *Plastic Ono Band* album, in which John recites a list of things in which he does not believe, including "Magic . . . I Ching . . . Bible . . . Tarot . . . Jesus . . . Buddha . . . mantra . . . [and] Gita." At the time the song was written, "Near-Death Experiences" and OOBEs had not yet become the stuff of cocktail-party conversation, but I

have always felt that if "God" had been written a few years later, John would have included them as well. On the other hand, in his last interview in *Playboy,* he characterized himself as "a most religious fellow . . . religious in the sense of admitting there is more to it than meets the eye . . . there is more that we still could know. I think . . . magic is just a way of saying science we don't know yet or we haven't explored yet." On the third hand, a man who refused to believe in either creationism *or* evolutionism (or, for that matter, in cancer) might well have considered near-death experiences underresearched.

2) Most of those who recount NDEs mention the presence of predeceased loved ones. Those would surely include John's mother Julia (run over by a drunken off-duty cop), his father Fred (died of cancer), original Beatle Stu Sutcliffe (died of cerebral hemorrhage), Beatles manager Brian Epstein (accidental overdose of Carbitrol) and Beatles roadie/companion Mal Evans (shot by police in Los Angeles).

3) John, author of "In His Own Write" and "A Spaniard in the Works," always believed that a good pun is in the *oy* of the beholder.

4) It seems to me that John, confronted with a Paul McCartney twenty-four years older than when last seen, would quite naturally mistake him for his father, James McCartney (pianist and former leader of the Jim Mac Jazz Band), in whose living room at Forthlin Road he and Paul had taught each other to play the guitar. (At the time of this writing, James McCartney is alive and well.)

5) Obviously a reference to the "Paul-is-dead" hysteria which swept the world in October 1969. Ironically, at that point Paul was alive, but the Beatles as a group were dead.

6) Many have commented on the physical resemblance between John and Julian Lennon, his first son by Cynthia

Powell Lennon. Julian will be forty-one by the time of the story, and just as likely as "Mister Mac" to be mis-identified by a man two dozen years dead. "The family Jules" is a typical Lennon pun, referring to a Paul McCartney nickname for Julian, of which more later.

7) The relationship between John and Julian was less than ideal when John was killed. Relevant quotes from "The Playboy Interviews With John Lennon and Yoko Ono": (Playboy Press, 1981) "I got rights to see him on his holidays and all that business and at least there's an open line still going. It's not the best relationship between father and son, but it is there . . . Julian and I will have a relationship in the future . . . I'm just sort of a figure in the sky, but he's obliged to communicate with me, even when he probably doesn't want to . . . I'm not going to lie to Julian. Ninety percent of the people on the planet, especially in the West, were born out of a bottle of whis-key on a Saturday night, and there was no intent to have children . . . I don't love Julian any less as a child. He's still my son, whether he came from a bottle of whiskey or because they didn't have pills in those days. He's here, he belongs to me, and he always will." It seems to me that Julian's emotions at the hypothetical revival of his father would be so mixed as to preclude immediate expression.

8) "Mother" was John's pet name for Yoko Ono.

9) I'm on shaky ground here, and my wife is annoyed with me for having failed to depict John and Yoko's legendary love as transcending death and time. I have no idea what Ms. Ono's opinions are on cryogenics; I have only the gut feeling that she is a very practical and intelligent woman who, her husband having been mur-dered before her eyes, would "declare him dead" in her mind and get on with her life, no matter what technological wizardry others might attempt. And if the attempt *did* pay

off, I believe she would be perceptive enough to approach a reunion twenty-four years later with caution, if at all. Please feel free to disagree; this story is my own dream, and you are perfectly welcome to your own.

10) The reference is to the song Paul wrote, "She Came in Through the Bathroom Window," shortly after meeting Linda Eastman McCartney. This paragraph is sheer science-fiction speculation. I have no evidence to suggest that Paul and Linda's marriage will not last another two and a half decades—other than general statistics on rock-star marriages, which are not relevant; statistics are *never* relevant to a marriage. I sincerely hope the speculation turns out to be false; this is just how it came out in my dream.

11) Obviously a reference to Sean Ono Lennon, John and Yoko's son. John stopped making music and dropped out of public life for five years to be a full-time parent to Sean.

12) Frankly, I cannot understand the continued failure of *this* particular science-fiction speculation to come true. Unless they keep him in solitary forever, it surely will one day . . . if he doesn't chicken out and do the job himself first. Again, though, this is a speculation that I personally hope will *not* come true, and if by chance you happen to be a prisoner who is in a position to slip a shank into Mark Chapman, I urge you to restrain yourself. Johnny was into peace; he wouldn't like it.

13) These are the three most commonly given reasons for the assassination; it may be that all three are true to some extent. Chapman himself claims that he overheard, as it were, an irritated God muttering, "Who will rid me of this troublesome John Lennon?"; I am intrigued to hear that a judge has refused to accept this as *prima facie* evidence of insanity. I keep remembering accounts of

Chapman's days as a born-again Christian: when the song "Imagine" was released with the line, "Imagine . . . nothing to kill or die for/and no religion, too," he and his friends used to chant, "Imagine no John Lennon."

14) The song "I'm Scared," written during the black period when John and Yoko were estranged, will be found on the album *Walls and Bridges*. The quote here is from one of John's most powerful middle eights: "Hatred and jealousy/gonna be the death of me/I guess I knew it right from the start/Sing out about love and peace/don't wanna see the red raw meat/the green-eyed, goddam, straight from the heart."

15) In October 1968, Paul McCartney paid a surprise visit to Cynthia and Julian Lennon. Cynthia was suing John for divorce, Yoko was pregnant, six-year-old Julian was confused and unhappy. Paul sang him a song he had made up on the way over in the car, to cheer him up, called "Hey, Jules." By the time it was recorded, it was "Hey, Jude." "Remember to let (her) under your skin/Then you'll begin/to make it better."

16) One of the best-known and most articulate proponents of cryogenic stasis is Robert Anton Wilson, co-author of the Illuminati novels and author of many fine fact and fiction books. Mr. Wilson's daughter Luna was beaten to death during a robbery several years ago; her body is cryogenically preserved.

17) If I have to tell you who George and Ringo are, perhaps we should just forget the whole thing.

18) In "The Playboy Interviews," John took a few angry potshots at George Harrison and his then-new book, *I, Me, Mine* (cf. pp. 126–28). He does, however, finish, "I am slightly resentful of George's book, but don't get me wrong—I still love those guys . . . I don't want to start another whole thing between me and George just because of the way I feel today."

19) Obviously a reference to what is probably the single most famous Beatle utterance of all, the most frequently misquoted and misunderstood thing John Lennon ever said: "We're more popular than Jesus now." He made it quite plain in that famous interview (with Maureen Cleave in the London *Evening Standard*) that he had nothing against Jesus, but only against some of his "thick" followers. "They're the ones who ruin it for me," he said. Sure enough, one of them ruined it all for him.

20) Surely you get the reference to "I Want To Hold Your Hand."

21) Again we are in the realm of speculation. In "The Playboy Interviews," John gets off several digs and potshots at Paul; in the title-by-title survey of Beatle tunes, for instance, he recalls countless instances when he helped Paul out with a given song, and few or no instances in which Paul helped *him*. Indeed at one point he charges rather vaguely that McCartney sometimes "sabotaged" Lennon's songs in the studio. I have before me a clipping from the *Dartmouth* (Nova Scotia) *Free Press,* unfortunately unattributed, headed, "John Still Liked Me, After All," which quotes an interview with Paul in the *Times* of London: " 'I certainly wasn't responsible for splitting up the Beatles as some people suggest.' . . . [Paul] also said he and Lennon didn't dislike one another—as many suggested. But he did acknowledge that Lennon's public criticism of him in the early 1970s shocked and hurt him . . . he rarely answered Lennon's challenges because he had little chance of matching his former partner's renowned wit. Lennon . . . actually liked him, McCartney said. *'From a purely selfish point of view, if I could get John Lennon back, I'd ask him to undo this legacy he's left me*. I'd ask him to tell everyone what he told Yoko in the privacy of his own room. Yoko and I talk on the phone a lot nowadays since his death, and what she says tells me

something very important: John still liked me, after all.' "
(Italics mine.) I think it is also significant in this connection that when a British radio station recently asked Paul to pick his ten favorite songs of all time, his choice for number one was a Lennon song from *Double Fantasy*, "Beautiful Boy," written to Sean.

22) John died at age forty; the reference here is obviously to Paul's song "When I'm Sixty-four," with its tag line, "Will you still need me?/Will you still feed me?/When I'm sixty-four."

23) John always maintained that Paul was particularly good at coming up with the middle eight—in "A Day In The Life," for instance, the inspired "Woke up, fell out of bed . . ." section.

24) "Scrambled Eggs" was the original working title of the tune that later became better known as "Yesterday."

In connection with Number 23 above, I must tell you that my original title for this story was "Middle Eight." "Rubber Soul" (a reference of course to the Beatles' album of the same name) was *The Best of Omni* editor Don Myrus's idea, and I think it is brilliant. There's something just, I don't know, cosmically appropriate in the notion of John Lennon's soul bouncing like a bad check. Thanks, Don.

Father Paradox

Carmody made sure that the guard would remain unconscious, then straightened and regarded the door with the closest thing to elation that he had felt in a long time. A part of him, since he was a moral man, felt sorrow and guilt for the pain of the fallen guard—and for the trail of other unconscious guards he had left behind him on his way to this door. But then, he reminded himself, very shortly the pain of all those public servants would—quite literally—vanish as if it had never been.

For behind the door was the world's first, and so far only, time machine.

Its existence was not common knowledge—or it would have been guarded much too well for Carmody to have come this far. But at present a bare handful of academics and military people knew that a time machine existed.

But what none of them realized—what Carmody alone had been in a position to realize—was that the machine was also the world's first and so far only *perfect* means of suicide.

The would-be suicide is presented with at least two major problems. First, of course, it *hurts*. There *is* no truly painless form of suicide. And to the extent that one minimizes physical pain, and thus shock, one maximizes the psychological horror of those last instants before the end. The last dreams of a sleeping-pill suicide, for instance, must surely be nightmares.

The second problem facing a would-be suicide with anything like a moral sense is that the suicide never solves his problems by dying, but merely transfers them to someone else. Loved ones, friends, relatives, bystanders, the stranger who bags the body or scrapes up the remains, the many strangers who read the rising suicide statistics and are disheartened thereby, all have to take on the karmic burden that was too heavy for its original bearer. Suicide is not simply a cop-out, but a rip-off, and Carmody was grown-up enough to know that.

But his wife and children were gone for good and his job was blown and his life was shit, and beyond that door was the perfect—the *only* perfect—solution to his problem, and so Carmody stepped over the guard and went through the door.

He was stunned by the simplicity of the time machine. It was a wire cage the shape and dimension of a bath-shower enclosure. The wire was narrow-guage. Inside the cage was a conventional computer console which seemed to have its own power source. The only odd hardware between it and cage was a black box the size of a Brazil nut. The room held nothing else but folding chairs. Carmody put away his pistol.

He sat at the console. It would tell him nothing about the interior of the black box without a security code he did not know—but it was willing to supply him with operating instructions. Within five minutes he knew how to send himself to a precise point in space and time. He selected the north forty of his father's farm in upper New York State for a geographical locus, and a day nine and a half months before his own birth for his chronological locus.

Carmody had read enough science fiction to be familiar with the classic Grandfather Paradox of time travel. He had always wondered whether it was some sort of unresolved collective-unconscious oedipal conflict which was responsible for the apparently universal decision to select the grandfather for the starring role in the conundrum. Why, since it would serve the purpose of the paradox equally well, should a hypothetical time traveler not slay his own father? (Or, for that matter, mother or grandmother?) Why go back *two* branches of the time-tree, and involve more extraneous relatives?

For Carmody the choice was clear. He had always hated his father, a sour, embittered old man who had always been cold to Carmody, and who had beaten Carmody's beloved mother every day of his life.

And so Carmody punched the *execute* key (failing to see the pun in that), and the room outside the time cage was replaced by a field of corn.

His father was checking the young ears for corn-borer infestation. When the cage materialized before him he most obligingly fainted.

Carmody himself was nearly as startled. The face of the unconscious man was unmistakably that of his father—but changed, even more than he had expected and allowed for. Age had written none of the sourness and bitterness that Carmody remembered on these features yet; the man looked optimistic and strong and good.

He shrugged and got on with the business at hand. Stepping out of the time-cage and onto the warm, soft soil of 1946, he stood over his unconscious father and removed his pistol from his pants pocket.

It was the ideal suicide. When the bullet crashed through his father's brain, Carmody himself—and all his problems, all his karma—would cease to exist, to *ever have existed*. How could that *hurt*—either himself or anyone else? He would literally erase himself from the fabric of history, root and branch, as Time healed itself around the wound he had made. His mother would never even know that she had been spared a lifetime of beatings . . . and a son who had grown up to be a disappointment.

He was aware, of course, of the theoretical possibility that his action might cause all of reality to disappear. But in the first place, this struck him as being unlikely—and in the second place he had to admit that the disappearance of the universe would solve his problem just as thoroughly. No one would suffer. Ever again. He pulled the trigger, and the man at his feet died.

And nothing else happened. He stood, still extant and suicidal, over a corpse with a smoking gun in his hand, and failed to dematerialize. "So the father paradox doesn't obtain after all," he mused. "Oh, the hell with it." He got back into the time cage and went home to 1987, where he ultimately committed a conventional suicide which hurt a good deal and saddened many other people. He never knew that at the moment his victim had died, his mother, a mile away in the farmhouse, was explaining to the hired man that because her husband's war wound had made him sterile, the hired man had damned well better pull out in time.

Carmody's last thought was that he was a particularly unlucky bastard, and he never knew how right he was.

True Minds

Locating her was no trouble at all. He tried the first bar that he came to, and as he cleared the door the noise told him that he had found her.

Behind the bar, the proprietor glanced around and recognized Paul, and his expression changed radically. He had been in the midst of punching a phone number; now he cleared the screen and came over to Paul.

"Hi, Scotty."

"Another one, Mr. Curry?" He jerked a thumb over his shoulder toward the back of the bar. Just around a corner and out of sight, a small riot seemed to be in progress; as Scott pointed, a large man sailed gracefully into view and landed so poorly that Paul decided he had been unconscious before he hit. The ruckus continued despite his absence.

"Afraid so, Scotty. I'm sorry."

"Jesus Christ. It's bad enough when they cry, but what the hell am I supposed to do with *this*? I dunno, I'm old

169

fashioned, but I liked it back when ladies had to be ladylike.''

A half-full quart of scotch emerged from the rear of the room at high speed and on a flat trajectory. It took out the mirror behind the bar and at least a dozen other bottles.

Paul almost smiled. "That is, and always has been, ladylike," he said, nodding toward the source of airborne objects. "What you mean is, you liked it better when, if it came to it, you could beat them up."

"Is that what I mean? Maybe it is. Mr. Curry, why in hell don't he just *tell* them?"

"Think about it, Scotty," Paul advised. "If it were you . . . would *you* tell them?"

"Why—" the innkeeper began, and paused. He thought about it. "Why—" he began again, and again paused. "I guess," he said at last, "I wouldn't at that." The sound of breaking glass took him back from his thoughts. "But honest to God, Mr. Curry, you gotta *do* something. I'm ready to call the heat—and I *can't*. You know who she is. But what if I don't report it and somebody gets—"

A scream came from the back, a male voice, but so high and shrill that both men clenched their thigh muscles in empathy.

"—see?" Scotty finished.

"You're covered," Paul told him. "From here on it's my problem," and he legged it for the source of the commotion.

As he rounded the corner she was just disposing of the last bouncer. The man had height, mass, and reach over her, but none of them seemed to be doing him any good. He was jackknifed forward, chin outthrust, in perfect position from her point of view; she was slapping him with big roundhouse swings, alternating left and right, slapping his unshaven face from side to side. Paul could not decide whether the bouncer was too preoccupied with his aching testicles to be aware of the slaps, or whether he welcomed them as an aid to losing consciousness. If the latter, his strategy worked—one last terrific left rolled up his eyes and put him down and out before Paul had time to intervene.

Paul Curry was, if the truth be known, terrified. He was slightly built, and lacked the skill, temperament, and training for combat which had not been enough to help the sleeping bouncer. Utensil, he thought wildly, where is there a utensil? Say, a morningstar. Nothing useful presented itself.

But love can involve one in strange and complex obligations, and so he moved forward emptyhanded.

She pivoted to face him, dropped into a crouch. He stopped short of engagement range and displayed the emptiness of his hands. "Miss Wingate," he began. He saw her eyes focus, watched her recognize him, and braced himself.

She left her crouch, straightened to her full height, and in the loudest voice he had ever heard coming from a woman she roared, *"He doesn't know* ANYTHING *about love!"*

And then—he would never forget it, it was one of the silliest and most terrible things he had ever seen—she clenched her right fist and cut loose, a short, vicious chop square on the button. Her own button. She went down harder than the bouncer had.

Scotty stuck his head gingerly around the corner. "Nice shot, Mr. Curry. I didn't know you could punch like that."

Paul thought, I am in a Hitchcock movie. Briefly he imagined himself trying to explain to the bartender that Anne Wingate had punched herself out. "Well," he said, "you've never pissed me off, Scotty. Give me a hand, will you?"

They got her onto a chair, checked pulse and pupils,

failed to bring her around with smelling salts. "All right," Paul said at last, "I'll take her to my place and she can sleep it off." The bartender looked unhappy. "Don't worry, Scotty. I'm a gentleman."

"I know that, Mr. Curry," Scotty said, looking scandalized. "But what do I—"

"There'll be no beef to you," Paul said. "I'll see to it. She was never here, right?"

Scotty looked around at the carnage. "I'll say it was a platoon of Marines."

"That'll work."

"Mr. Curry, honest to God, if Senator Wingate comes down on me, forty years of squeeze goes right down the—"

"The Senator will never hear a word about this, Scotty. Trust me."

Paul was painfully aware that his promise was backed by nothing at all. By the time the cab arrived he was feeling pessimistic—he insisted that the driver prove to him that his batteries held adequate charge. It is not necessarily a disaster to run out of juice, even in an Abandoned Area; one simply buttons up and waits for the transponder to fetch the police. But if one is in the company of the unconscious daughter of an extremely powerful man at the time, one can scarcely hope to stay out of the newstapes.

The batteries were indeed charged; the offended driver insisted that Paul prove he had the fare. As Paul and Scotty were loading her into the cab, she opened one eye, murmured, "Not a single *thing*," and was out again. The trip was uneventful; even when the driver was forced to skirt Eagle turf, they drew only desultory small arms fire. She slept through it all.

Luck was with him; she did not begin vomiting until just as he was getting her out of the cab. Nonetheless he tipped the cabbie extra heavily, both by way of apology and to encourage amnesia. Mollified, the driver waited until Paul had gotten her safely indoors before pulling away.

She was half awake now. He managed to walk her most of the way to the bathroom. She sat docilely on the commode while he got her soiled clothes off. He knew she would return to full awareness very shortly after the first blast of cold shower hit her, and he was still determined not to be beaten up by her if he could avoid it. So he sat her down in the tub, made sure everything she would need was available, slapped the shower button and sprinted from the room while the water was still gurgling up the pipes. He was halfway to his laundry unit when the first scream sounded. It was the opening-gun of a great deal of cacophony, but he had thoughtfully locked the bathroom door behind him; the noise had ceased altogether by the time he had coffee and toast prepared.

He went down the hall, unlocked the bathroom door. "Miss Wingate," he said in a firm, clear voice, "the coffee is ready when you are."

The response was muttered.

"Beg pardon?"

"I said, Philip Rose doesn't know one goddamned thing about love."

"The coffee will stay hot. Take your time." He went back to the kitchen and poured himself a cup. In about five minutes she came in. She wore the robe he had left for her. Her hair was in a towel. Very few people can manage the trick of being utterly formal and distant while dressed in robe and towel, but she had had expert training from an early age. She did not tell him how seldom she did this sort of thing, because she assumed he knew that.

"May I have some coffee, Mr. Curry?"

He watched the steadiness of her hand as she picked up the cup, and wondered if, given her money, he could buy himself physical resilience like that, or if a person just had to be born with it.

"Thank you for looking after me," she said. "I'm sorry I've been such a bother. I've put you to no end of expense and difficulty and I . . . not the *first* damned thing about it. This is very good coffee, Mr. *How* can you work for a phoney like that?"

"I liked you better drunk."

"I beg your pardon?"

"And if you call Mr. Rose a phoney again, Miss Wingate, I will as politely as possible punch you in the mouth." Or die trying, he added to himself.

She took her time answering. "I apologize, Mr. Curry. I am a guest under your roof. Forgive my bad manners." She looked suddenly sheepish. "This really is excellent coffee. Are my clothes salvageable?"

He was getting used to her Stengelese conversational style. "There was no difficulty and your apology is accepted and I'm pleased you like the coffee and he knows a great deal more about love than anyone alive and your clothes are in the laundry. Did I leave anything out?"

She looked stubborn and drank her coffee. He poured more, and passed her her purse so that she could have a cigarette. "Don't worry," he said as she lit up. "The aspirins should take effect any minute."

She almost choked on smoke. "How do you know I took aspirins?" she asked sharply.

He raised an eyebrow. "Afraid I spied on you in my own bathroom? Miss Wingate, how do you think you got in the tub? I don't strip all my guests, but you were covered with vomit. Look, you got hurt and then drunk and then crazy, and then you passed out and woke up in a squall of icewater. If your head doesn't hurt, you're dead. There are aspirin in my medicine chest, clearly marked, and I assume you have an instinct for self-preservation."

She wore an odd expression, as if there were something extraordinary or dismaying about what he had said. "Oh," she said finally in a small voice. "Again I apologize."

"De nada, Miss Wingate."

"Anne."

"Paul."

"Paul, why do I get the impression that none of this is new to you?"

He poured himself another cup. "New to me?"

"You're too competent, too skilled at coping with troublesome drunken women. I'm not the first, am I?"

He laughed aloud, surprising himself. "Anne, you are not the twenty-first. I've been Mr. Rose's personal secretary for about ten years, and I would say that one of you manages to get past me every six or seven months, on the average." He frowned. "Too many." And thought, but you *looked* intelligent and stable.

"And you say he knows about love." She put down her cup, got up and paced. She came to his powered cookstool; the proper height for counter and cabinet work; a pedal for each wheel, heel for reverse, toe for forward. She sat on it and heel-and-toed it into rotating. It was a whole-body fidget, annoying to watch.

"Anne, love rides his back like a goblin. It lives in his belly like a cancer. He wears it like a spacesuit in a hostile environment. It wears him like a brakedrum wears shoes. I can't tell whether he generates love or the other way around." His voice was rising; he was irritated by her continued rotation on the stool. "I think everybody knows that. Everybody who can read."

She stopped the stool suddenly, with her back to him. "Was there ever anything that 'everybody knew' that turned out to be so?"

His irritation increased. "I worry about anyone under eighteen who isn't a cynic—and anyone over eighteen who is. There are *thousands* of things that everybody knows that are true. Falling off a cliff will hurt you. It gets dark at night. Snow is cold. Philip Rose knows about love. Damn it, you've read his books.''

"Yes, I've read his fucking books!" she yelled at his refrigerator.

Something told him that now was the time to shut up. He sat where he was, elbows on the table, pinching his lower lip between his thumbs, and looked at her back. It was some time before she spoke, but he did not mind the wait.

"When I was eight years old," she said at last, "my Aunt Claire gave me one of his juveniles. *Latchkey Kid*. It smacked me between the eyes."

He nodded uselessly.

"I'd always been loved. So thoroughly, so completely, so automatically that both I and the people who loved me took it for granted. The book made me understand what it *felt* like not to be loved. That would have been enough for most writers. But Rose went further. He made me love Cindy, even though she wasn't very likeable, and he made me see how even she could find love, even in a world like hers. He wasn't famous then, he only had a dozen or so books out.

"The next one I tried was *Tommy's Secret*. I don't suppose I could quote you more than a chapter or so at a time without referring to the text. For my tenth birthday I asked for a hard-cover set of everything he had ever written. My father was scandalized—it wasn't expensive enough—so I let him buy me two sets. That way I had one copy to preserve, immaculate, and one I could mark up and underline and dog-ear. Soon I found I needed a third set. Some writers you want to keep, special and private, for yourself and a few close friends. Rose I gave away to anyone who didn't duck fast enough.

"There is a story he wrote, 'A Cup of Loneliness,' that is the only reason I didn't kill myself when I was sixteen."

Unseen, Paul nodded again.

"By then I was old enough to realize how much I owed Aunt Claire. Unfortunately I realized it at her funeral. After a while I decided that I was repaying her by giving Philip Rose to other people. I mailed copies of his books to every critic and reviewer I could find. In college I got three credits of independent study for a critical analysis of Rose's lifework to date that must have taken me forty-eight hours to put on paper. My professor got it published. I began to realize just how much weight my father's name carried, and I used it, to see that Philip Rose's career prospered. Eventually I had persuaded enough influential people to 'discover' him that public awareness of him started to grow.

"Part of that was selfish. He was obscure, next to nothing was known about him as a person in any references I could find. I wanted to know about him, about his life, about where he had been and what he had done and whether or not he had had enough love in his own life."

Paul nodded a third time and lit one of her cigarettes.

"He didn't accept visitors and didn't give interviews and didn't return biographical questionnaires from Who's Who in Books and didn't put more than he could help in his 'About the Author' blurbs. All I knew was that it said in the back of *Broken Wings* that he was married, and then the PR for the next one, *A Country We Are Privileged to Visit,* mentioned that he lived alone in this city. It never occurred to me to actually approach him myself, any more than it would occur to most people to look up the President." (Curry happened to know that the President had been Anne Wingate's godfather.) "But I threw reporters and scholars at him until I realized I was wasting his time and mine. If *People* magazine can't get past you to him, no one can. I suppose I could have just put a good agency onto researching him, but the idea of setting detectives on Philip Rose is grotesque.

"I decided that I would make him famous, and sooner or later he would simply have to open up. Not that I claim to be responsible for his fame—even I'm not that arrogant. He was already certain to be a legend in his own lifetime—but I speeded up the process. And it didn't work worth a damn. Not since Salinger has a writer been so famous, so loved, and so little known. You cover him well. I still don't know what went wrong with his marriage—or even what her name was.

"Finally I decided there was only one way to thank the man who had taught me everything I know about love. It's because of him that I studied lovemaking, so that I could give my lovers a gift that was something more than a commonplace. It's because of him that I'm still involved in politics. It's because of him that I don't hate my father. It's because of him that I don't hate myself."

Paul interrupted for the first time. "You don't hate yourself, Anne, because he taught you how to forgive."

She banged her fist against the stool's flank. *"How can I forgive him for what he did?"*

He kept his own voice soft and low. "Don't you mean, How can I forgive him for what he didn't do?"

"Damn it, he didn't have to *do* anything. Just lay back and let me do the doing—"

"And that wouldn't be doing something? You say you've studied lovemaking: is there any such thing as a passive partner? Aside from necrophilia and rubber dolls? You wanted him to *do* you the favour of accepting pleasure from you. You're young and very beautiful: perhaps you've never met a man who wouldn't count that a privilege. You made your offer, and he declined politely—I'll bet my life it was politely—and so you decided to make him an offer he couldn't refuse. And learned the sad truth: that there is *no* offer a man cannot refuse if he must.''

"Why 'must'? There was no obligation of any kind, expressed or implied—if he's half the telepath his books make him seem, he must have known that. All I wanted to do was say thanks.''

"You *did* thank him. And then before he could say 'you're welcome,' you tried to ram your thanks down his throat, or down yours, or whatever, and made him throw you out. There's an old John Lennon song, 'Norwegian Wood.' I've always felt that he changed the title to avoid censorship. I think the song is about the nicest compliment a man can receive from a woman. Isn't it good?: *knowing she would*. But that message can be conveyed from twenty feet away, by body language. Only children need it confirmed by effort and sweat, that's what Lennon was trying to say. Damn it, Anne, haven't you ever been turned down?''

"Not like *that*!''

"You gave Mr. Rose exactly two choices: be raped or be rude. I wasn't there, but I *know*. Otherwise he would not have been rude.''

"But—''

"Anne, I've been through this before, and I must say they usually take it better than you. But once every couple of years or so we get one so young and so blind with need that he has to be rude to turn her off. It always upsets him.''

"Damn you,'' she yelled.

"Anne, the first step to forgiving yourself is facing up to what you've done wrong. Or did you think that your own upset was only hurt pride and frustration?''

"And how do you handle the dumb young insistent ones?'' she asked bitterly, and spun the stool around to face him. He saw tear tracks. "Take the Master's sloppy seconds?"

"I lie to them, generally," he said evenly. "I talk to them until I get an idea of which excuse they're willing to be sold, and then I sell it to them. If it seems necessary, I figure out what sort of bribe or threat it will take to keep their mouths shut, and provide that. As for myself, I prefer bed partners who know as much about love as they do about lovemaking."

She flinched, but said nothing. She was studying his face.

"You say you've read all his books," he went on. "Do you recall reading in any of them a definition of 'love'? As opposed to lust or affection or need or any of a dozen other cousins?"

"No, I don't think he's ever defined it, in so many words."

"You're right. But there *is* a single, concise definition that runs through everything he ever wrote. He never wrote it down because it had already been done, by another writer, about whom Mr. Rose feels much the same way that you feel about him."

"The old man in free fall? The science fiction writer?"

"That's right. You *have* done your homework. He defined love as 'that condition in which the welfare and happiness of another are essential to your own.' "

She thought that over. "Make your point."

"Is that what you claim motivated you?"

Her eyes closed. Her expression smoothed over. She was looking deep inside for the answer. After twenty seconds she half opened her eyes. "Yes, partly," she said slowly. "More than half. I wanted to be personally sure he was happy and well—to make him happy myself, to be there and know that it was so."

"By giving him something he doesn't want."

"Damn it, he needs it—he must!"

"Ah, the old standby of the teenage male: 'Continence is unhealthy.' Anne, in your experience, do priests and monks tend to die young?"

"But why would *he* want to be celibate?"

"Did it ever occur to you that he might not have any choice? Let me tell you a story that is none of your—"

She shook her head. "Now you're doing what you said a moment ago—lying, giving me a plausible excuse. Some story about a war wound, or a tragic accident, or a wasting disease. Save it, please. Philip Rose's work could *not* have been produced by any kind of a eunuch. Furthermore, I *know* better. He had to be *very* rude to get rid of me. I got close enough to be sure that all his equipment was in place and functioning." She smiled bitterly. "I don't care much for puns, but I assure you: Philip rose."

So did his eyebrows. "My respect for you has jumped another notch. I'm impressed. And, frankly, intrigued. And mildly annoyed at the low respect in which you seem to hold me. I have not lied to you yet, and I wasn't going to start. The story I was—"

"Why not?"

"Do you want to hear this story or not?"

His volume made her start. She must have spent a lot of time on the road; the small involuntary movements of her feet, brake, clutch, accelerator, made the chair pivot back and forth spasmodically, so that as her head nodded yes, her body said no.

Neither of them could help giggling at that; it broke some of the tension, leaving both with half smiles. She waited in silence, determined not to interrupt again, while he chose his words.

This took him longer than it should have. He found that he was staring at her eyelashes. They were so long and perfectly formed that he had assumed them false. Now he saw that they were real. He tore his gaze from them, fixed it on his own hands, whereupon he discovered that they were fidgeting, caressing each other. He forced them to be still—and his foot started tapping on the floor.

"You are certainly under twenty-five," he said, "so you cannot have been born earlier than 1970. Which does not," he added, "mean that you're ignorant of prior times. I know you are something of a historian. But you're not likely to have an intuitive feel for an era you haven't lived through."

He saw the ever-so-slight tightening of those muscles used to keep the mouth shut. Her mouth was as distracting as her eyes.

"Philip Rose," he went on doggedly, "was born in 1934. He didn't marry until he was twenty-five—that made it 1959. Marriage then was something different from marriage today. Which actually may not be all that relevant—Mr. Rose has never been a slave to convention. He has always, I think, made his own rules.

"Maybe that's the point I'm trying to make. If you are the kind of man who makes his own rules, in 1959, you *keep* the rules you make for yourself. That's the dilemma that Situational Ethics blundered into—if you can change them situationally, they're not rules; if you can't they're a straitjacket. What I mean is, Mr. Rose might change his own personal rules—but once he's made a promise, he'll keep it. No matter how much he might—or might not—regret making it.

"So in 1959 he married Regina Walton. There were several unconventional things about the marriage, and one very conventional thing.

"The first unconventional thing was the age difference. She was nearly ten years older than he, already well established in her field. The second unconventional thing—for the time—was that she kept her own last name. At his

urging. A Rose by any other name, and so forth. The final
unconventional thing was that they wrote their own wedding vows—and that was the thing that hurt.

"Can you see that? How that would make a difference
to him? The conventional marriage ceremony of that time
was an utterly standardized legal contract with ritual trap-
pings. Everyone took the same vows, with minor varia-
tion, and as you took them you knew they could be
dissolved in thirty days in Reno. If you must mouth a
certain formula in order to cohabit legally, then, if you
should ever change your mind, you can rationalize that it
wasn't a 'real' promise. But the two of them wrote their
own vows, thinking them through very carefully first—so
they left themselves no loopholes at all.

"Which is a shame, because of the one conventional
part I mentioned. Their contract is quite specific: lifetime
sexual fidelity is spelled out. Old fashioned death-do-us-
part monogamy.

"Conventional for the time: even though divorce was
common then, term marriage was emphatically not. Oh,
people got married knowing that 'forever' might translate,
'until we change our minds'—but they didn't get married
at all unless they at least *hoped* for forever.

"But Philip and Regina *meant* it. They were practical
romantics: they did not want a deal they could quit when
the going got tough. They carefully left themselves no
escape clauses."

Involuntarily, she interrupted for the first time. "Foolish."

"Shut your stupid mouth," he said quietly. "It is not
for you to criticize them."

She bit her lip.

"I read just the other week, the average term marriage
runs three years, and the average 'lifetime' marriage now
lasts about nine or ten years. The Rose-Walton union has
lasted forty years so far."

He might just as well have kicked her in the belly. Her breath left her explosively, her hands and feet flew up from their resting places, snapped back. She drew air convulsively in through both nose and mouth, slumped down again in her chair and cried, "No!" She jumped up and began pacing around the room, turning to face him as she paced. "No. It's not possible! I would have *heard, some*thing— and there was no trace of a woman's hand in that apartment, I'm *certain* of that, damn it, the first thing I *thought* of was someone else." As she convinced herself, she began to get mad at him. "You lying son of a—"

"You don't listen very well," he said, enough edge on his voice to get through to her. "I said they were practical romantics. I said they thought it through. Her profession sometimes made long trips necessary, and his work-habits made him a homebody. They agreed to be faithful forever— but they did *not* promise to live together always."

She stopped pacing. She blinked those marvelous eyelashes so rapidly that he fancied he could feel the breeze. Then she shut her eyes and frowned.

"For more than twenty-five years," he continued, "all went well and more than well and better than that. I don't know why they never had children—I never will unless he chooses to tell me—but they don't seem to have suffered from the lack of children. They were never apart for more than three or four months at a time, and when they were together they were more together than most people ever get to be. He says that they supplied each other's missing parts, that between them they made up one good and sane human being. You said yourself he's a telepath. Anyone may have a taste of telepathy, but it takes a really good marriage to develop it to anything like his level."

He paused, and was silent in thought for a time, and she waited patiently.

"Then the hammer fell on them.

"Her field was immunology, and she was one of its leaders. It was a natural interest for her—she was loaded with serious allergies herself, the kind that have to be wrestled with permanently and can kill you if you get careless. When the European Space Station went up, it was a natural for her. What better place could there be to do medical research than a totally and permanently sterile environment? So she bullied and squeezed her way into a tour as the ESS's first resident physician. She and her husband thought it would be a pleasant vacation from her own allergies. I assume you know what happened to most of the first-year ESS personnel."

She was gaping, perhaps for the first time in her life. "You are telling me that 'Dr. R.V. Walton' is Regina Wal . . . is *Philip Rose's wife?*"

"Trapped in space by free-fall adaptation—one of the unlucky fourteen pioneers. She can never come home again."

"Oh my God." Her eyes were open so wide that the lashes now appeared normal size. She swayed where she stood, and her hands made little seeking gestures for something to clutch. They settled on the robe she wore, and if he needed any further proof of the extent of the impact on her, he had it, for as she clenched at the pockets of the robe it parted, baring her up to the belt, and she failed to notice. "Oh filthy *God*," she cried. "Oh, couldn't he—"

"Not unless the fucking Space Taxi ever gets off the drawing boards," he said bitterly. "Ten years overdue already. The Shuttles are space trucks, big rough brutes. All his life Philip Rose has had a bad heart valve. He's in great shape for a man of sixty-five. He'll probably live another ten or fifteen years, here on Earth. But there's never been a day in his life when he could have survived a Shuttle blastoff."

She looked up at the ceiling. She looked down at the

floor, and absently pulled the robe closed. She looked from side to side. She sat on the floor and stuck out her lower lip and burst into tears.

He went on his knees beside her, holding her in one strong arm and stroking her hair. She cried thoroughly and easily and for a long time, and when she was done she stopped. "And they still . . . how could. . . ."

"You know," he told her, "you did him a hell of a big favour, helping him get famous. The money came along just in time, Anne—his phone bill was getting to be a bonecrusher."

"You mean—"

"Every night they spend at least an hour on the phone together, talking, sharing their respective days, sometimes just looking at each other. With a three-quarter-second time lag." He shook her gently. "Anne, listen to me: it's sad, but it's not *that* sad. They live. They work. They have time together every day, more than some doctors' spouses—or writers' spouses—get by on. They just can't touch. They are, incredible as it may seem to you and me, both quite happy. In all the years I have known them, I've never heard either of them complain about the situation, not ever. Maybe there aren't many people who could maintain and enjoy a relationship like that. But they were already each other's other leg when she first went up into orbit. When one of them dies, the other will go within a month—but meanwhile what they have is enough for them."

She sat with her head bowed. Slowly, stiffly she got to her feet. He helped her and stood himself. He began gathering up dirty cups and dishes.

"Where's your laundry?"

"Down the hall there," he said, "just past the coat closet. Your clothes will be ready to wear by now. I'll call you a cab."

She was back, dressed and face repaired, by the time the

cab showed on the door-screen. "Paul," she said formally, heading for the door, "I want to thank—"

He held up his hand. "Wait just one minute, please."

She paused, clearly already gone in her mind but trying to be politely attentive.

"Back when I first met Mr. Rose, before I knew his situation, I made my own pass. Tentatively, because I knew he was old-fashioned in some ways. But I made it clear that as his personal secretary and his fan I would do *anything* he wanted. He was flattered. Turned me down, of course, but it has made for a kind of intimacy between us, that we might never have shared otherwise. So I'm in a position to tell you something you have no business knowing. He won't mind, and I think I know you well enough now to believe that it may be comfort of a kind to you. Do you know what he is doing now? Seventy percent certainty?"

She shook her head.

"He's on the phone with Regina. It's that time of night. He's telling her about your encounter, embellishing in spots, perhaps, and they are masturbating together."

She stood stock still, expressionless, for perhaps ten seconds. And then she smiled. "Thank you, Paul. It is a comfort."

And she left. He watched the door monitor until he was certain she had entered the cab safely.

A week later his phone blinked. He looked over the caller—and accepted at once. "Anne! Hello!"

"One question," she said briskly. "When the robe came open, you didn't look. Not even a glance. Are you gay-only?"

He caught the robe reference at once; the question took him a second. "Eh? Oh . . . I see. Emphatically no. It's just that I only look at skin that's being shown to me."

She nodded. "Thought so. Wanted to be sure." She

smiled. "I know why you didn't lie to me. I'm going to be very busy for a long time. Be patient."

And the screen went dark, leaving him mystified.

Two years later he was talking to one of the dozens of reporters who crammed the pressroom at Edwards Air Force Base.

"—takes off just like a conventional plane," he was saying, "no more takeoff stress than a 797—so Mr. Rose should have no trouble at all. I think it's going to add twenty years to his life."

"What I can't figure," the reporter said, "is how incredibly *fast* the thing got pushed through. Two years from a standing start, wham, the damned thing is out of R & D, into production, and up in the air." He turned his head to watch the big monitor screen which showed the new Space Taxi climbing, endlessly climbing. "Two years ago it was too expensive and impractical. Now it's halfway to ESS and your boss has a firm reservation for the fourth flight in a couple of months. *Some*body in congress made a big muscle . . . but why wouldn't he cash in on the PR? I go back to the Shuttle days, Mr. Curry, and that was like pulling teeth. This went so quick it almost scares me."

Paul nodded. "Yep, it's a wonder, all right," he said, and then he said, "Excuse me, Phil," very abruptly, and seemed to teleport across the crowded pressroom.

She was waiting for him, exquisite in white and blue.

"Hello, Paul."

"Hello, Anne."

"Two years is a long time."

"Yes." He gestured at the huge monitor. "Short time for a project like that, though. You did a good job."

She smiled. "Today, for the first time in two years, my father is off the hook."

He smiled back. "I pity your enemies."

"You didn't lie to me, two years ago, because you were in love with me." The way she said it was somewhere between a question and an accusation.

"That's right."

"Are you sexually or romantically encumbered now?"

"No."

"Then there is some skin I'd like to show you."

"Yes."

"Should we have dinner before or after, do you think?"

An observer might have said that she read her answer on his face, but it was really nothing of the sort.

Satan's Children

A beginning is the end of something, always.

Zaccur Bishop saw the murder clearly, watched it happen—although he was not to realize it for over an hour.

He might not have noticed it at all, had it happened anywhere but at the Scorpio. The victim himself did not realize that he had been murdered for nearly ten minutes, and when he did he made no outcry. It would have been pointless: there was no way to demonstrate that he was dead, let alone that he had been killed, nor anything whatever to be done about it. If the police had been informed—and somehow convinced—of all the facts, they would have done their level best to forget them. The killer was perhaps as far from the compulsive-confessor type as it is possible to be: indeed, that was precisely his motive. It is difficult to imagine another crime at once so public and so clandestine. In any other club in the world it would have been perfect. But since it happened at the Scorpio, it brought the world down like a house of cards.

The Scorpio was one of those clubs that God sends every once in a while to sustain the faithful. Benched from the folkie-circuit for reasons he refused to discuss, a musician named Ed Finnegan somehow convinced the owners of a Chinese restaurant near Dalhousie University to let him have their basement and an unreasonable sum of money. (Finnegan used to claim that when he vacationed in Ireland, the Blarney Stone tried to kiss him.) He found that the basement comprised two large windowless rooms. The one just inside the front door he made into a rather conventional bar—save that it was not conventionally overdecorated. The second room, a much larger one which had once held the oil furnace (the building predated solar heat), he painted jet black and ceilinged with acoustic tile. He went then to the University, and to other universities in Halifax, prowling halls and coffeehouses, bars, and dormitories, listening to every musician he heard. To a selected few he introduced himself, and explained that he was opening a club called Scorpio. It would include, he said, a large music room with a proper stage and spotlight. Within this music room, normal human speech would be forbidden to all save the performers. Anyone wishing food or drink could raise their hand and, when the waitress responded, point to their order on the menu silk-screened into the tablecloth. The door to this room, Finnegan added, would be unlocked only between songs. The PA system was his own: six Shure mikes with boomstands, two Teac mixers, a pair of 600-watt Toyota amps, two speaker columns, four wall speakers, and a dependable stage monitor. Wednesday and Thursday were Open Mike Nights, with a thirty-minute-per-act limit, and all other nights were paying gigs. Finnegan apologized for the meagerness of the pay: little more than the traditional all-you-can-drink and hat privileges. The house piano, he added, was in tune.

Within a month the Scorpio was legend, and the Chinese restaurant upstairs had to close at sunset—for lack of parking. There have always been more good serious musicians than there were places for them to play; not a vein for the tapping but an artery. Any serious musician will sell his or her soul for an intelligent, sensitive, *listening* audience. No other kind would put up with Finnegan's house rules, and any other kind was ejected—at least as far as the bar, which featured a free jukebox, Irish coffee, and Löwenbräu draft.

It was only because the house rules were so rigidly enforced that Zack happened to notice even that most inconspicuous of murders.

It happened in the spring of his twenty-fourth year. He was about to do the last song in his midevening solo set; Jill sat at a stageside table nursing a plain orange juice and helping him with her wide brown eyes. The set had gone well so far, his guitar playing less sloppy than usual, his voice doing what he wanted it to, his audience responding well. But they were getting restive: time to bottle it up and bring Jill back onstage. While his subconscious searched its files for the right song, he kept the patter flowing.

"No, really, it's true, genties and ladlemen of the audio radiance, I nearly had a contract with Chess Records once. Fella named King came to see me from Chess, but I could see he just wanted old Zack Bishop for his pawn. He was a screaming queen, and he spent a whole knight tryin' to rook me, but finally I says, 'Come back when you can show me a check, mate.' " The crowd groaned dutifully, and Jill held her nose. Lifting her chin to do so exposed the delicate beauty of her throat, the soft grace of the place where it joined her shoulders, and his closing song was chosen.

"No, but frivolously, folks," he said soberly, "it's nearly time to bring Jill on back up here and have her sing a few—but I've got one last spasm in me first. I guess you could say that this song was the proximate cause of Jill and me getting together in the first place. See, I met this lady and all of a sudden it seemed like there was a whole lot of things we wanted to say to each other, and the only ones I could get out of my mouth had to do with, like, meaningful relationships, and emotional commitments, and how our personalities complemented each other and like that.'' He began to pick a simple C-Em-Am-G cycle in medium slow tempo, the ancient Gibson ringing richly, and Jill smiled. ''But I knew that the main thing I wanted to say had nothing to do with that stuff. I knew I wasn't being totally honest. And so I had to write this song.'' And he sang:

> Come to my bedside and let there be sharing
> Uncounterfeitable sign of your caring
> Take off the clothes of your body and mind
> Bring me your nakedness . . . help me
>   in mine . . .
>
> Help me believe that I'm worthy of trust
> Bring me a love that includes honest lust
> Warmth is for fire; fire is for burning . . .
> Love is for bringing an ending . . .
>   to yearning
>
> For I love you in a hundred ways
> And not for this alone
> But your lovin' is the sweetest lovin'
> I have ever known

He was singing directly to Jill, he always sang this song directly to Jill, and although in any other bar or coffee-house in the world an open fistfight would not have distracted his attention from her, his eye was caught now by a tall, massively bearded man in black leather who was insensitive enough to pick this moment to change seats. The man picked a stageside table at which one other man was already seated, and in the split second glance that Zack gave him, the bearded man met his eyes with a bold, almost challenging manner.

Back to Jill.

> Come to my bedside and let there be giving
> Licking and laughing and loving and living
> Sing me a song that has never been sung
> Dance at the end of my fingers and tongue

> Take me inside you and bring up your knees.
> Wrap me up tight in your thighs and then squeeze
> Or if you feel like it you get on top
> Love me however you please, but please . . .
>   don't stop

> For I love you in a hundred ways
> And not for this alone
> But your lovin' is the sweetest lovin'
> I have ever known

The obnoxious man was now trying to talk to the man he had joined, a rather elderly gentleman with shaggy white hair and ferocious moustaches. It was apparent that they were acquainted. Zack could see the old man try to shush his new tablemate, and he could see that the bearded man was unwilling to be shushed. Others in the audience were also having their attention distracted, and resenting it. Mentally gritting his teeth, Zack forced his eyes away and threw himself into the bridge of the song.

I know just what you're thinking of
There's more to love than making love
There's much more to the flower than the bloom
But every time we meet in bed
I find myself inside your head
Even as I'm entering your womb

The Shadow appeared as if by magic, and the Shadow was large and wide and dark black and he plainly had sand. None too gently he kicked the bearded man's chair and, when the latter turned, held a finger to his lips. They glared at each other for a few seconds, and then the bearded man turned around again. He gave up trying to talk to the white-haired man, but Zack had the funny idea that his look of disappointment was counterfeit—he seemed underneath it to be somehow *satisfied* at being silenced. Taking the old man's left hand in his own, he produced a felt-tip pen and began writing on the other's palm. Quite angry now, Zack yanked his attention back to his song, wishing fiercely that he and Jill were alone.

So come to my bedside and let there be loving
Twisting and moaning and thrusting and shoving
I will be gentle—you know that I can
For you I will be quite a singular man . . .

Here's my identity, stamped on my genes
Take this my offering, know what it means
Let us become what we started to be
On that long ago night when you first came with me

Oh lady, I love you in a hundred ways
And not for this alone
But your lovin' is the sweetest lovin'
I have ever known

The applause was louder than usual, sympathy for a delicate song shamefully treated. Zack smiled half-ruefully at Jill, took a deep draught from the Löwenbräu on the empty chair beside him, and turned to deliver a stinging rebuke to the bearded man. But he was gone, must have left the instant the song ended—Shadow was just closing the door behind him. The old man with the absurd mous- taches sat alone, staring at the writing on his palm with a look of total puzzlement. Neither of them knew that he was dead. The old man too rose and left the room as the applause trailed away.

To hell with him, Zack decided. He put the beer down at his feet and waved Jill up onto the stage. "Thank you folks, now we'll bring Jill back up here so she and I can do a medley of our hit . . ."

The set went on.

The reason so many musicians seem to go a little nutty when they achieve success, demanding absurd luxuries and royal treatment, is that prior to that time they have been customarily treated like pigs. In no other branch of the arts is the artist permitted so little dignity by his merchandisers and his audience, given so little respect or courtesy. Ed Finnegan was a musician himself, and he understood. He knew, for instance, that a soundproof dressing room is a pearl without price to a musician, and so he figured out a cheap way to provide one. He simply erected a single soundproof wall, parallel to the music room's east wall and about five feet from it. The resulting corridor was wide enough to allow two men with guitars to pass each other safely, long enough to pace nervously, and silent enough to tune up or rehearse in.

And it was peaceful enough to be an ideal place to linger after the last set, to recover from the enormous expenditure of energy, to enjoy the first *tasted* drink of the night, to hide from those dozens of eyes half-seen through the spotlight glare, to take off the sweat-soaked image and lounge around in one's psychic underwear. The north door led to the parking lot and was always locked from the outside; the south door opened onto stage right, and had a large sign on its other side that said clearly, "If the performers wish to chat, sign autographs, accept drinks or tokes or negotiate for your daughter's wedding gig, they will have left this door open and you won't be reading this. PLEASE DO NOT ENTER. DON'T KNOCK IF YOU CAN HELP IT. RESPECT US AND WE'LL MAKE BETTER MUSIC. Thank you—Finnegan."

It was sanctuary.

Zack customarily came offstage utterly exhausted, while Jill always finished a gig boiling over with nervous energy. Happily, this could be counterbalanced by their differing metabolic reactions to marijuana: it always gave Zack energy and mellowed Jill. The after-gig toke was becoming a ritual with them, one they looked forward to unconsciously. Tonight's toke was a little unusual. They were smoking a literal cigar of grass, GMI's newest marketing innovation, and assessing the validity of the product's advertising slogan: "It doesn't get you any higher—but it's more fun!"

Zack lay on his back on the rug, watching excess smoke drift lazily up from his mouth toward the high ceiling. An internal timer went off and he exhaled, considered his head. "Let me see that pack," he said, raising up on one elbow. Jill, just finishing her own toke, nodded and passed over both cigar and pack.

Zack turned the pack over, scanned it and nodded. "Brilliant," he said. He was beginning to come out of his postperformance torpor. He toked, and croaked "Fucking brilliant," again.

Jill managed to look a question while suppressing a cough.

He exhaled. "Look," he said. " 'Guaranteed 100% pure marijuana.' See what that means?"

"It means I'm not crazy, I really *am* stoned."

"No, no, the whole cigar business. Remember the weather we had last spring? Half the GMI dope fields got pasted with like thirty-two straight days of rain, which is terrific for growing rope and rotten for growing smoke. Stalks like bamboo, leaves like tiny and worth squat, dope so pisspoor you'd have to smoke a cigar-full of it to get off. So what did they do?" He grinned wolfishly. *"They made cigars.* They bluffed it out, just made like they planned it and made cigars. They're pure grass, all right—but you'd have to be an idiot to smoke a whole cigar of *good* grass. And by Christ I'll bet they pick up a big share of the market. These things *are* more fun."

"What do you think that is?" Jill asked. "*Why* is it more fun? Is it just the exaggerated oral trip?"

"Partly that," he admitted. "Oh hell, back when I smoked tobacco I knew that cigars were stronger, cooler, and tastier—I just couldn't afford 'em. But these aren't much more expensive than joints. Breaks down to about a dime a hit. Why, don't you like 'em?"

She took another long toke, her expression going blank while she considered. Suddenly her eyes focused, on him. "Does it turn you on to watch me smoke it?" she asked suddenly.

He blushed to his hairline and stammered.

"Honesty, remember? Like you said when you sang our song tonight. Trust me enough to be honest."

"Well," he equivocated. "I hadn't thought about . . ." He trailed off, and they both said "bullshit" simultaneously and broke up. "Yeah, it turns me on," he admitted.

She regarded the cigar carefully, took a most sensuous

toke. "Then I shall chain smoke 'em all the way home," she said. "Here." She handed him the stogie, then began changing out of her stage clothes, making a small production out of it for him.

Eight months we've been living together, Zack thought, *and she hasn't lost that mischievous enthusiasm for making me horny. What a lady!* He put the cigar in his teeth, waggled it and rolled his eyes. "Why wait 'til we get home?" he leered.

"I predict another Groucho Marx revival if those things catch on." Her bra landed on top of the blouse.

"I like a gal with a strong will," he quoted, "or at least a weak won't." He rose and headed for her. She did not shrink away—but neither did she come alive in his arms.

"Not here, Zack."

"Why not? It was fun in that elevator, wasn't it?"

"That was different. Someone could come in."

"Come on, the place is closed, Finnegan and the Shadow are mopping up beer and counting the take, nobody's gonna *fuck a duck.*"

Startled, she pulled away and followed his gaze. A shining figure stood in the open doorway.

She was by now wearing only ankle-length skirt and panties, and Zack had the skirt halfway down her hips, but she, and he, stood quite still, staring at the apparition. It was several moments after they began wishing for the power of motion that they recalled that they possessed it; moments more before they used it.

"It was true," the old man said.

He seemed to shine. He shimmered, he crackled with an energy only barely visible, only just intangible. His skin and clothes gave the impression of being on the verge of bursting spontaneously into flame. He shone as the Christ must have shone, as the Buddha must have shone, and a

Kirlian photograph of him at that moment would have been a nova-blur.

Zack had a sudden, inexplicable and quite vivid recollection of the afternoon of his mother's funeral, five years past. He remembered suddenly the way friends and relatives had regarded him as strangers, a little awed, as though he possessed some terrible new power. He remembered feeling at the time that they were correct—that by virtue of his grief and loss he was somehow charged with a strange kind of energy. Intuitively he had *known* that on this day of all days he could simply scream at the most determined and desperate mugger and frighten him away, on this day he could violate traffic laws with impunity, on this day he could stare down any man or woman alive. Coming in close personal contact with death had made him, for a time, a kind of temporary shaman.

And the old man was quite dead, and knew it.

"Your song, I mean. It was true. I was half afraid I'd find you two bickering, that all that affection was just a part of the act. Oh thank *God*."

Zack had never seen anyone quite so utterly relieved. The old man was of medium height and appeared to be in robust health. Even his huge ungainly moustaches could not completely hide the lines over half a century of laughter and smiles. His complexion was ruddy, his features weatherbeaten, and his eyes were infinitely kindly. His clothes were of a style which had not even been revived in years: bell-bottom jeans, multicoloured paisley shirt with purple predominating, a double strand of beads and an Acadian scarf-cap sloppily tied. He wore no jewellery other than the beads and no make-up.

A kind of Hippie Gepetto, Zack decided. *So why am I paralyzed?*

"Come in," Jill said, and Zack glanced sharply at her, then quickly back. The old man stepped into the room, leaving the door ajar. He stared from Zack to Jill, and back again, from one pair of eyes to the other, and his own kindly eyes seemed to peel away onion-layers of self until he gazed at their naked hearts. Zack suddenly wanted to cry, and that made him angry enough to throw off his trance.

"It is the custom of the profession," he said coldly, "to knock and shout, 'Are you decent?' Or didn't you see the sign there on the door?"

"Both of you are decent," the old man said positively. Then he seemed to snap out of a trance of his own: his eyes widened and he saw Jill's half-nakedness for the first time. *"Oh,"* he said explosively, and then his smile returned. "Now I'm supposed to apologize," he twinkled, "but it wouldn't be true. Oh, I'm sorry if I've upset you—but that's the last look I'll ever get, and you're lovely." He stared at Jill's bare breasts for a long moment, watched their nipples harden, and Zack marvelled at his own inability to muster outrage. Jill just stood there . . .

The old man pulled his eyes away. "Thank you both. Please sit down, now, I have to say some preposterous things and I haven't much time. Please hear me out before you ask questions, and please—please!—believe me."

Jill put on the new blouse and jeans, while Zack seated himself from long habit on the camel-saddle edge of his guitar case. He was startled to discover the cigar still burning in his hand, stunned to see only a quarter-inch of ash on the end. He started to offer it to the old man; changed his mind; started to offer it to Jill; changed his mind; dropped the thing on the carpet and stepped on it.

"My name is Wesley George," the old man began.

"Right," Zack said automatically.

The old man sighed deeply. "I haven't much time," he repeated.

"What" *the hell would Wesley George be doing in*

Halifax? Zack started to say, but Jill cut him off sharply with "He's Wesley George and he doesn't have much time" and before the intensity in her voice he subsided.

"Thank you," George said to Jill. "You *perceive* very well. I wonder how much you know already."

"Almost nothing," Jill said flatly, "but I know what I know."

He nodded. "Obviously you've both heard of me; Christ knows I'm notorious enough. But how much of it stuck? Given my name, how much do you know of me?"

"You're the last great dope wizard," Zack said, "and you were one of the first. You used to work for one of the 'ethical' drug outfits and you split. You synthesized DMT, and didn't get credit for it. You developed Mellow Yellow. You made STP safe and dependable. You develop new psychedelics and sell 'em cheap, sometimes you give 'em away, and some say you're stone nuts and some say you're the Holy Goof himself. You followed in the footsteps of Owsley Stanley, and you've never been successfully busted, and you're supposed to be richer than hell. A dealer friend of mine says you make molecules talk."

"You helped buy the first federal decrim bill on grass," Jill said, "and blocked the cocaine bill—both from behind the scenes. You founded the Continent Continent movement and gave away five million TM pills in a single day in New York."

"Some people say you don't exist," Zack added.

"As of now, they're right," George said. "I've been murdered."

Jill gasped; Zack just stared.

"In fact, you may have noticed it done," Wesley said to Zack. "You remember Sziller, the bearded man who spoiled your last solo? Did you see him write this?"

George held his left hand up, palm out. A black felt-tip

pen had written a telephone number there, precisely along his lifeline.

"Yeah," Zack agreed. "So what?"

"I dialed it a half hour ago. David Steinberg answered. He said that once he had a skull injury, and the hospital was so cheap they put a *paper* plate in his head. He said the only side effect was that every sunny day he *had* to go on a picnic. I hung up the phone and I knew I was dead."

"Dial-a-Joke," Jill said wonderingly.

"I don't get it," said Zack.

"I was supposed to meet Sziller here tonight—in the bar, after your set. I couldn't understand why he came into the music room and tried to talk to me there. He knew better. He *wanted* to be shushed, so he'd have to write his urgent message on my hand. And the urgent message was literally a joke. So what he really wanted was to write on my hand with a felt-tip pen."

"Jesus," Zack breathed, and Jill's face went featureless.

"In the next ten or fifteen minutes," George said conversationally, "I will have a fatal heart attack. It's an old CIA trick. A really first-rate autopsy might pick up some traces of a phosphoric acid ester—but I imagine Sziller and his people will be able to prevent that easily enough. They've got the building surrounded; I can't get as far as my car. You two are my last hope."

Zack's brain throbbed, and his eyelids felt packed with sand. George's utter detachment was scary. It said that Wesley George was possessed by something that made his own death unimportant—and it might be catching. His words implied that it was, and that he proposed to infect Zack and Jill. Zack had seen *North By Northwest*, and had no intention of letting other people's realities hang him out on Mount Rushmore if there were any even dishonourable way to dodge.

But he could *perceive* pretty well himself, and he knew

that whatever the old man had was a burden, a burden that
would crush him even in death unless he could discharge
it. Everything that was good in Zack yearned to answer the
call in those kindly eyes; and the internal conflict—almost
entirely subconscious—nearly tore him apart.

There was an alternative. It would be easy to simply
disbelieve the old man's every word. Was it plausible that
this glowing, healthy man could spontaneously die, killed
by a bad joke? Zack told himself that Hitler and Rasputin
had used just such charisma to sell the most palpable
idiocies, that this shining old man with the presence of a
Buddha was only a compelling madman with paranoid
delusions. Zack had never seen a picture of Wesley George.
He remembered the fake Abby Hoffman who had snarled
up the feds for so long. He pulled scepticism around
himself like a scaly cloak, and he looked at those eyes
again, and louder and more insistent even than Jill's voice
had been, they said that the old man was Wesley George
and that he didn't have much time.

Zack swallowed something foul. "Tell us," he said,
and was proud that his voice came out firm.

"You understand that I may get you both dipped in soft
shit, maybe killed?"

Zack and Jill said, "Yes," together, and glanced at
each other. This was a big step for both of them: there is
all the difference in the world between agreeing to live
together and agreeing to die together. Zack knew that
whatever came afterward, they were married as of now,
and he desperately wanted to think that through, but there
was no time, no time. *What's more important than death
and marriage?* he thought, and saw the same question on
Jill's face, and then they turned back as one to Wesley
George.

"Answer me a question first," the old man said. Both
nodded. "Does the end justify the means?"

Zack thought hard and answered honestly. Much, he was sure, depended on this.

"I don't know," he said.

"Depends on the end," Jill said. "And the means."

George nodded, content. "People with a knee-jerk answer *either* way make me nervous," he said. "All right, children, into your hands I place the fate of modern civilization. I bring you Truth, and I think that the truth shall make you flee."

He glanced at his watch, displayed no visible reaction. But he took a pack of tobacco cigarettes from his shirt, lit one, and plainly gave his full attention to savouring the first toke. Then he spoke, and for the first time Zack noticed that the old man's voice was a pipe organ with a double bass register, a great resonant baritone that Disraeli or Geronimo might have been proud to own.

"I am a chemist. I have devoted my life to studying chemical aspects of consciousness and perception. My primary motivation has been the advancement of knowledge; my secondary motive has been to get people high—as many people, as many ways as possible. I think the biggest single problem in the world, for almost the last two decades, has been morale. Despairing people solve no problems. So I have pursued better living through chemistry, and I've made my share of mistakes, but in the main I think the world has profited from my existence as much as I have from its. And now I find that I am become Prometheus, and that my friends want me dead just as badly as my enemies.

"I have synthesized truth.

"I have synthesized truth in my laboratory. I have distilled it into chemical substance. I have measured it in micrograms, prepared a dozen vectors for its use. It is not that hard to make. And I believe that if its seeds are once sown on this planet, the changes it will make will be the biggest in human history.

"Everything in the world that is founded on lies may die."

Zack groped for words, came up empty. He became aware that Jill's hand was clutching his tightly.

" 'What is truth?' asked jesting Pilate, and would not stay for answer. Neither will I, I'm afraid—but I ought to at least clarify the question. I cannot claim to have objective truth. I have no assurance that there is such a thing. But I *have* subjective truth, and I *know* that exists. I knew a preacher once who got remarkable results by looking people square in the eye and saying, 'You do *too* know what I mean.' "

A spasm crossed the old man's face and his glowing aura flickered. Zack and Jill moved toward him as one, and he waved them away impatiently.

"Even those of us who pay only lip service to the truth know what it is, deep down in our hearts. And we all believe in it, and know it when we see it. Even the best rationalization can fool only the surface mind that manufactures it; there is something beneath, call it the heart or the conscience, that knows better. It tenses up like a stiff neck muscle when you lie, in proportion to the size of the lie, and if it stiffens enough it can kill you for revenge. Ask Richard Corey. Most people seem to me, in my cynical moments, to keep things stabilized at about the discomfort of a dislocated shoulder or a tooth about to abscess. They trade honesty off in small chunks for pleasure, and wonder that their lives hold so little *joy*. Joy is incompatible with tensed shoulders and a stiff neck. You become uneasy with people in direct proportion to how many lies you have to keep track of in their presence.

"I have stumbled across a psychic muscle relaxant."

"Truth serum's been around a long time," Zack said.

"This is no more pentothal than acid is grass!" George thundered, an Old Testament prophet enraged. He caught himself at once—in a single frantic instant he seemed to extrude his anger, stare at it critically, tie it off, and amputate it, in deliberate steps. "Sorry—rushed. Look: pentothal will—sometimes—get you a truthful answer to a direct question. *My* drug imbues you with a strong desire to get straight with all the people you've been lying to regardless of the consequences. Side effects include the usual accompaniments of confession—cathartic relief, euphoria to the point of exaltation and a tendency to babble— and a new one: visual colour effects extremely reminiscent of organic mescaline."

He winced again, clamped his jaw for a moment, then continued.

"That alone might have been enough to stand the world on its ear—but the gods are jollier than that. The stuff is water-soluble—damn near anything-soluble—and skin-permeable and as concentrated as hell. Worse than acid for dosage, and it can be taken into the body just about every way there is. For pentothal you have to actually shoot up the subject, and you have to hit the vein. My stuff—Christ, you could let a drop of candle wax harden on your palm, put a pinpoint's worth on the wax, shake hands with a man and dose him six or seven hours' worth. You could put it on a spitball and shoot it through a straw. You could add it to nail polish or inject it into a toothpaste tube or roll it up in a joint or simply spray it from an atomizer. Put enough of it into a joint, in a small room, and even the nonsmokers will get off. The method Sziller has used to assassinate me would work splendidly. There may be some kind of way to guard against it—some antidote or immunization—but I haven't found it yet. You see the implications, of course."

At some point during George's speech Zack had reached the subconscious decision to believe him implicitly. With doubt had gone the last of his paralysis, and now his mind was racing faster than usual to catch up. "Give me a week and a barrel of hot coffee and I think I could reason out most of the major implications. All I get now is that you can make people be truthful against their will." His expression was dark.

"Zack, I know this sounds like sophistry, but that's a matter of definition. Whoa!" He held up his hands. "I know, son, I know. The Second Commandment of Leary: 'Thou shalt not alter thy brother's consciousness without his consent.' So how about retroactive consent?"

"Say again."

"The aftereffects. I've administered the drug to blind volunteers. They knew only that they were sampling a new psychedelic of unknown effect. In each case I gave a preliminary 'attitude survey' questionnaire with a few buried questions. In fourteen cases I satisfied myself that the subject would probably *not* have taken the drug if he or she had known its effect. In about three-quarters of them I damn well knew it.

"The effects were the same for all but one. All fourteen of them experienced major life upheaval—usually irreversible and quite against their will—while under the effects of the drug. They all became violently angry at me after they came down. Then all fourteen stormed off to try and put their lives back together. Thirteen of them were back within a week, asking me to lay another hit on them."

Zack's eyes widened. "Addictive on a single hit. Jesus."

"No, *no!*" George said exasperatedly. "It's not the drug that's addictive, dammit. *It's the truth that's addictive.* Every one of those people came back for, like, three-four hits, and then they stopped coming by. I checked up on the ones I was in a position to. They had just simply rearranged their lives on solid principles of truth and honesty and began to live that way all the time. *They didn't need the drug anymore*. Every damn one of them thanked me. One of them fucked me, sweetly and lovingly—at my age.

"I was worried myself that the damned stuff might be addictive. So I had at least as many subjects who *would* probably have taken the drug knowingly, and *all* of them asked for more and I told them no. Better than three-fourths of them have made similar life adjustments on their own, without any further chemical aid.

"Zack, living in truth *feels good*. And it sticks in your memory. Like, it's a truism with acid heads that you can never *truly* remember what tripping feels like. You *think* you do, but every time you trip it's like waking up all over again, you recognize the head coming on and you dig that your memories of it were shadows. *But this stuff you remember!* You're left with a vivid set of memories of just exactly how good it felt to not have any psychic muscles bunched up for the first time since you were two years old. You remember joy; and you realize that you can recreate it just by not ever lying anymore. That's goddam hard, so you look for any help you can get, and if you can't get any you just take your best shot.

"Those people ended up happier, Zack.

"Zack, Jill . . . a long long time ago a doctor named Watt slapped me on the ass and forced me to live. It was very much against my will; I cried like hell and family legend says I tried to bite him. Now my days are ended, and taking it all together I'm very glad he went to the trouble. He had my retroactive consent. It wasn't his fault anyhow: my parents had already forced me to exist, before I had a will for it to be against—and they have my retroactive consent. Many times in my life, good friends and even strangers have kicked my ass where it needed kicking; at least twice women have gently and compassionately kicked me out—all against my will, and they all have my retroactive consent, god bless 'em. Can it be immoral to dose folks if you get no complaints?''

"What about the fourteenth person?" Jill asked.

George grimaced. "Touché."

"Beg pardon?"

"Nothing's perfect. The fourteenth man killed me."

"Oh."

The temperature in the room was moderate, but George was drenched with sweat; his ruddy complexion was paling rapidly.

"Look, you two make up your own minds. You can help them haul me out to the ambulance in a few minutes and then walk away and forget you ever met me, if that's what you want. But I have to ask you: please, *take over this karma for me*. Someone has to, one way or the other: I seriously doubt that the drug will ever be found again."

"Is there like a set of instructions for the stuff?" Zack asked. *Involved*, his head told him. "Notes, molecule diagrams—" *Somebody's getting infuckingvolved . . .*

"Complete instructions for synthesis, and about ten liters of the goods, in various forms. That's about enough to give everything on earth with two legs a couple of hits apiece. I tell you, it's easy to make. And it's *fucking* hard to stumble across. If I die, it dies with me, maybe forever. Blind luck *I* found it, just blind—"

"Where?" Zack and Jill interrupted simultaneously.

"Wait a minute, you've got to understand. It's in a *very* public place—I thought that was a good idea at the time, but . . . never mind. The point is, from the moment you pick up the stuff, you must be very very careful. They don't have to physically touch you—try not to let anyone come near you if you can help it, anyone at all—"

"I'll know a fed when I see one," Zack said grimly, "north *or* south."

"No, NO, not feds, not *any* kind of feds! Think that way and you're dead. It wasn't feds that killed me."

"Who then?" Jill asked.

"In my line of work, I customarily do business with a loosely affiliated organization of non-Syndicate drug dealers. It has no name. It is international in scope, and if it ever held a meeting, a substantial fraction of the world's wealth would sit in one room. I offered them this drug for distribution, before I really understood what I had. Sziller is one of the principals of the group."

"Jesus God," Zack breathed. "*Dealers* had *Wesley George* snuffed? That's like the apostles offing Jesus."

"One of them did," George pointed out sadly. "Think it through, son: dope dealers can't afford honesty."

"But—"

"Suppose the feds did get hold of the stuff," Jill suggested.

"Oh."

"Or the Syndicate," George agreed. "Or their own customers, or—"

"What's the drug called?" Jill asked.

"The chemical name wouldn't mean a thing to some of the brightest chemists in the world, and I never planned to market it under that. Up until I knew what it was I called it The New Batch, and since then I've taken to calling it TWT. The Whole Truth." Suddenly urgency overtook him and he was angry again. "Listen, fuck this," he blazed. "I mean fuck all this garbage. OK? I haven't got time to waste on trivia. Will you do the important thing; will you take on the karma I've brought you? Will you turn Truth loose on the world for me? Please, you aaaAAAA-AAHHH-EE *shit*." He clutched at his right arm, screamed again and fell to the floor.

"We promise, we promise," Jill was screaming, and Zack was thundering, "Where, *where?* Where, dammit?"

and Jill had George's head on her lap and Zack had his hands and they clenched like steel and *"Where"* he shouted again, and George was bucking in agony, breathing in with great whooping gargles and breathing out with sprays of saliva, jaw muscles like bulging biceps on his face, and "Hitch" he managed through his teeth, and Zack tried, "Hitch. Hitchhike, *a locker at the hitching depot"* very fast and then added "Key in your pocket?" and George borrowed energy from his death struggle to nod twice, "Okay, right Wesley, it's covered, man," and George relaxed all over at once and shat his pants. They thought he was dead, then, but the blue-grey eyelids rolled heavily up one last time and he saw Jill's face over his, raining tears. "Nice tits . . ." he said ". . . Thanks . . . children. . . thanks . . . sorry," and in the middle of the last word he did die, and his glowing aura died with him.

The Shadow was standing in the doorway, filling it full, breathing hard. "I heard the sound, man, what—oh holy *shit*, man. What the fuck *happenin'* here?"

Zack's voice was perfect, his delivery impeccable, startled but not involved. "What can I tell you, Shadow? The old guy comes back to talk blues and like that and his pump quits. Call the croaker, will you? And pour me a triple."

"Shee-it," the Shadow rumbled. "Nev' a dull night aroun' this fuckin' joint. Hey, *Finnegan!* Finnegan, god damn it." The big black bouncer left to find his boss.

Zack found a numbered key in George's pants, and turned to Jill. Their eyes met and locked. "Yes," Jill said finally, and they both nodded. And then together they pried Zack's right hand from the clutching fingers of the dead dope wizard, and together they made him comfortable on the floor, and then they began packing up their instruments and gear.

* * *

Zack and Jill held a hasty war council in the flimsy
balcony of their second-floor apartment. It overlooked a
yard so small it would have been hard put not to, as Zack
loved to say, and offered a splendid view of the enormous
oil refining facility across the street. The view of Halifax
Harbour which the architect had planned was forever hidden now behind it, but the cooling breezes still came at
night, salt-scented and rich. Even at two A.M. the city was
noisy, like a dormitory after lights out, but all the houses
on this block were dark and still.

"I think we should pack our bags," Zack said, sipping
coffee.

"And do what?"

"The dealers must know that Wesley brought a large
amount of Truth with him—he intended to turn it over to
them for distribution. They don't know *where* it's stashed,
and they must be shitting a brick wondering who else
does. We're suspect because we're known to have spoken
with him, and a hitching depot is a natural stash—so we
don't go near the stuff."

"But we've *got* to—"

"We will. Look, tomorrow we're *supposed* to go on
tour, right?"

"Screw the tour."

"No, hon, look! This is the smart way. We do just
exactly what we would have done if we'd never met
Wesley George. We act natural, do the tour as planned—we
pack our bags and *go down to the hitching depot* and take
off. But some friend of ours—say, John—goes in just
ahead of us and scores the bag. Then we show up and
ignore him, and by and by the three of us make up a full
car for somebody, and after we're out of the terminal and
about to board, out of the public eye, John changes his
mind and fades and we take over the bag. Zippo bang, off
on tour."

"I'll say it again. Screw the tour. We've got more important things to do."

"Like what?"

"?"

"What do *you* wanna do with the stuff? Call the reporters? Stand on Barrington Street and give away samples? Call the heat? Look. We're proposing to unleash truth on the world. I'm willing to take a crack at that, but I'd like to live to see what happens. So I don't want to be connected with it publicly in any way if I can help it. We keep our cover and do our tour—and we sprinkle fairy dust as we go."

"Dose people, you mean?"

"Dose the most visible people we can find, and make damn sure we don't get caught at it. We're supposed to hit nineteen cities in twenty-eight days, in a random pattern that even a computer couldn't figure out. I intend to leave behind us the god-damndest trail of headlines in history."

"Zack, I don't follow your thinking."

"Okay." He paused, took a deep breath, slowed himself visibly. "Okay . . . considering what we've got here, it behooves me to be honest. I have doubts about this. Heavy doubts. The decision we're making is incredibly arrogant. We're talking about destroying the world, as we know it."

"To hell with the world as we know it, Zack, it stinks. A world of truth *has* to be better."

"Okay, in my gut something agrees with you. But I'm still not sure. A world of truth may be better—but the period of turmoil while the old world collapses is sure going to squash a lot of people. Nice people. Good people. Jill, something *else* in my gut suspects that *maybe even good people need lies sometimes*.

"So I want to hedge my bets. I want to experiment first and see what happens. To do that I have to make another arrogant decision: to dose selected individuals, cold-bloodedly and without giving them a chance, let alone a vote. Wesley experimented himself, with a lab and volunteers and procedure and tests, until he proved to his satisfaction that it was okay to turn this stuff loose. Well, I haven't got any of that—but I have to establish to *my* satisfaction that it's cool.''

"Do you doubt his results?" Jill asked indignantly.

"To *my* satisfaction. Not Wesley's, or even yours, my darling, or anyone else's. And yes, frankly, I have some doubts about his results.''

Jill clouded up. "How can you—"

"Baby, *listen to me.* I believe that every word Wesley George said to us was the absolute unbiased truth as he knew it. But *he himself had taken the drug.* That makes him suspect.''

Jill dropped her eyes. "That retroactive consent business bothered me a little too.''

Zack nodded. "Yeah. If everybody comes out of prefrontal lobotomy with a smile on his face, what does that prove? If you kidnapped somebody and put a droud in their head, made 'em a wirehead, they'd thank you on their way out—but so what? Things like that are like scooping out somebody's *self* and replacing it with a new one. The new one says thanks—but the old one was *murdered.* I want to make *sure* that Homo veritas is a good thing—*in the opinion of Homo sapiens.*

"So I propose that neither of us take the drug. I propose that we abstain, and take careful precautions not to accidentally contaminate ourselves while we're using it. We'll dose others but not ourselves, and then when the tour is over—or sooner if it feels right—we'll sit down and look over what we've done and how it turned out. Then if we're still agreed, we'll take a couple of hits together and call CBC News. By then there'll be so much evidence they'll have to believe us, and then . . . then the word will be out. Too far out for the dealers to have it squashed or discredited. Or the government.''

''And then the world will end.''

''And a new one will begin . . . but first we've got to *know*. Am I crazy or does that make sense to you?''

Jill was silent a long time. Her face got the blank look that meant she was thinking hard. After a few minutes she got up and began pacing the apartment. ''It's risky, Zack. Once the headlines start coming they'll figure out what happened and come after us.''

''And the only people who know our schedule are Fat Jack and the Agency. We'll tell 'em there's a skip tracer after us and they'll both keep shut—''

''But—''

''Jill, this ain't the feds after us—it's a bunch of dealers who dasn't let anybody know they exist. They *can't* have the resources they'd need to trace us, even if they did know what city we were in.''

''They might. A dealers' union'd have to be international. That's a lot of weight, Zack, a lot of money.''

''Darlin'—if all you got is pisspoor dope . . .'' He broke off and shrugged.

Jill grinned suddenly. ''You make cigars. Let's get packed. More coffee?''

They took little time in packing and preparing their apartment for a long absence. This would be their third tour together; by now it was routine. At last everything that needed doing was done, the lights were out save for the bedside lamp, and they were ready for bed. They undressed quickly and silently, with no flirting byplay, and slid under the covers. They snuggled together spoon fashion for a few silent minutes, and then Zack began rubbing her neck and shoulders with his free hand, kneading with guitarist's fingers and lover's knowledge. They had not yet spoken a word of the change that the events of the evening had brought to their relationship, and both knew it, and the tension in the room was thick enough to smell. Zack thought of a hundred things to say, and each one sounded stupider than the last.

"Zack?"

"Yeah?"

"We're probably going to die, aren't we?"

"We're positively going to die." She stiffened almost imperceptibly under his fingers. "But I could have told you that yesterday, or last week." She relaxed again. "Difference is, yesterday I couldn't have told you positively that we'd die *together*."

Zack would have sworn they were inextricably entwined, but somehow she rolled round into his arms in one fluid motion, then pulled him on top of her with another. Their embrace was eight-legged and whole-hearted and completely nonsexual, and about a minute of it was all their muscles would tolerate. Then they drew apart just far enough to meet each other's eyes. They shared that, too, for a long minute, and then Zack smiled.

"Have you ever noticed that there is no position or combination of positions in which we do *not* fit together like nesting cups?"

She giggled, and in the middle of the giggle tears leaked from her laughing eyes. "Oh, Zack," she cried, and hugged him again. "I love you so much."

"I know, baby, I know," he murmured in her ear, stroking her hair. "It's not every day that you find something worth dying for—*and* something worth living for. Both at the same time. Christ, I love you."

They both discovered his rigid erection at the same instant, and an instant later they discovered her sopping wetness, and for the first time in their relationship their loins joined without manual aid from either of them. Together they sucked air slowly through their teeth, and then he began to pull his head back to meet her eyes and she stopped him, grabbing his head with her hands and pushing her tongue into his ear. His hips arched reflexively, his hands clutched her shoulders, her legs locked round his, and the oldest dance began again. It was eleven A.M. before they finally slept, and by that time they were in someone else's car, heading, ironically enough, north by northwest.

It's the best way out of Halifax.

The reader wishing a detailed account of Zack and Jill's activities over the next month can find it at any library with a good newstape and newspaper morgue. The reader is advised to bring a lunch. At any time of year the individual stories that the two folksingers sowed behind them like depth charges would have been hot copy—but God had ordained that Wesley George drop dead in August, smack in the middle of the Silly Season. The news media of the entire North American Confederation went into grateful orgasmic convulsions.

Not all the stories made the news. The events involving the Rev. Schwartz in Montreal, for instance, were entirely suppressed at the time, by the husbands involved, and have only recently come to light. When militant radical leader Mtu Zanje, the notorious "White Mau Mau," was found in Harlem with bullets from sixteen different unregistered guns in him, there was at that time nothing to connect it with the other stories, and it got three inches on page forty-three.

Indeed, the most incredible thing in retrospect is that no one, at the time, connected *any* of the stories. Though each new uproar was dutifully covered in detail, not one journalist, commentator or observer divined any common denominator in them until the month was nearly up. Confronted with the naked truth, the people of North America did not recognize it.

But certainly every one of them saw it or heard about it, in living colour stereo and thirty-six point type and four-channel FM, in weekly news magazines and on documentary shows, in gossip columns and radio talk shows, in political cartoons and in comedians' routines. Zack and Jill strongly preferred to examine their results from a distance, and so they tended to be splashy.

In St. John, New Brunswick, they hit an elderly and prominent judge who had more wrinkles than a William Goldman novel, while he was sitting in open court on a controversial treason case. After an astonishing twenty-seven-minute monologue, the aged barrister died in a successful attempt to cover, with the sidearm he had snatched from his bailiff, the defendant's escape. Zack and Jill, sitting in the audience, were considerably startled, but they had to agree that only once had they seen a man die happier: the judge's dead face was as smooth as a baby's.

In Montreal (in addition to the Rev. Schwartz), they managed to catch a Conservative MP on his way to a TV studio and shake his hand. The programme's producer turned out to have seen the old movie *Network*—he kept the politician on the air, physically knocking down the programming director when that became necessary. The MP had been—er—liberally dosed; after forty-five minutes of emotional confession he began specifically outlining the secret dreams he had had ever since he first took office, the really *good* programs he had constructed in his imagination but never dared speak aloud, knowing they could never be implemented in the real world of power blocs and interest groups. He went home that night a broken but resigned man, and woke up the next morning to confront a landslide of favourable response, an overwhelming mandate to implement his dreams. To be sure, very

very few of the people who had voted for him in the last election ever did so again. But in the *next* election (and every subsequent election involving him) the ninety percent of the electorate who traditionally never vote turned out almost to a person. The producer is now his chief aide.

In Ottawa they tried for the Prime Minister, but they could not get near him or near anything that could get near him. But they did get the aging Peter Gzowski on *Morningside.* He too chanced to have seen *Network,* and he had much more survival instinct than its protagonist: the first thing he did upon leaving the studio was to make an extensive tape recording and mail several dubs thereof to friends with instructions for their disposal in the event of his sudden death. Accordingly he is still alive and broadcasting today, and there are very few lids left for him to tear off these days.

Outside Toronto Zack and Jill made their most spectacular single raid, at the Universal Light and Truth Convocation. It was a kind of week-long spiritual olympics: over a dozen famous gurus, swamis, reverends, Zen masters, Sufis, priests, priestesses and assorted spiritual teachers had gathered with thousands of their followers on a donated hundred-acre pasture to debate theology and sell each other incense, with full media coverage. Zack and Jill walked through the Showdown of the Shamen and between them missed not a one. One committed suicide. One went mad. Four denounced themselves to their followers and fled. Seven denounced themselves to their followers and stayed. Four wept too hard to speak, the one the others called The Fat Boy (although he was middle-aged) bit off his tongue, and exactly one teacher—the old man who had brought few followers and nothing for sale—exhibited no change whatsoever in his manner or behaviour but went home very thoughtfully to Tennessee. It is now known that he could have blown the story then and there, for he was a telepath, but he chose not to. The single suicide bothered Jill deeply; but only because she happened to know of and blackly despise that particular holy man, and was dismayed by the pleasure she felt at his death. But Zack challenged her to name one way in which his demise either diminished the world or personally benefited her, and she came tentatively to accept that her pleasure might be legitimate.

They happened to arrive in Detroit just before the annual meeting of the Board of Directors of General Motors. Madame President absent-mindedly pocketed the cigar she found on the back seat of her Rolls that morning, though it was not her brand, and it had been saturated with enough odourless, tasteless TWT to dose Madison Square Garden. It is of course impossible to ever know exactly what transpired that day in that most sacrosanct and guarded and unpublic of rooms—but we have the text of the press release that ensued, and we do know that all GM products subsequent to 1994 burn alcohol instead of gasoline, and exhibit a sharp upward curve in safety and reliability.

In Chicago Zack and Jill got a prominent and wealthy realtor-developer and all his tame engineers, ecologists, lawyers and other promotion experts in the middle of a public debate over a massive rezoning proposal. There are no more slums in Chicago, and the developer is, of course, its present mayor.

In Cleveland they got a used car salesman, a TV repairman, a plumber, an auto mechanic, and a Doctor of Philosophy in one glorious afternoon.

In New York they got Mtu Zanje, quite by accident. The renegade white led a force of sixteen New Black Panthers in a smash-and-grab raid on the downtown club where Zack and Jill were playing. Mtu Zanje personally took Jill's purse, and smoked a cigar which he found therein on his way back uptown. Zack and Jill never learned of his death or their role in it, but it is doubtful that they would have mourned.

In Boston they concentrated on policemen, as many as they could reach in two mornings and afternoons, and by the time they left that town it was rocking on its metaphorical foundations. Interesting things came boiling up out of the cracks, and most of them have since decomposed in the presence of air and sunlight.

In Portland, Maine, Zack figured a way to plant a timed-release canister in the air-conditioning system of that city's largest Welfare Centre. A great many people voluntarily left the welfare rolls over the ensuing month, and none have yet returned—or starved. There are, of course, a lot of unemployed caseworkers . . .

And then they were on their way home to Halifax.

But this is a listing only of the headlines that Zack and Jill left behind them—not of everything that happened on that trip. Not even of everything important; at least, not to Zack and Jill.

In Quebec a laundry van just missed killing them both, then roared away.

In Ottawa they went out for a late night walk just before a tremendous explosion partially destroyed their motel. It had apparently originated in the room next to theirs, which was unoccupied.

In Toronto they were attacked on the streets by what might have been a pair of honest muggers, but by then they were going armed and they got one apiece.

In Detroit the driver of the cab they had taken (at ruinous expense) to eliminate a suspected tail apparently went mad and deliberately jumped a divider into high-speed oncoming traffic. In any car crash, the Law of Chaos prevails, and in this instance it killed the driver and left Zack and Jill bruised and shaken but otherwise unharmed.

They knew enemy action when they saw it, and so they

did the most confusing thing they could think of: stopped showing up for their scheduled gigs, but kept on following the itinerary. They also adopted reasonably ingenious disguises and, with some trepidation, stopped travelling together. Apparently the combination worked; they were not molested again until they showed up for the New York gig to break the pattern, and then only by Mtu Zanje, which they agreed was coincidence. But it made them thoughtful, and they rented several hours of complete privacy in a videotape studio before leaving town.

And on the road to Boston they each combed their memory for friends remembered as One Of The Nice Ones, people they could trust, and in that city they met in the Tremont Street Post Office and spent an hour addressing and mailing VidCaset Mailer packs. Each pack contained within it, in addition to its program material, a twenty-second trailer holding five hundred hits of TWT in blotter form—a smuggling innovation of which Zack was sinfully proud.

They had not yet taken TWT themselves, but their decision was made. They agreed at the end of that day to take it together when they got back to Halifax. They would do it in the Scorpio, alone together, in the dressing room where Wesley George had died.

They waited until well after closing, after Finnegan and the Shadow had locked up behind them and driven away the last two cars in the parking lot. Then they waited another hour to be sure.

The night was chill and still, save for the occasional distant street sounds from more active parts of town. There was no moon and the sky was lightly overcast; darkness was total. They waited in the black together, waiting not for any particular event or signal but only until it felt right, and they both knew that time without words. They were more married already than most couples get to be in a lifetime, and they were no longer in any hurry at all.

When it was time they rose from their cramped positions behind the building's trash compactor and walked stealthily around to the front of the building to the descending stairway that led to the outer door of the dressing room. Like all of Finnegan's regulars they knew how to slip its lock, and did so with minimal noise.

As soon as the door clicked shut behind them, Jill heaved a great sigh, compounded of relief and fatigue and déjà vu. "This is where it all started," she breathed. "The tour is over. Full circle."

Zack looked around at pitch blackness. "From the smell in here, I would guess that it was Starship Earth played here tonight."

Jill giggled. "Still living on soybeans, too. Zack, can we put the light on, do you think?"

"Hmmm. No windows, but this door isn't really tight. I don't think it'd be smart, hon."

"How about a candle?"

"Sold. Let me see—ouch!—if the Starship left the— yeah, here's a couple." He struck the light, and started both candles. The room sprang into being around them, as though painted at once in broad strokes of butter and chocolate. It was, after a solid month of perpetually new surroundings, breathtakingly familiar and comfortable. It lifted their hearts, even though both found their eyes going at once to the spot on which Wesley George had fallen.

"If your ghost is here, Wesley, rest easy, man," Zack said quietly. "It got covered. And we're both back to do truth ourselves. They killed you, man, but they didn't stop you."

After a pause, Jill said, "Thank you, Wesley," just as quietly. Then she turned to Zack. "You know, I don't even feel like we *need* to take the stuff, in a place."

"I know, hon, I know. We've been more and more honest with each other, opened up more every day, like the truth was gonna come sooner or later so we might as well get straight now. I guess I know you better than I've ever known any human, let alone any woman. But if fair is fair and right is right we've *got* to take the stuff. I wouldn't have the balls not to."

"Sure. Come on—Wesley's waiting."

Together they walked hand in hand, past the cigar-burn in the rug, to Wesley's dying place. The whisper of their boots on the rug echoed oddly in the soundproof room, then faded to silence.

"The door was open that night," Jill whispered.

"Yeah," Zack agreed. He turned the knob, eased the door open and yelped in surprise and fright. A bulky figure sat on the stage ten feet away, half-propped against an amp, ankles crossed before it. It was in deep shadow, but Zack would have known that silhouette in a coal cellar. He pushed the door open wider, and the candlelight fell on the figure, confirming his guess.

"Finnegan!" he cried in relief and astonishment. "Jesus Christ, man, you scared me. I swear I saw you leave an hour ago."

"Nope," said the barkeep. He was of medium height and stocky, bald as a grape but with fuzzy brown hair all over his face and neck. It was the kind of face within which the unbroken nose was incongruous. He scratched his crinkly chin with a left hand multiply callused from twenty years of guitar and dobro and mandolin and fiddle, and grinned what his dentist referred to as the Thousand Dollar Grin. "You just thought you did."

"Well shit, yeah, so it seems. Look, we're just sort of into a little head thing here if that's cool, meant to tell you later . . ."

"Sure."

A noise came from behind Zack, and he turned quickly to Jill. "Look, baby, it's Finn—"

Jill had not made the noise, nor did she make one now. Sziller had made the noise as he slipped the lock on the outside door, and he made another one as he snapped the hammer back on the silenced Colt. It echoed in the dressing room. Zack spun back to Finnegan, and the barkeep's right hand was up out of his lap now and there was a .357 Magnum in it.

Too tired, Zack thought wearily, *too frigging tired. I wasn't cautious enough and so it ends here.*

"I'm sorry, Jill," he said aloud, still facing Finnegan.

"I," Finnegan said clearly and precisely, "am a bi-federal agent, authorized to act in either the American or the Canadian sector. Narcotics has been my main turf for years now."

"Sure," Zack agreed. "What better cover for a narc than a musician?"

"This one," Finnegan said complacently. "I always hated being on the road. Halifax has always been a smuggler's port—why not just sit here and let the stuff come to me? All the beer I can drink—"

Sziller was going through the knapsack Jill had left by the door, without taking his eyes or his gun off them for an instant.

"So how come you're in bed with Sziller?" Zack demanded. Sziller looked up and grinned, arraying his massive beard like a peacock's tail.

"George blew my cover," Finnegan said cheerfully. "He knew me from back when and spilled the soybeans. If he'd known you two were regulars here he'd likely have warned you. So after Sziller did him in and then . . . found out he had not adequately secured the goods . . . he naturally came straight to me."

"Finnegan's got a better organization than we do," Sziller

chuckled. His voice was like a lizard's would sound if lizards could talk. "More manpower, more resources, more protection."

"And Sziller knew that TWT would mean the end of me too if it got out. He figured that our interest coincided for once—in a world of truth, what use is a narc? How can he work?"

Much too goddam tired, Zack told himself. *I'm hallucinating*. Finnegan appeared to be winking at him. Zack glanced to see if Jill were reacting to it, but her eyes were locked on Sziller, whose eyes were locked on her. Zack glanced swiftly back, and Finnegan still appeared to be winking, and now he was waving Zack toward him. Zack stood still; he preferred to die in the dressing room.

"He took a gamble," Finnegan went on, "a gamble that I would go just as far as he would to see that drug destroyed. Well, we missed you in Quebec and Ottawa and Toronto, and you fooled us when you went to Portland instead of your gig in Bangor, but I guess we've got you now."

"You're wrong," Jill said, turning to glare at Finnegan. "It's too late. You're both too late. You can kill us, but you can never recall the truth now."

"People forget headlines," Sziller sneered confidently. "Even a month of headlines. Nothing."

"You're still wrong," Zack said, staring in confusion from Sziller to Jill to the gesticulating Finnegan. "We put about thirty tapes and TWT samples in the mail—"

"Jerks," Sziller said, shaking his head. "Outthought every step of the way. Look, sonny, if you want to move a lot of dope with minimum risk, where do you get a job?" He paused and grinned again. "The Post Office, dummy."

"No," Zack and Jill said together, and Finnegan barked "*Yes*," quite sharply. They both turned to look at him.

"You can bug any room with a window in it, children,"

he said wearily. "And that dressing room, of course, has always been bugged. Oh, *look,* dammit."

He held up a VidCaset Mailer pack with broken seals, and at *last* they both started forward involuntarily toward it, and as he cleared the dressing room doorway Zack finally caught on, and he reached behind him and an incredible thing happened.

It must be borne in mind that both Zack and Jill had, as they had earlier recognized, been steadily raising the truth level between them for over a month, unconsciously attempting to soften the blow of their first TWT experience. The Tennessee preacher earlier noted had once said publicly that all people are born potentially telepathic—but that if we're ever going to get any message-traffic capacity, we must first shovel the shit out of the Communications Room. This room, he said, was called by some the subconscious mind. Zack and Jill had almost certainly been exposed to at least threshold contamination with TWT, and they were, as it happens, the first subjects to be a couple and very much in love. They had lived together through a month that could have killed them at any time, and they were already beginning to display minor telepathic rapport.

Whatever the reasons, for one fractioned instant their hands touched, glancingly, and Jill—who had seen none of Finnegan's winking and almost nothing of his urgent gestures—knew all at once exactly what was about to happen and what to do, and Zack *knew* that she knew and that he didn't have to worry about her. Sziller was close behind them; there was no time even for one last flicker-glance at each other. They grinned and winked together at Finnegan and Zack dove left and Jill dove right and Sziller came to the doorway with the Colt extended, wondering why Finnegan hadn't fired already, and there was just time for his face to register *of course, he has no silencer* before Finnegan shot him.

A .357 Magnum throwing a 120-grain Supervel hollow-point can kill you if it hits you in the foot, from hydrostatic shock to the brain. Sziller took it in the solar plexus and slammed back into the dressing room to land with a wet, meaty thud.

The echoes roared and crackled away like the treble thunder that comes sometimes with heat lightning.

"I'm kind of more than your garden-variety narc," Finnegan said calmly. "Maybe you guessed."

"Yes," Jill said for both of them. "A few seconds ago. To arrange that many convincingly bungled hits, you've got to be *big*. But you took a big chance with that cab driver."

"Hell, he wasn't mine. The guy just happened to flip—happens all the time."

"I believe you," she said, again for the two of them.

"People will have heard that shot," Zack suggested diffidently.

"Nobody who wasn't expecting it, son," Finnegan said, and sighed. "Nobody who wasn't expecting it."

Zack nodded. "Question?"

"Sure."

"How come you're still holding that gun out?"

"Because both of you still have yours," the government man said softly.

No one moved for a long frozen moment. Zack was caught with his right hand under him; in attempting to conceal the gun he had lost the use of it. Jill's was behind a crouching leg, but she left it there.

"We don't figure you, Ed," she said softly. "That's all. You see that, don't you?"

"Of course," he said. "So lighten up on the iron and by and by we'll all go get ham and eggs at my place. I'll teach you that song about Bad-Eye Bill and the Eskimo gal.''

"You're not relaxing us worth a shit, Finnegan," Zack grated. "Talk. How big *are* you?"

Finnegan pursed his lips, blew a tiny bubble between them. "Big. Bigger than narcotics. Bifederality leaves a lot of gaps. I guess you could say I'm The Man, Zaccur old son. For our purposes, anyway. Oh, I have superiors, including the President *and* the Prime Minister. I'm so clever and nimble none of them is even afraid of me. I think the PM rather likes me. It's important that you know how heavy I am—it'll help you believe the rest.''

He paused there, and Zack said "Try us," in a gentler tone of voice.

Finnegan looked around him at the darkened music room, at shadowy formica-toadstool tables bristling with chair legs, at the great hovering-buzzard blot that was the high spotlight, at a stage full of amplifiers and piano like stolid dwarves and a troll come to sit in judgement on him, at the mocking red glow of the sign over the door that claimed it was an exit. He took a deep breath, and spoke very carefully.

"Did you ever wonder why a man takes on a job like mine?" He wet his lips, "He takes it on because it's a job that someone has to do, and he sees that the man doing it is a bloody bungling butcher playing James Bond with the fate of the world. Can you see that? I hated his job as much as I hated him, but I understood that in a world like this one, *some*body *has* to do that job. Somebody just plain *has* to do that job, and I decided that no one in sight could do a better job than me. So I forced him to retire and I took his job. It is a filthy pig fucker of a job, and it has damaged me to do it—but *somebody had to*. Look, I have done things that horrify me, things that diminish me, but I did good things, too, and I have been striving every minute toward a world in which my job didn't exist, in which nobody had to shoulder that load. I've been working to put myself out of a job, without the faintest shred of hope, for over ten years—and now it's Christmas and I'm free, I'm fucking *FREE*. That makes me so happy that I could go down to the cemetery and dig up Wes and kiss him on the mouldy lips, so happy I'll feel just *terrible* if I can't talk you two out of killing me.

"My job is finished, now—nobody knows it but you and me, but it's all over but the shouting. And in gratitude to you and Wes I intend to use my last gasp of power and influence to try and keep you two alive when the shit hits the fan."

"Huh?"

"I kind of liked your idea, so I let your VidCaset packs go through. But first I erased 'em and rerecorded. Audio only, voice out of a voder, nothing identifying you two. That won't fool a computer for long, they're all friends of yours, but it buys us time."

"For what?" Jill asked.

"Time to get you two underground, of course. How would you like to be, oh, say, a writer and her husband in Colorado for six months or so? You'd look good as a blonde."

"Finnegan," Zack said with great weariness, "this all has a certain compelling inner consistency to it, but you surely understand our position. Unless you can prove any of this, we're going to have to shoot it out."

"Why you damned fools," Finnegan blazed, "what're you wasting time for? You've got some of that stuff with you—*give me a taste.*"

There was a pause while the pair thought that over. "How do we do this?" Jill asked at last.

"Put your guns on me," Finnegan said.

They stared.

"Come on, dammit. For now that's the only way we can trust each other. Just like the world out there—guns at each other's heads because we fear lies and treachery, the sneak attack. Put your fucking guns on me, and in an hour that world will be on its way out. *Come on!*" he roared.

Hesitantly, the two brought up their guns, until all three weapons threatened life. Jill's other hand brought a tiny stoppered vial from her pants. Slowly, carefully, she advanced toward Finnegan, holding out the truth, and when she was three feet away she saw Finnegan grin and heard Zack chuckle, and then she was giggling helplessly at the thought of three solemn faces above pistol sights, and all at once all three of them were convulsed with great racking whoops of laughter at themselves, and they threw away their guns as one. They held their sides and roared and roared with laughter until all three had fallen to the floor, and then they pounded weakly on the floor and laughed some more.

There was a pause for panting and catching of breath and a few tapering giggles, and then Jill unstoppered the vial and upended it against each proffered fingertip and her own. Each licked their finger eagerly, and from about that time on everything began to be all right. Literally.

An ending is the beginning of something, always.

Not Fade Away

I became aware of him five parsecs away.

He rode a nickel-iron asteroid of a hundred metric tonnes as if it were an unruly steed, and he broke off chunks of it and hurled them at the stars, and he howled.

I manifested at the outer periphery of his system and waited to be noticed. I'm sure he had been aware of me long before I detected him, but he affected not to see me for several weeks, until my light reached him.

I studied him while I waited. There was something distinctly odd about his morphology. After a while I recognized it: he was wearing the original prototype, the body our ancestors wore! I looked closer, and realized that it was the only body he had ever worn.

Oh, it had been Balanced and spaceproofed and the skull shielded, of course. But he looked as if when Balancing was discovered, he had been just barely young enough for the process to take. He must have been one of the oldest of the Eldest.

But why keep that ridiculous body configuration? It was fairly large planets, and rather poorly to that. For a normal environment, everything about it was wrong. I saw that he had had the original sensory equipment improved for space conditions, but it was still limited and poorly placed. Everything about the body was laid out bilaterally and unidirectionally, creating a blind side. The engineering was all wrong, the four limbs all severely limited in mobility. Many of the joints were essentially one-directional, simple hinges.

Stranger still, the body was grotesquely, comically overmuscled. Whenever his back happened to be turned to his star, the forty-kilo bits of rock he hurled achieved system escape velocity—yet he was able to keep that asteroid clamped between his great thighs. What individual needs that much strength in free space?

Oddest of all, of course, his mind was sealed.

Apparently totally. I could get no reading at all from him, and I am a very good reader. He must have been completely unplugged from the Bonding, and in all my three thousand years I have met only four such. He must have been as lonely as any of our ancestors ever was. Yet he knew that the Bonding exists, and refused it.

A number of objects were tethered or strapped to his body, all of great age yet showing signs of superb maintenance. It took me several days to identify them all positively as utensils, several more to realize that each was a weapon. It takes time for things to percolate down out of the Race Memory, and the oldest things take the most time.

By then he was ready to notice me. He focused one of his howls and directed it to me. He carefully ignored all the part of me that is Bonded, addressing only my individual ego, with great force.

"GO AWAY!"

"Why?" I asked reasonably.

"GO AT ONCE OR I WILL END YOU!"

I radiated startled interest. "Really? Why would you do that?"

"OH, GAAAH . . ."

There was a silence of some hours.

"I will go away," I said at last, "if you will tell me why you want me to."

His volume was lower. "Do you know who I am?"

I laughed. "How could I know? Your mind is sealed."

"I am the last warrior."

"Warrior? Wait now . . . 'warrior.' Must be an old word. 'Warrior.' Oh—*oh*. You kill and destroy. Deliberately. How odd. Are you going to destroy me?"

"I may," he said darkly.

"How might I dissuade you? I do not believe I am old enough to die competently yet, and I have at least one major obligation outstanding."

"Do you lack the courage to flee? Or the wit?"

"I shall attempt to flee if it becomes necessary. But I would not expect to succeed."

"Ah. You fear me."

" 'Fear' . . . no. I recognize the menace you represent. I repeat: how might I dissuade you from ending me? Is there something I can offer you? Access to the Bonding, perhaps?"

His reply was instant. "If I suspect you of *planning* to initiate the Bonding process with me, I will make your death a thing of unending and unspeakable agony."

I projected startlement, then masked it. "What can I do for you, then?"

He laughed. "That's easy. Find me a fair fight. Find me an enemy. If he or she is as strong as me, I will let you go unharmed. If stronger, I will give you all I own and consecrate my death to you."

"I'm not sure I understand."

"I am the *last* warrior."

"Yes?"

"When I chose my profession, warriors were common, and commonly admired. We killed or destroyed not for personal gain, but to protect a group of non-warriors, or to protect an idea or an ideal."

I emanated confusion. "Against what?"

His answer was days in coming. "Other warriors."

"How did the cycle get started?"

"Primitive men were all warriors. Then there came a time when the average man had to be forced to kill or destroy. Before long, he could no longer be forced. A Balanced human in free space cannot be coerced, only slain. Can you visualize circumstances which would impel you to kill?"

"Only with the greatest difficulty," I said. "But you enjoy it? You would find pleasure or value in killing me?"

A week passed. At last he smote his asteroid with his fist, sharply enough to cause rock to fly from its other side. "No. I lied. I will not kill you. What good is a fight you can't lose?"

"Why did you . . . 'lie'?"

"In order to frighten you."

"You failed."

"Yes. I know."

"Why did you wish to frighten me?"

"To compel you to my will."

"Hmmm. I believe I see. Then you do urgently wish to locate an enemy. I am baffled. I should have thought a warrior's prime goal to be the elimination of all other warriors."

"No. A warrior's prime goal is to overcome other warriors. I am the greatest warrior that our race has raised up.

I have not worked in over five thousand years. There is no one to overcome.''

"*Oh.*"

"Do you know what the R-brain is?"

"Wait. It's coming. Oh. I know what the R-brain *was*. The primitive reptile brain from which the human brain evolved."

"And do you know that for a considerable time early humans—true humans—possessed, beneath their sentient brains, a vestigial but powerful R-complex?"

"Of course. The First Great Antinomy."

"I have an R-complex."

I registered shock. "You cannot possibly be old enough."

I could sense his bitter grin before the sight of it crawled to me at lightspeed. "Do you notice anything interesting about this particular star-system?"

I glanced around. "Barring your presence in it, no."

"Consider that planet there. The third."

At first glance it was an utterly ordinary planet, used up like a thousand others in this out-of-the-way sector. But after only a few days I cried out in surprise. "Why . . . its period of rotation is *precisely* one standard day. And its period of revolution seems to approximate a standard year. Do you mean to tell me that that planet is . . . uh. . . ."

"Dirt," he agreed. "And that star is Sol."

"And you imply that—"

"Yes. I was born here. On that planet, in fact. At a time when all humans in the universe lived within the confines of this system—and used less than half the planets, at that."

"!!!"

"Do you still wonder that I shun your Bonding?"

"No. To you, with a reptile brain-stem, it must be the ultimate obscenity."

"Defenselessness. Yes."

"A thing which can be neither dominated nor compelled. And which itself will not dominate or compel . . . you must hate us."

"Aye."

"You could be healed. The reptile part of your brain could . . ."

"I could be gelded, too. And why not, since none will breed with me? Yet I choose to retain my gonads. And my R-complex."

"I see." I paused in thought. "What prevents you from physically attacking the Bond? I believe you could harm it greatly, perhaps destroy it."

"I repeat, what good is a fight you cannot lose?"

"Oh."

"In the old days . . . there was glory. There was a galaxy to be tamed, empires to be carved out of the sky, mighty enemies to challenge. Once I pulverized a star. With four allies I battled the Ten of Algol, and after two centuries broke them. Then were other sentient races found, in the inner neighbouring arm of the galaxy, and I learned the ways of fighting them." He paused. "I was honoured in those days. I was one of mankind's saviours." A terrible chuckle. "Do you know anything sorrier than an unemployed saviour?"

"And your fellows?"

"One day it was all changed. The brain had evolved. Man's enemies were broken or co-opted. War ended. The cursed Bonding began. At first we fought it as a plague swallowing our charges. But ere long we came to see that it was what they freely chose. Finally there came a day when we had only ourselves to fight."

"And?"

"We fought. Whole systems were laid waste, alliances were made and betrayed, truly frightening energies were released. The rest of mankind withdrew from us and forgot us.''

''I can see how this would be.''

''Man had no need of us. Man was in harmony with himself, and it was now plain that in all the galaxy there were no competing races. For a long time we had hope that there might lie enemies beyond this galaxy—that we might yet be needed. And so we fought mock-combats, preserving ourselves for our race. We dreamed of once again battling to save our species from harm; we dreamed of vindication.''

A long pause.

''Then we heard of contact with Bondings of sentient beings from neighbouring galaxies. The Unification began. In rage and despair we fell upon each other, and there was a mighty slaughter. There was one last false alarm of hope when the Malign Bonding of the Crab was found.'' His voice began to tremble with rage. ''We waited for your summons. And you . . . and you . . .'' Suddenly he screamed. ''YOU *CURED* THE BASTARDS!''

''Listen to me,'' I said. ''A neuron is a wonderful thing. But when a billion neurons agree to work together, they become a thing a billion times a billion times more wonderful—a brain. A mind. There are as many stars in this galaxy as there are neurons in a single human mind. More than coincidence. The galaxy has *become* a single mind: the Bonding. There are as many galaxies in this universe as there are stars in the average galaxy. Each has, or is developing, its own Bonding. Each of these is a neuron in the Cosmic Mind. One day soon Unification will be complete, and the universe will be intelligent. You can be part of that mind, and share in it.''

''*No*,'' he said emphatically. ''If I am part of the Cosmic Mind, then I am part of its primitive subconscious mind. The subconscious is useful only for preservation from outside threat. As your brain evolved beyond your ancestors' subconscious mind, your universal mind has evolved beyond me. There is nothing in the plenum that you need fear.'' He leaned forward in sudden pain, embraced his asteroid with his arms as well as his legs. I began moving closer to him, not so rapidly as to alarm him if he should look up, but not slowly.

"When we understood this," he said, "we warriors fell upon each other anew. Four centuries ago Jarl and I allied to defeat The One in Red. That left only each other. We made it last as long as we could. It was perhaps the greatest battle ever fought. Jarl was very, very good. That was why I saved him for last."

"And you overcame him?"

"Since then I have been alone." He lifted his head quickly and roared at the universe. "Jarl, you son of a bitch, *why didn't you kill me?*" He put his face again to the rock.

I could not tell if he had seen me approaching.

"And in all the years since, you have had no opponent?"

"I tried cloning myself once. Useless. No clone can have my experience and training; the environment which produced me no longer exists. What good is a fight you cannot lose?"

I thought for some time, coming ever closer. "Why do you not suicide?"

"What good is a fight you cannot lose?"

I was near now. "Then all these years you have prayed for an enemy?"

"Aye." His voice was despairing.

"Your prayer is answered."

He stiffened. His head came up and he saw me.

"I represent the Bonding of the Crab," I said then. "The cure was imperfect," and I did direct at him a laser.

I was near, but he was quick, and his mirror-shield

deflected my bolt even before he could have had time to absorb my words. I followed the laser with other energies, and he dodged, deflected, or neutralized them as fast as they could be mounted.

There was an instant's pause then, and I saw a grin begin slowly and spread across his face. He flung his own weapons into space.

"I am delivered," he cried, and then he shifted his mass, throwing his planetoid into a spin. When it lay between us, I thought he had struck it with both feet, for suddenly it was rushing toward me. Of course I avoided it easily—but as it passed, he darted around from behind it, where he had been hidden, and grappled with me physically. He had hurled the rock not with his feet, but with a reaction drive.

Then did I understand why he kept such an ancient bodyform, for it was admirably suited to single combat. I had more limbs, but weaker, and one by one my own weapons were torn from me and hurled into the void. Meanwhile mental energies surged against each other from both sides, and space began to writhe around us.

Mentally I was stronger than he, for he had been long alone, and mental muscles can be exercised only on another mind. But his physical power was awesome, and his ferocity a thing incomprehensible to me.

And now I see the end coming. Soon his terrible hands will reach my brain-case and rip it asunder. When this occurs, my body will explode with great force, and we shall both die. He knows this, and in this instant of time before the end, I know what he is doing, beneath his shield where I cannot probe. He is composing his last message for transmission to you, his people, his Bonding. He is warning you of mortal danger. He is telling you where to find his hidden clone samples, where to find the records he has made of everything he knows about combat, how to train his clones to be *almost* as good as he is. And he is feeling the satisfaction of vindication. *I could have told you!* he is saying. *Ye who knew not my worth, who have forgotten me, yet will I save you!*

This is my own last message to you, to the same people, to the same Bonding. It worked. He believes me. I have accomplished what you asked of me. He has the death he craved.

We will die together, he and I. And that is meet and proper, for I am the last Healer in the cosmos, and now I too am unemployed.

About the Author

Spider Robinson began writing science fiction in 1972. He and his wife, Jeanne (founder and Artistic Director of the modern dance company *Nova Dance Theatre*), collaborated to win the Hugo and Nebula Awards and the *Locus* Poll for Best Novella of 1977, for portions of their novel *Stardance*. By himself he has won the John W. Campbell Award for Best New Writer, two more Hugo Awards (most recently for the title story of this volume), the E.E. Smith Memorial Award for Speculative Fiction, the Pat Terry Memorial Award for Humorous Writing, and the *Locus* Poll for Best Critic. His first story collection, *Callahan's Crosstime Saloon*, was named a Best Book for Young Adults by the American Library Association.

He has worked at various times as a sewer guard, morgue attendant, soda jerk, human fire-alarm, folksinger/guitarist, real estate editor, process-server, shipping clerk, rent-a-cop, janitor, and small farmer. Although he comes from a good family, he admits to having (infrequently) committed both editorship and agentry (to *Locus*'s charge that he has committed criticism he cops a plea, claiming to have been merely a book reviewer with shoes on), but states that he has successfully rehabilitated himself.

He presently lives in Nova Scotia, with Jeanne, his daughter Luanna, and his computer Anne (a 512K Macintosh named after the secretary-*cum*-Fair Witness in Robert A. Heinlein's *Stranger in a Strange Land*). Their home is known as Tottering-on-the-Brink, and he has stolen other licks from Will Cuppy too.

HARRY HARRISON

Buy them at your local bookstore or use this handy coupon:
Clip and mail this page with your order

TOR BOOKS—Reader Service Dept.
P.O. Box 690, Rockville Centre, N.Y. 11571

Please send me the book(s) I have checked above. I am enclosing
$_____ (please add $1.00 to cover postage and handling).
Send check or money order only—no cash or C.O.D.'s.

Mr./Mrs./Miss _____
Address _____
City _____ State/Zip _____
Please allow six weeks for delivery. Prices subject to change without
notice.